MYSTIC
PARK

Also by Regina Hart

Finding Home series
Trinity Falls
Harmony Cabins
Wishing Lake

The Brooklyn Monarchs Trilogy
Fast Break
Smooth Play
Keeping Score

MYSTIC PARK

REGINA HART

Kensington Publishing Corp.
http://www.kensingtonbooks.com

DAFINA BOOKS are published by

Kensington Publishing Corp.
119 West 40th Street
New York, NY 10018

All Kensington Titles, Imprints, and Distributed Lines are available at special quantity discounts for bulk purchases for sales promotions, premiums, fund-raising, and educational or institutional use. Special book excerpts or customized printings can also be created to fit specific needs. For details, write or phone the office of the Kensington special sales manager: Kensington Publishing Corp., 119 West 40th Street, New York, NY 10018, attn: Special Sales Department, Phone: 1-800-221-2647.

Dafina and the Dafina logo Reg. U.S. Pat. & TM Off.

ISBN-13: 978-1-61773-566-0
ISBN-10: 1-61773-566-3
First Kensington Mass Market Edition: September 2015

eISBN-13: 978-1-61773-567-7
eISBN-10: 1-61773-567-1
First Kensington Electronic Edition: September 2015

10 9 8 7 6 5 4 3 2 1

Printed in the United States of America

To my dream team:

- *My sister, Bernadette, for giving me the dream.*
- *My husband, Michael, for supporting the dream.*
- *My brother Richard, for believing in the dream.*
- *My brother Gideon, for encouraging the dream.*

And to Mom and Dad, always with love.

CHAPTER 1

"How long will you be in town?" Dr. Vaughn Brooks's deep bedroom voice lifted Benita Hawkins from that place halfway between sleep and wakefulness.

She shifted under the sheets of Vaughn's king-sized bed and spooned into his warm naked body. "About one month. Aunt Helen said her former colleagues planned to make the announcement about the endowed chemistry chair they're naming in her honor either at the end of April or the beginning of May."

Doctor Helen Gaston—Ms. Helen to the residents of Trinity Falls, Aunt Helen to Benita—was a retired chemistry professor. She used to teach at Trinity Falls University. The endowed chair was a gift to the university from one of her former students.

"A month?" The Trinity Falls University music professor played her body like a virtuoso. His large, hot hand left a trail of electricity from her waist, over her hip, stopping at her thigh. His sleepy drawl played a sexy melody with her stomach muscles. "That's about thirty times longer than your usual visits." His hand moved again, back up her thigh, along her hip, past her waist to cup her breast.

Benita pressed into his hold. Her nipple pebbled. "I have a job back in Los Angeles, remember?"

"You work for yourself." Vaughn molded her breast in the palm of his hand. He whispered into her ear. "You can afford to be away longer than an overnight trip."

Benita swallowed a groan as Vaughn's caresses re-awakened her recently sated passion. "Overnight trips? Stop exaggerating."

Vaughn's hair-roughened chest moved against her back. "I'm not. When you came home for the Trinity Falls Sesquicentennial Celebration, you arrived Friday night and left Saturday."

Benita rolled over to face him. His left arm embraced her loosely. His erection flexed against her stomach. She rested her right hand on his bare broad shoulder and stared into his cocoa eyes. Her gaze roamed his beloved nutmeg features: well-shaped, clean-shaven head, high cheekbones, strong nose, full lips, and wicked goatee.

"As much as I'd like to spend a month with you every time I come back to Trinity Falls, I can't usually be away from work that long."

Vaughn sighed. "Benny, you have your own business. You're an entertainment lawyer and business manager. You can work from anywhere. You can work from here."

Familiar arguments. They'd been having them since Benita moved to L.A. three years ago. Why wouldn't he understand her need for more than Trinity Falls? "When my clients are in the middle of contract negotiations and business dealings, they don't want to wait a week, much less a month for me to weigh in on their contract offers."

"That's why you have e-mails, cell phones, and faxes.

You don't have to be in Los Angeles to negotiate for your clients."

"I've made a life for myself in L.A." She searched his almond-shaped eyes. Would he ever accept her need to spread her wings? "Since we were in high school, you knew I'd eventually leave Trinity Falls."

"Yes. You and Ean had that in common in high school. But Ean eventually came to his senses. He moved back two years ago." Vaughn rolled onto his back. Suddenly, the mood was gone.

Benita lay on her back as well. The late afternoon sun penetrated Vaughn's cream venetian blinds to illuminate his dark wood bedroom furnishings. "I guess it depends on your point of view. From my perspective, Ean lost his mind."

"No, he lost his father." Vaughn's retort was muted. "That's when he realized the rat race wasn't for him."

Ean Fever had been a year behind Vaughn and Benita at Heritage High School. Like Benita, Ean had earned a law degree. He'd made partner with a prestigious firm in New York City, the culmination of his childhood dream. Then his father had died of cancer. That's when Ean had thrown away the life he'd worked so hard for in New York. He'd returned to Trinity Falls and opened a little law practice in the town center. Nuts.

"Ean probably just needed a break." Benita had known Ean's father. Paul Fever's death had been a great loss for the community. She could only imagine how devastating it had been for the Fever family. "He didn't have to move back to Trinity Falls."

"You sound like your parents. What happened to the college student who spent her Christmas breaks and most of her summer vacations in Trinity Falls?"

Vaughn was right. Benita's parents had been very vocal about hating Trinity Falls. They'd had their reasons: nothing to do, nowhere to go, nothing to see, no one to talk to. As soon as she'd graduated from college, her parents had moved to Alexandria, Virginia. Benita had followed them before moving on to L.A. It was probably natural that she'd adopt at least some of their attitudes. But unlike her parents, she didn't hate her hometown. She just wanted more.

Benita turned her head on the fluffy pillow and studied Vaughn's profile. The softness of youth had hardened into the strong, determined lines of adulthood, complete with an attractive goatee. In high school, she'd been crazy about the boy. As a woman, she could easily fall in love with the man. Maybe she already had. But how foolish would that be if she wanted to build a life in L.A. while he stubbornly remained in Trinity Falls?

"If you really want to spend more time with me, you could move to L.A." Benita offered him a hopeful smile. But she may as well have saved herself the effort. They'd played this verbal game before.

Here we go again. The thought flickered across Vaughn's mind. His sigh was long and deep. Why did they keep rehashing this debate? "Trinity Falls is my home."

"We could be happy in L.A."

"You mean you could be happier if someone you knew was with you." Vaughn searched Benita's hazel brown eyes, noting the midnight ring around the irises. "There's a town full of people you know and who know you right here. You've given Los Angeles three years, Benny. If you're not happy there, it's time to come home."

Benita's eyes widened. "What makes you think I'm not happy in L.A.?"

"I've visited you six times. You're a different person when you're in Los Angeles. You're stressed and distracted."

She frowned. "I thought you enjoyed visiting me."

Vaughn shook his head against the pillow. "I want to be with you. But when we're in Los Angeles, you're mentally somewhere else. You're checking e-mails, texting, or answering a hundred calls a day. And when we're out, you're less interested in us than in who might see us."

Benita seemed to become more tense with every accusation Vaughn aimed at her. "I didn't know you felt this way."

Vaughn lifted her chin. He held her troubled gaze. "Didn't you?"

"If you want to get to the top, you have to be willing to put in the time. And I want to get to the top."

As an answer, that didn't tell him anything. "What are you willing to sacrifice to get there?"

"Why do I have to sacrifice anything?"

Vaughn climbed from the bed. The chill in his bedroom prompted him to reclaim his jeans from the thick navy carpeting. He pulled them on before turning back to Benita. She walked toward him, bold, beautiful, and completely naked. At five feet, five inches in height, Benita was a small woman. But she had long, toned limbs. Her body was slender. Her breasts were full, the nipples pouting toward him. Her hips were round and swayed in a mesmerizing rhythm. When she bent forward to collect her blue jeans and matching purple underwear, she wiped Vaughn's mind clean.

She straightened, meeting his gaze with wary hazel eyes that still captivated him after eighteen years. Her dark brown hair was tousled in waves around her heart-stoppingly beautiful face. Had she somehow cast a spell on him? Was that the reason he'd put his life on hold these past three years as he waited—praying—for her to return to Trinity Falls?

Vaughn watched her slip on her underwear and fasten her bra. He didn't want to start this next conversation. He'd rather fly to the moon, dive to the bottom of the ocean, or grade finals and projects. But she didn't leave him a choice. "We can't go on this way, Benny." Vaughn's voice was gruff with reluctance.

"What do you mean?" Benita hesitated in the act of pulling on her form-fitting jeans.

Vaughn struggled to get the words out. "Our relationship isn't working for me. I'm almost forty—"

"You're only thirty-five."

"Which is almost forty. I want to get married, buy a house, raise a family."

"I want the same things." Benita fastened her jeans, then bent to reclaim her orange lightweight sweater.

"But you don't want them here."

"Trinity Falls isn't enough for me." Benita pulled on her sweater. "You know I've always wanted more."

Her words hurt even more than he'd thought they would. They turned his world on its behind, making it seem as though the ground beneath his wall-to-wall navy carpeting shifted. "Then I'm not enough for you."

Benita's lips parted in surprise. "That's not true."

"Then come home and build a life with me."

"Why are you so resistant to moving to L.A.? You

could do so much more with your music there: teach, produce, write, perform. Or all of those things."

"I can do all those things here."

"In Trinity Falls?" Benita sounded skeptical. "L.A.'s concert venues hold more people than this town's entire population."

"I won't argue that Los Angeles has more of everything: people, theaters, traffic, smog, crime, earthquakes—"

"So it's not the Garden of Eden." Benita held up her right hand, palm outward. She was like a very small, somewhat irritated traffic officer. "Still you can do so much more there. You could *be* so much more there."

"I can do and be everything I want right here at home." Vaughn pulled on his dark gray jersey.

"That's always been your problem." Frustration leaked into Benita's words. "You've always been willing to settle. You've never had any dreams or aspirations."

"I have dreams, Benny." Vaughn reined in his temper. "But I've put them on hold for you."

"I never asked you to do that."

"I've been waiting for you to return to your senses and come home."

"And I've been waiting for you to join me in L.A."

They'd reached the impasse. He'd been expecting it, but still he wished they could have avoided it. Vaughn locked his legs, hoping the act would prevent him from dropping to his knees and begging her to reconsider. Otherwise, he'd have to make a tough decision of his own. "I don't want a long-distance relationship. I need to move on with my life here in Trinity Falls."

It was a stretch to call what they had a relationship. It was more like periodic hookups during Benita's quick visits home or the few times he'd gone to Los Angeles.

But even as Vaughn spoke the words, something was drawing him to Benita like a magic spell.

"Why won't you give L.A. a chance?" The tears pooling in her eyes tore at his heart.

"Los Angeles is changing you. You're not the woman I know when you're there." She wasn't the caring, considerate woman he'd fallen in love with when they were teenagers, the woman he'd fallen in love with all over again as adults.

"So this is it?" She lifted her chin.

"I'm sorry, Benny." He strode from the room, giving her time alone to finish dressing. Giving himself time alone to deal with his breaking heart.

Early Monday morning, Vaughn thought himself alone in Trinity Falls University's auditorium. He sat on the faux black leather cushioned bench before the university's eighteen-year-old Steinway baby grand piano. His fingers danced over its ivory keys, running up and down the chords, calling forth an evocative ballad. A love song, one of his original pieces, swelled from the notes and sketched images on his mind: Benita, laughing, loving, breaking his heart. He drove the piece past its crescendo, then allowed the music to fade and, finally, to end.

The applause startled him.

Vaughn's eyes shot open. His gaze swung around the room until he spotted Dr. Peyton Harris, standing in the second row.

"Encore!" The petite history professor stopped clapping and maneuvered her way onto the auditorium's aisle. She approached him, her caramel eyes twinkling in her honey-and-chocolate-cream, heart-shaped face. "Is this Untitled Opus Number Six or does this one have a name?"

Vaughn smiled at his friend's reference to the last time she'd found him at the piano. He checked his watch. It was almost half past seven in the morning. His first class wasn't until nine. Peyton's must be earlier.

"'Forever Love.'" He couldn't stop tinkering with it.

Peyton stopped beside the piano. Her curly bright brown hair bounced just above her shoulders. "That's intriguing."

"Thank you." Vaughn rose from the bench. He escorted Peyton from the auditorium.

It was a large room in Butler Hall, the university's administrative building and one of the oldest buildings on campus. It was named after the university's founder, Clara Butler. The auditorium's three sections of approximately six hundred mahogany chairs were bolted in place. The red cement floor gave the impression of carpeting climbing subtly toward the doors. Long, narrow gothic windows were carved into the walls just below the high ceiling, giving the auditorium a cathedral-like appearance. In front of the room, a concert pit stretched between the audience and the mahogany stage.

He could feel the history that filled the sweeping space: plays and concerts that had taken place during the almost century and a half since the auditorium's debut, actors and musicians who'd performed, audiences that had been entertained and inspired.

"How are your plans for your musical progressing?" Peyton's question pushed the ghosts of performances past back into the corners of his mind.

"I appreciate your not-so-subtle encouragement." Vaughn smiled at the university's newest faculty member.

Peyton had arrived in Trinity Falls in July via New York City. She was now dating Darius Knight, one of Vaughn's childhood friends and the town newspaper's managing editor. The journalist was a lucky man.

"That's not an answer." Peyton gave him a chastising look.

"I'm ready to start production." He forced the words past the uncertainty weaving doubts in his mind.

"You don't sound ready. What's holding you back?"

Vaughn paused in the hallway just outside the auditorium. Benita's refusal to return to Trinity Falls still hurt. "I'm not sure I can do this alone."

Peyton stopped beside him. "Producing a musical is a lot of work. I'm sure you'll need help."

Vaughn hesitated. "Would you have time to help me?"

"Me?" Peyton's winged eyebrows flew toward her hairline.

"I know it's a lot to ask. I'll understand if you're busy."

"I want to help"—Peyton spread her arms—"but I don't know anything about producing a play."

"You did a great job cochairing the fund-raising committee for the Guiding Light Community Center last winter."

Peyton dropped her arms. "Fund-raising is a lot different from the theater. I can throw a party. But you need someone who knows what's involved in producing a performance."

Once again, Benita invaded Vaughn's mind. In high school, they'd been members of their drama club. Now she worked in the entertainment industry. She had years of experience with performances: contracts, budgets, schedules, logistics. But he shut down that road before he traveled too many miles. He had to let go of Benita. She'd made him realize that two days ago.

"I'll try it alone first. Maybe I can handle it." Vaughn began walking in the direction of Peyton's office near the end of the hallway.

"Isn't there someone in Trinity Falls who's been involved with plays?"

"We don't have a community theater."

The building was just coming awake with other faculty members preparing for early morning classes. Vaughn gave a nod of greeting to housekeeping staff as he escorted Peyton down the hall. It was the last full week of March. Midterms were behind them. Spring break was around the corner. The air was brittle with tension as the school year rocketed toward finals week.

"I don't think it's a good idea for you to produce this play on your own." Peyton sounded worried. "Why don't you make a list of the things that need to be done, then give us assignments so we can help you?"

The "us" Peyton referred to were their mutual friends, most of whom had known each other since childhood. They were each other's Constant Cavalry. If ever one of them was in a bind, all he or she had to do was call. "If I get overwhelmed, I'll consider that."

Peyton stopped, prompting Vaughn to halt beside her. "There's no 'if' about it. You're going to need help. It took a lot of courage to get to this point. I don't want you to become discouraged and give up on your dream. You've worked too hard."

Peyton spoke with the passion of someone who knew what it was like to gather one's courage for a leap of faith. She'd taken a similar leap when she'd left her familiar life in New York City to start over in Trinity Falls, Ohio.

Vaughn smiled. "I promise that, if I need help, I'll ask."

"All right." Peyton gave him a dubious look. "But I'm going to stay on you about this."

"Fair enough."

But Peyton wouldn't need to. This musical wasn't his only goal. Vaughn was hitting the Play button on his life and putting himself back on the market. If Benita wasn't going to be part of his future, he'd find someone who was interested.

CHAPTER 2

"Are you going to spend your entire visit moping around my home?" Ms. Helen spoke with her back to Benita Monday afternoon.

Benita frowned from the threshold of her great-aunt's kitchen. She wasn't moping around. *Am I?*

She took in the small, neat figure of the elderly woman standing in front of the kitchen sink. Her great-aunt Helen filled her kettle with water before moving on to her stove. She wore an oversized vivid floral-patterned blouse over sage green yoga pants. Pink ballet slippers protected her dainty feet.

"I'm going to mope around Harmony Cabins tomorrow." Benita lowered herself onto a seat at the kitchen table. "I want to check on Audra. I'll probably shift my moping to Books and Bakery Wednesday."

"At least you have a plan." Ms. Helen fired up the burner under the kettle, then faced Benita. "I hope you snap out of it before we meet with Foster on Friday. If he sees you looking so sulky, he'll think I'm not feeding you."

Benita smiled at the idea. "Aunt Helen, I don't think anyone would think I'm missing meals."

"What's wrong?" Her great-aunt's thin, arched eyebrows knitted with concern. She joined Benita at the table. "Did you and Vaughn argue?"

"Vaughn?" Benita kept her expression blank.

"You remember Vaughn." Ms. Helen spoke with the patience of a nurse, comforting an amnesiac. "He's the nice young man you dated in high school. He teaches music at the university now. You have sex with him at least once every time you return to Trinity Falls."

Shock wiped Benita's mind clean. "You know about that?"

"This is Trinity Falls." Ms. Helen rose from her seat at the table and crossed to the cabinet beside her stove. "Did you really think no one would notice?"

"People are talking about us?"

"I don't know about all that." Her great-aunt took three mugs from her cupboard and set them on the counter. "Probably, although there are plenty of other things to talk about in this town."

"Oh. My. God." Benita's gaze swept the kitchen without seeing the bright green walls and ivory cabinets that made the room seem spacious and cheery. "Why didn't Vaughn tell me?"

"I wouldn't have." Ms. Helen selected tea bags from a separate cupboard and placed one in each mug.

"Why not?" Benita's gaze lifted to the back of Ms. Helen's head. Her great-aunt had pinned her snow white hair into a neat, thick chignon.

"What does it matter if people are talking about you? Your visits are so brief. You're not usually here long enough to hear the gossip."

Ms. Helen checked the clock on the wall across the kitchen. Benita followed her gaze. It was a couple of minutes before noon. She puzzled at her great-aunt's actions. Why was she preparing three mugs of tea when there were only two of them in her house? Was she right to be concerned about the older woman's health and her ability to continue living on her own?

Benita started to ask about the third mug of tea when the kettle came to a boil. Ms. Helen turned off the burner just as the front doorbell rang.

"I'll get it." Ms. Helen gave Benita a critical look. "Try to look pleasant, dear. We don't want our company to think I've been beating you."

"Yes, Aunt Helen." Benita stood to trail her relative to the foyer. Ms. Helen's soft laughter floated back to her. Benita shook her head at her relative's twisted sense of humor.

Ms. Helen stood on her toes to check her peephole before releasing her locks. She stepped back, pulling the front door wide. "Alonzo, how nice of you to stop by."

"It's good to see you, Ms. Helen." Their guest's warm baritone rumbled across the threshold before he entered the foyer. Ms. Helen closed and locked the door behind him.

Sheriff Alonzo Lopez was old enough to be Benita's father, but that didn't detract one bit of her appreciation for his exotic good looks. He removed his brown campaign hat, revealing his still-dark, wavy hair. His tall, lean, broad-shouldered frame was impressive in his sheriff's uniform: brown shirt, black tie, and green gabardine pants. Or maybe it was his build that made the uniform look impressive.

His dark, coffee-colored eyes smiled at her. "Welcome home, Benita. How are you?"

"Fine, thank you, Sheriff. And you?"

"I can't complain." The understatement of the year, considering the happiness and well-being Benita felt radiating from him in waves.

"No, you can't, considering you're marrying one of the most wonderful people in Trinity Falls. Congratulations." Benita watched with delight as Alonzo's smile spread into a grin. She felt a twinge of envy.

According to her great-aunt, Alonzo had been in love with Doreen Fever—now the mayor of Trinity Falls as well as manager of the café at Books & Bakery—since they were in high school. Now nearing retirement, the sheriff was finally going to marry the great love of his life. In contrast, Benita had just broken up with her high school sweetheart. Wasn't life something?

"Doreen is *one* of the most wonderful people in town." Alonzo's expression softened at the mention of his fiancée. "Your great-aunt is equally a treasure."

Benita smiled in agreement. "You shouldn't let Aunt Helen hear you say that, though. It'll go straight to her head."

"Save your backhanded compliments." Ms. Helen waved a small, seemingly frail hand. "Would you like some tea, Alonzo?"

Benita frowned as she recalled the three mugs of tea on the counter beside her great-aunt's stove.

"If it's not too much trouble." Alonzo tucked his campaign hat under his arm.

"No trouble at all." Ms. Helen led them back to her kitchen. "We were just about to have some ourselves."

Alonzo waited for Benita to follow her great-aunt

before accompanying them to the kitchen. How had Ms. Helen known to prepare three mugs of tea? Had she known Alonzo was on his way? But she'd seemed surprised to find him on her doorstep. Benita shrugged the mystery aside. She had enough weighing on her mind. Vaughn had broken up with her after eighteen years of their on-again-off-again romance. And she needed to find a way to convince Ms. Helen to move into an assisted living home.

About half an hour later, Benita cleared the table after their tea with Alonzo and prepared a light lunch for Ms. Helen and her. She slid a glance toward her great-aunt, who was enjoying a second mug of chai tea. Her relative seemed in good spirits after the sheriff's report on his department's morning activities. In Los Angeles, Benita was bombarded with news bulletins about drive-by shootings, home invasions, and murders. In contrast, this morning, the Trinity Falls Sheriff Department had freed a toddler whose head had been stuck in a staircase banister. Deputies had investigated a prank at Heritage High School involving students who'd nailed shut the teachers' break room. Alonzo suspected the perpetrators to be the same ones who'd nailed shut the high school's exterior doors last Halloween. Benita was reassured that the national crime wave hadn't spread to Trinity Falls.

"Never a dull moment in Trinity Falls, is there?" Benita was only half joking.

She lowered the burner under the pot of homemade chicken soup she'd prepared for dinner last night. The air swelled with the scents of seasonings and fresh vegetables. Benita pulled her homemade wheat bread from the refrigerator to make sandwiches as she waited for the soup to boil. She was rarely inspired to cook like this in L.A. Why was that?

"That's what I keep telling you." Ms. Helen crossed to the dishwasher to add her mug to the machine. "Do you need help preparing lunch?"

"No, I've got it."

"That's what I love about your visits." Ms. Helen returned to her seat at the kitchen table. "As brief as they are, I never have to do anything while you're here. You wait on me hand and foot."

"Actually, Aunt Helen, that's one of the things I wanted to speak with you about. I'm concerned about your living alone."

"Why? Because of the recent crime spree? Now you know how I feel about your living in Los Angeles."

Benita's living in Los Angeles was a different matter from her great-aunt living on her own *anywhere*. But Ms. Helen wouldn't take kindly to that sentiment. "I realize Trinity Falls is comparatively safe."

Ms. Helen snorted. "You mean, compared to anyplace else you've ever lived?"

Benita ignored her relative's commentary. She pulled from the refrigerator sliced chicken breast, honeyed ham, and cheddar cheese. "The fact is, Aunt Helen, I'm concerned that you're getting older. You need help getting around and taking care of things."

"According to whom?"

Benita looked around at her great-aunt. Ms. Helen seemed more curious than angry. Benita quickly constructed the sandwiches, then turned off the stove. "No one's said anything, at least not to me. This is a concern *I've* had for a while."

"Benita, I'm a scientist. If you want to convince me of your hypothesis, you're going to have to offer something more than your feelings."

Had the temperature in the kitchen dropped about twenty degrees? Benita filled two bowls with the chicken soup. She carried one of the bowls and a sandwich to Ms. Helen, then returned for her own dishes.

"Aunt Helen, how old are you?" Benita sank onto a chair at the kitchen table.

"I'm old enough to know when someone doesn't have the facts to support their premise." Ms. Helen gestured toward Benita with her soup spoon. "You claim I'm too old to live on my own, but you don't know my age."

"Aunt Helen, I—"

"What examples can you offer to validate your concern?"

Benita hadn't thought this through. She spread her napkin on her lap, trying to buy time. It didn't help. "I can't think of any."

"Then why are we having this conversation?" Ms. Helen spooned up some soup. "You say I look as though I need help. Well, science has proven that looks can be deceiving." The retired university chemistry professor proceeded to eat her lunch in stony silence. Her displeasure was obvious in the set of her shoulders.

Benita swallowed a sigh of despair. Vaughn had ended their relationship. Ms. Helen was irritated with her. How many other people in her hometown would she alienate before returning to L.A. in a month's time?

* * *

"I don't know how I'm going to do it." Doreen's fingers trembled with the need to rip out her hair Tuesday morning. All of it. By the roots.

Megan McCloud, her employer, dear friend, and her son's girlfriend—soon-to-be-fiancée?—was lending a sympathetic ear as Doreen voiced her anxieties. It was coming up on seven in the morning. Megan was keeping Doreen company in Books & Bakery's kitchen before the store opened at eight A.M. It was a habit they'd developed when Doreen had first started working for Megan almost three years ago. The bookstore owner wore a warm gold pencil-thin skirt with a hem that ended just above her knees. Her maple brown scoop-neck blouse complimented her cinnamon skin.

The kitchen was a bakery chef's dream—or at least it was Doreen's dream. The modest white and silver room was bright and lined with modern industrial equipment. All of the appliances were clean and well cared for, and everything was positioned within her reach.

"You don't have to plan your wedding all by yourself, Doreen." Megan spoke from her usual perch on one of the two honey wood chairs nestled into the corner of the kitchen.

"I'm just trying to wrap my mind around it." Doreen measured flour, salt, and cinnamon into a mixing bowl. "It's been years since I've attended a wedding."

"Me, too." Megan smoothed back her shoulder-length dark brown hair. "My last single friend got married a couple of years ago."

Doreen gave Megan a brief look before returning her attention to her Trinity Falls Fudge Walnut Brownie mixture. *Turn off the Mommy Radar*. Time enough to worry about Megan and her son, Ean's, relationship when she and her fiancé, Sheriff Alonzo Lopez, returned from their honeymoon. Urgh, the honeymoon. Another thing to add to the task list. And they would have one or Alonzo would rue the day, especially after everything he was putting her through to plan their wedding on his impossible time frame.

"Alonzo did agree to wait until June." Doreen measured cocoa, nutmeg, and butter into the electric mixer. "He'd originally wanted a May wedding."

"That's an additional four weeks." Megan seemed satisfied.

Doreen wasn't. "I don't understand why he couldn't wait until *next* June." She let the blender run before continuing. "He proposed in January. Six months isn't enough time to enjoy the engagement much less plan a wedding."

"But, Doreen, Alonzo's already waited forty-three years." Megan's tone was indulgent.

Whose side was she on? But the knowledge that Alonzo had loved her so much for so long gave her a warm, dreamlike feeling. She held on to the sensation a moment longer.

"That's the reason he wants a traditional wedding." Doreen combined the contents of her two ingredients bowls. Then she wrapped in a cup and a half of wheat flour. She spread the brownie batter into the pretreated baking pan. "He said he'd waited too long to settle for the justice of the peace."

"He has a point."

Yes, he does. Doreen didn't want to celebrate their love with a rushed ceremony, either. Wasn't there something halfway between a shotgun wedding and the ceremony from *The Sound of Music*?

"He can't have it both ways." Tension twisted the muscles in Doreen's shoulders. "He can't have a big, traditional wedding on a justice-of-the-peace schedule. There's just too much to do."

"But you don't have to do it all yourself." Behind her, Megan's voice was persuasive. "Ean and I can help you. I'm sure Audra, Jackson, Peyton, and Darius would be happy to help as well."

Megan had listed four of their closest friends, two couples who were showing signs of moving toward their own happily-ever-after soon.

"I bought one of those bridal magazines. Even with help, there's a lot to get done in three months." Doreen settled the baking pan with the brownie mixture in the oven, then closed the door. She wiped her hands on her chef's apron.

Earlier, Doreen had transferred her first batch of pastries to one of the display cases in the dining area just outside the kitchen. Their scent—sugar, chocolate, fruits, and frosting—combined with the aromas of the brownie batter she'd just placed in the oven.

"Just tell us what to do."

"Alonzo and I have other responsibilities, too." Doreen turned to face Megan. "I have this café. Alonzo's the sheriff and I'm mayor now."

"I know." Megan spread her arms. "But you don't have to be Wonder Woman and Alonzo doesn't have to be Superman. You both have plenty of friends and we'd be happy to lend a hand."

Doreen's stubborn self-reliance made it difficult to accept help. "You're all so busy, too." She gestured toward Megan. "You're doing even more for the café now that I'm also mayor. Ean's practice has taken off.

Jackson's back at the newspaper while he's renovating his cabins. And Audra's on deadline with a new song-writing contract."

"All right, Doreen. But if you change your mind, let us know." Megan crossed her arms. "I really would like to help and I'm sure the others would, too."

Doreen forced a smile. "Thank you for listening. I needed to get that off my chest."

She must be mad to reject Megan's offer. She had a little more than twelve weeks to plan and prepare her wedding. Let the full-on panic begin.

CHAPTER 3

Hours later, Doreen returned to the customer counter, preparing for Books & Bakery's lunch crowd. Her mood had improved somewhat after sharing breakfast with friends at the café.

"Doreen." Nessa Linden's arrival brought back some of her tension.

The Trinity Falls Town Council president stood on the other side of the café's counter. Nessa was a skinny woman of average height. Her bone-straight dark brown hair was styled in a conservative bob that framed her narrow face and swung above her thin shoulders. She'd coupled navy slacks and a matching jacket with a cream blouse.

"How are you, Nessa?" *And what are you doing here?* On the rare occasions the council president came to Books & Bakery, the encounters were not pleasant.

"I'd be happier if I didn't have to go to such lengths to meet with you to discuss town business." Nessa adjusted the strap of her brown handbag on her shoulder.

Doreen kept a firm grasp on her patience. "What do you mean?"

"It's only eleven o'clock in the morning." Nessa swept a hand to indicate the diner. "Do you think I like to take my lunch break an hour early just to speak with you?"

"I didn't ask you to." Doreen was confused. "I'm here from six in the morning until three in the afternoon. You can join me for coffee in the morning or take a later lunch."

"I shouldn't have to wait in line with your customers to discuss official town business."

"You're welcome to stop by my house on your way home from work." Doreen had just given Nessa three alternatives to an early lunch. Still the council president's features remained pinched in disapproval.

Nessa's brown eyes narrowed. "Are you sure you have time to be mayor?"

Doreen wasn't in the mood for the other woman's games. "How can I help you, Nessa?"

The council president straightened and looked down her nose at Doreen. "I've heard rumors that Alonzo plans to retire when his term ends in January. Is that true?"

"Rumors from whom?"

"Does that matter? Is Alonzo planning to retire?"

"You'll need to ask him." Doreen would neither confirm nor deny the rumors. Alonzo was her fiancé, but his retirement plans were his business to discuss. He'd announce them when he was ready. She wasn't going to do it for him.

"You don't know?" Nessa sounded skeptical. "You're

going to marry the man. Shouldn't you know his future plans, whether he's going to be gainfully employed?"

Doreen checked her silver and pearl Movado wristwatch. The item had been a gift from her son. It was almost half past eleven. The bread still had some time to bake in the oven. Pots of chicken noodle soup and New England clam chowder were both keeping warm on the stove. But she wouldn't be prepared for the lunch crowd until Nessa left. "Why are you asking about Alonzo's plans?"

"He's the town's sheriff." Nessa's laughter was condescending. "If he's decided not to run for another term, we should all be concerned. Don't you agree?"

"Even if Alonzo retired, the town won't be left without a sheriff." Doreen propped a hip against the counter. "Several people already have started campaigning for the position."

In her peripheral vision, Doreen noticed the increased number of customers browsing the titles on the bookstore's shelves as they made their way to the café. Lunch time.

Nessa followed Doreen's gaze. "Am I taking you away from something important?"

"We both work full-time jobs in addition to our responsibilities to the town."

"But along with your mayoral duties and your café, you're planning a wedding. How's that going, by the way?"

"Fine, thank you. Is there anything else I can do for you?" Doreen glanced behind Nessa toward her arriving customers. The older couple Megan had hired to help part-time at the café took their positions behind the cash register.

"Yes." Nessa checked her gold wristwatch. She glanced at the sign on the wall behind the counter, announcing the day's special. "I'll take a cup of chicken noodle soup and a half roast beef on rye to go. And you can add a Trinity Falls Fudge Walnut Brownie to that."

"I'll just be a moment." Doreen turned toward the kitchen. She exchanged greetings with her part-time assistants.

Minutes later, she returned to the register with a paper bag containing Nessa's soup, sandwich, and a slice of the brownie.

The council president met her at the register to pay for her lunch. "If we continue meeting here to discuss town matters, I'll become heavier and poorer. Is that your intent?"

Was Nessa making a joke? Doreen gave the other woman a smile and the benefit of the doubt. "I offered alternatives to lunch at the café."

"Those were convenient for you." Nessa accepted her change.

Doreen fisted her palm behind the register. "Let me know when you come up with something that better suits your schedule."

"I'll do that."

Doreen watched Nessa leave. She was tempted to write off the other woman as a miserable person whose mission in life was to be a thorn in the side of every Trinity Falls mayor. But Ramona McCloud, the former mayor, insisted Nessa had never given her any trouble.

Either Ramona was an exception to Nessa's plan or Nessa's mission was personal to Doreen. Had she done something to offend the council president?

The sound of a key in the front door lock Tuesday afternoon eased some of Benita's tension—only some. She stood in the archway between Ms. Helen's foyer and living room, waiting for her great-aunt to walk through the door.

"Where have you been?" Benita strained to keep an even tone.

Ms. Helen froze with her hand on the doorknob. She stared at Benita as though she'd never seen her before. "Who are you? My mother?" The older woman locked the door, muttering about family members who acted like prison guards.

"I got back from lunch at Books and Bakery, and you weren't here." Benita tracked Ms. Helen's progress across the foyer and through the living room. She followed her great-aunt into the kitchen. "You didn't leave a note. I didn't know where you were or when you'd be back."

"You live in Los Angeles. You never know where I am or when I'll be back." Ms. Helen crossed to the stove and plucked the tea kettle from the front burner. She carried it to the sink. "Why is today different?"

"Because, for the next month, I'm living with you in your house." Benita wondered if her head would explode. She'd never been so worried as when she'd come home and found her great-aunt missing. "The next time you leave the house when I'm not home, could you please leave me a note so I know where you are?"

"No." Ms. Helen filled the kettle with water from the faucet, then returned it to the front burner. "Would you like some tea?"

Benita caught her breath. *No?* "What do you mean no?"

"No, I won't write a note when I leave the house whether or not you're home." Ms. Helen turned on the flame beneath the kettle. "Tea? I won't ask again."

"Yes, please." Benita crossed to the kitchen table. She drummed her fingers on its surface. What could she say to convince her great-aunt not to disappear without a trace in the future? "Why won't you leave me a note?"

"I know you, Benny. Next you'll want to know who I'm with, what I'm doing, and when I'll be back. You and I aren't doing that." Ms. Helen pulled tea bags, sweeteners, mugs, and teaspoons from the cupboards and drawers. "I'm not asking you to let me know where you are every minute of the day. I'd appreciate the same respect."

"This isn't a matter of respect. It's about your safety." Benita sighed her frustration. "I'm not an elderly woman, wandering the town alone. I can look after myself."

"So can I." Ms. Helen leaned against the counter beside the stove. Her obstinate look conveyed her refusal to be reasoned with.

Benita dropped the subject. For now. "How was your afternoon?"

"Is this where you pump me for information?" Ms. Helen gave her a knowing smile. "I was at the Guiding Light Community Center."

"I could've taken you there, if I'd known you were going." *Subtle?*

Ms. Helen arched a thin gray brow. "I have a car. I drove myself."

Stubborn. Benita struggled with a smile. She admired her great-aunt. She liked to think she'd inherited some of Ms. Helen's determination. "Did you have lunch with friends?"

"You could say that." The kettle whistled. Ms. Helen turned off the stove and filled the mugs with hot water. "I had a lunch meeting with Vaughn and the center's director."

Vaughn. The sound of his name made her heart leap like a schoolgirl with a painful crush. "What was the meeting about?"

"Vaughn wants to produce a play at the center." Ms. Helen carried the two mugs of tea to the table. She handed one to Benita before sitting.

"What kind of play?" The scent of lemons rose from the steaming mug. Vaughn had been composing songs for a script. As far as she knew, he wasn't anywhere near finished, though.

"It's a musical." Ms. Helen stirred sweetener into her tea.

"A musical?" Benita froze. Her mind went blank.

"It makes sense." Ms. Helen sipped her tea. "He's a band director."

Benita's tea was forgotten. Her mind spun with questions, almost too many to hold. *When had he finished his musical? How was he going to produce it? Who was*

*going to assist him with it? What can I do to help him?
Why hadn't he told me?*

"I knew about his musical." Benita poured two packets of sweetener into her mug. Her hands barely trembled. "He's been working on it for years. I just hadn't realized he'd finished it. Or that he hoped to perform it at the community center."

"It sounds interesting. The story's based on Caribbean folklore."

"It's a love story about a mortal man, a farmer, who falls in love with a water fairy. The villain is a water spirit, Mama D'Leau, who's part woman and part serpent." Benita drank her tea. It helped.

Ms. Helen took another sip. "He's holding an audition April twenty-second."

Sadness twisted into temper. Benita shook her head in disbelief. "He used to talk about his script all the time. I just don't understand why he didn't tell me he'd finally finished it."

"I do." Ms. Helen shrugged. "He spends time with you maybe three weeks out of the year."

Benita's eyes widened. She released her mug and spread her hands. "We call each other all the time. We e-mail. We even Skype."

"And you think that sustains a relationship?" Ms. Helen leaned into the table. "He's not leaving Trinity Falls and you're not leaving Los Angeles, so what kind of a relationship do you really have?"

"I've asked him to move to L.A. with me."

"And he's asked you to come home to Trinity Falls." Ms. Helen sat back, shaking her head with apparent disappointment. "Relationships are about compromises. One of you is going to have to compromise and I think it should be you."

Benita's lips parted with shock. "Why me?" She could have sworn her great-aunt supported her need to follow her dream.

"Everyone you love and everything you care about is in this town."

"What about my career?"

"You don't enjoy it nearly as much as you pretend."

Am I really that transparent? Benita dropped her gaze to the table. "How did you know?"

"You didn't plan a month's stay in Trinity Falls just to help me celebrate my upcoming endowed chair." Ms. Helen pushed back her chair and crossed to the sink. "You're here to decide what you want to do now and where you want to do it."

"I know where I want to live." Benita regarded the tiny woman's back.

Ms. Helen washed her mug, then set it on her drain board. "You may think you do."

Benita watched her great-aunt leave the kitchen. The woman thought she knew everything. That was a family trait. Ms. Helen was right that Benita had grown increasingly disenchanted with her career as an entertainment lawyer and celebrity business manager. But she was wrong if she thought Benita had changed her mind about living in L.A. She intended to put down roots there. What did she need to do to convince Vaughn to join her?

* * *

"I'm announcing my retirement in December."
Alonzo watched as surprise, confusion, then disappointment swept across Deputy Juan Ramirez's tan features.

The two men sat in Alonzo's office Wednesday morning drinking coffee. Juan sat in one of the gray visitor's
chairs on the other side of his desk. He'd worked with the
younger man for three years, since he'd been elected
sheriff. In that time, they'd become friends.

"Is this your April Fool's joke? It's not funny." Juan
cradled his white coffee mug against his torso.

"It's not April Fool's Day." It was only Wednesday,
March twenty-fifth. The muscles twisting in Alonzo's
gut eased as he thought of his retirement. "And I'm not
joking. I'm serious."

"I can't believe you're planning to retire. Are you
sure?"

"I'm sixty-six years old. I've earned it." Alonzo lowered his gaze to his coffee. He was using one of the
sheriff's office's mismatched ceramic mugs. This one
was black. It was easier not to be distracted by coffee
stains in your mug when you couldn't see them.

"Sixty-six isn't dead, Sheriff." Juan straightened on
the chair. "Why do you want to retire?"

"I thought you'd be happy." Alonzo grinned at the
deputy, whose youthful features belied his thirty-seven
years of age. "Now you won't have to campaign against
me to remove this old man from office and make room
for more youthful energy and ideas."

"I don't want to be sheriff." Juan snorted a laugh.

"You should consider it." Alonzo sobered. "You'd make
a good one."

"We have a good one." Juan spread his arms. "Marrying Doreen doesn't mean you have to give up your career."

"I'm ready to start this new chapter of my life."

"What's in it?"

"Making myself worthy of Doreen."

"What do you mean?"

He'd said more than he'd intended. But maybe another law enforcement officer could understand. Alonzo settled his gaze on a corner of his office and let his mind play scenes from his past. "Doreen has spent her whole life helping to build this community. She's served on committees to raise money for the schools, the volunteer fire department. She led the Sesquicentennial Celebration Committee."

"She pushed for a lot of improvements in the town, including the lights in Freedom Park." Juan shifted on his chair. "But what does that have to do with you?"

"She's helped people." Alonzo heaved a sigh. "I've hurt people, a lot of them."

"You've protected communities." Juan's tone was firm.

"At what cost?" Alonzo wiped his hand across his brow. Gun battles, screams, death, and blood—that's what he had to live with, thanks to his past.

"I know you've seen a lot more action than I have. But I also know that everything you've done was to protect people in the communities you served."

"There's blood on my hands, Juan." Alonzo's voice was low. "Until I wash them clean, I won't feel worthy of someone like Doreen."

"You're a good man, Sheriff." Juan's words were adamant. "I know that and so does Doreen."

"Doreen doesn't know about my past." Alonzo sighed again. He should have confessed everything to her before he'd proposed. That would have been the honorable thing to do before asking her to spend the rest of her life with him. But he hadn't had the courage to take the risk.

"Then tell her." Juan shrugged his broad shoulders. "You'll see that her opinion of you won't change. She loves you."

Alonzo's gaze slid away. Would she still love him once she knew about his past?

CHAPTER 4

"So, who's going to sit in my chair?" Ms. Helen settled onto one of the four crimson red cushioned seats ringing the small honey wood circular conversation table in Dr. Foster Gooden's office.

It was the last Friday morning in March. Benita had joined Foster and Ms. Helen at Trinity Falls University to discuss the endowed chemistry chair a wealthy alumna was gifting to the university in Ms. Helen's honor.

Benita sat beside her great-aunt and allowed her gaze to roam the room. The vice president for academic affairs' office was modest in size, masculine in appearance, and compulsive in order. A thin layer of anxiety covered the office as though all was not as well with the university as the administration would have you believe.

She turned away from her perusal of Foster's family photographs. He'd sacrificed one whole bookshelf to the captured memories.

Benita grinned at Ms. Helen. "'The Doctor Helen Gaston Endowed Chemistry Chair.' This is a tremendous honor, not just for my great-aunt but for our entire family."

Ms. Helen squeezed Benita's left hand where it lay on the table beside her. Her voice swelled with laughter. "If it's such an honor for the family, why are you the only one here?"

"Everyone else is afraid of you." Benita slid the older lady a look. "You told us not to come. I'm the only one who didn't listen."

Foster chuckled. "We're glad you could make it, Benita." He turned to Ms. Helen. "We haven't made a formal announcement to the faculty about the chair yet. We want you to be present for the announcement and involved in selecting the professor for the position."

The vice president's consideration for her great-aunt warmed Benita. "That's very thoughtful of you, Doctor Gooden. Thank you."

Ms. Helen spoke over Benita, waving a dismissive hand. "That's not necessary, Foster. You and the science division chair can select the professor."

Foster shook his head. "We want your input, Doctor Gaston. So does the donor."

"Well, that's just ridiculous." Ms. Helen's gaze moved from Foster to Benita, then back. "It's kind of her to offer the endowment. And I'm honored that she's named it after me. But you and the science division chair know your faculty. You can choose someone without my input."

Benita only half heard her great-aunt's objections. "What can you tell us about this donor? She sounds very interesting."

"Doctor Lana Penn was one of Doctor Gaston's students." Foster nodded toward Ms. Helen. "She's now founder, president, and chief chemical engineer of Penn

Research Laboratories, an international pharmaceutical research company. She credits Doctor Gaston with her success."

Benita gaped at her great-aunt. "I've heard of Penn Research Laboratories."

Ms. Helen shrugged. "You and at least three and a half billion other people, half the population of the world."

Benita blew an impatient breath. "But you were her chemistry professor. She said *you're* the reason for her success."

"Baloney." Ms. Helen sucked her teeth. "*She's* the reason for her success. I didn't earn her doctorate; she did. I didn't found Penn Research Laboratories; she did."

Foster raised his hands. "We can argue to what extent you affected her success, but the fact is she credits you for it." He let his hands fall to the table. "Because of that, she's offered the university a lot of money, including the endowed chemistry chair."

"I've toured the campus recently. The university can use her generosity." Ms. Helen's tone was dry.

The TFU vice president shifted on his seat. "Yes, well, many colleges and universities are going through difficult financial times. Enrollment is down around the country, especially here in the Midwest."

Benita turned to her great-aunt. "If all she's asking in exchange is that you identify the professor for the endowed chair, you should do it. It's a small request."

"Actually, that's not all she's asking." Foster folded his hands. "She wants to host a banquet in your honor in recognition of the endowment."

Ms. Helen began shaking her head even before Foster finished speaking. "No fuss, Foster."

"But Doctor Gaston—"

"I said no fuss." Ms. Helen shrugged her purse onto her shoulder and stood.

Benita tugged her great-aunt's arm to pull her back to her seat. "Aunt Helen, I didn't travel the twenty-four hundred miles from L.A. to Trinity Falls just to sit in Foster's office with you. No offense, Foster."

"None taken." Foster raised both hands again.

Ms. Helen crossed her arms. "I told you not to come."

"And I told you having an endowed chair named after you is a big deal." Benita grabbed hold of her patience.

"You're the one who's making it a big deal, not me." Ms. Helen was the embodiment of obstinacy.

Benita wasn't fazed. "Did it ever occur to you that this banquet isn't just about you? It's about the university and Doctor Penn as well. She wants to host an event in your honor. Give her a break and let her do it."

Ms. Helen opened her mouth to argue. Benita arched a challenging brow.

Ms. Helen looked away. "I'll think about it. I'm not making any promises."

Benita nodded. "Fair enough."

Foster looked from Ms. Helen to Benita with an expression of amazement. "Well, all right. Great. Just so you know, Doctor Penn will be here on April seventeenth to discuss the endowed chair and the banquet."

"I'll check my calendar." Ms. Helen sniffed.

"Aunt Helen, that's three weeks from now." Benita stood and looked to Foster. "We're free. Just let us know the time and location."

Foster rose to his feet. "Ladies, thank you for coming. I'm looking forward to working with both of you as well as Doctor Penn to launch the Doctor Helen Gaston Endowed Chemistry Chair."

Ms. Helen grunted. "I'm sure you are."

"I'm glad you were here." Foster spoke to Benita in a low tone. "I don't think I could have convinced her to even consider the banquet. Doctor Gaston is a very strong personality."

Benita turned back to Foster as Ms. Helen left his office without her. "You mean stubborn. It'll be an interesting couple of weeks." She turned to track down her great-aunt.

Ms. Helen was right outside Foster's door. She gave Benita a cool look from sharp ebony eyes. "If you're done managing my schedule, can we leave now?"

Benita led Ms. Helen down the stairs. "Aunt Helen, Doctor Penn is traveling hundreds of miles and giving the university a great deal of money. You can give her one hour of your time."

She fell into step beside Ms. Helen as they crossed the hallway to the exit. The walls were covered with brochures detailing student services and posters promoting education abroad trips, seminars, and presentations. She pushed through the exit at the end of the hallway and held the door for Ms. Helen to join her.

Her great-aunt stopped beside Benita's rental car. She freed her smartphone from her purse. "I need to text Alonzo. There's no need for his standing noon check-in today." She spoke as she tapped her keypad. "I don't want him to convene a search party or call highway patrol when I'm not there."

Benita fished her car keys from her handbag. "I thought his visits were too predictable."

"They are. And so are Megan and Ean's, Doreen's and Darius's daily visits." Ms. Helen dropped her smartphone back into her purse, then turned toward the heart of the university, its Oval.

"Where are you going?" Benita fisted her car key and hurried after the older woman.

"I want to stop by Vaughn's office before going home." The retired professor spoke over her shoulder as she started across the Oval toward another academic building.

"Aunt Helen, I didn't realize you wanted to pay visits to university professors while we were here." Benita's muscles chilled with the thought of seeing Vaughn now. *I'm not ready!*

"Well, now you know." Ms. Helen didn't slow down nor did she look at Benita. She just kept walking.

Benita was growing desperate. It wouldn't take long to reach Freeman Hall and Vaughn's office. The Oval wasn't large. "It's only eleven o'clock. He's probably in class."

"No, I called before we came to TFU. He's expecting us."

He's expecting us? I wasn't expecting him. Benita was momentarily speechless. The building drew closer and closer. "Why didn't you tell me you wanted to meet with him?"

"Because I knew you'd overreact. I didn't want to deal with it until I absolutely had to." Ms. Helen paused to face Benita. "Vaughn and I are still friends even though the two of you aren't together anymore."

Benita fisted her palms to keep from wringing her hands. "Aunt Helen, I'm sorry, but I'm not ready to see him."

Ms. Helen jerked her chin toward the west side of campus. "Then buy yourself a cup of tea at the student center. I won't be long."

Benita wanted to take this easy way out. She wasn't proud of that. "Are you sure?"

"I'm sure." Her great-aunt raised her hand and cupped Benita's left cheek. "You'll do this when you're ready."

Benita raised her eyes toward Freeman Hall in the near distance. Vaughn was waiting inside. She could picture him, his long, leanly muscled body seated behind his old-fashioned wooden desk. His movie star good looks and soap-and-cedar scent. Her palms itched to caress his smooth nutmeg skin and handsome goatee. She wanted to taste him again.

Benita stepped back. Her great-aunt's hand dropped away. "I'll take your suggestion and get that cup of tea."

She turned and hurried toward the student center. She'd see Vaughn again. Trinity Falls was way too small to imagine she wouldn't. Hopefully, she'd be stronger when they ran into each other. At least stronger than she was today—because the next time she saw him, she intended to win him back.

CHAPTER 5

"You've been pretty quiet lately. Is everything OK?" Doreen attempted a casual tone as she and Alonzo tidied the dining room and kitchen after dinner Friday night.

She closely watched her fiancé of more than three months. This wasn't the first time she'd asked him about his sudden and uncharacteristic brooding. He probably wouldn't be any more forthcoming today than he'd been the other four times. Still it was worth a try.

"Everything's fine." Alonzo's faint smile wasn't reflected in his coffee eyes. "I'm just tired."

Doreen swallowed a sigh. Men. Why was it they always thought they had to deal with their problems alone? She changed the subject. "I bought my wedding dress today."

"That's nice."

A bit more enthusiasm wouldn't have been unseemly. She led him from the kitchen to the family room where she'd laid out her lists, pamphlets, and schedule for their wedding plans. "Have you rented your tuxedo?"

"Not yet."

Her tension began to build. Doreen took a deep, cleansing breath. "When do you think you'll get to that?"

"Soon."

"That's what you said last week." Doreen settled onto the sofa. Alonzo sat beside her. "I'm confused. I thought you wanted to get married in June. That's just under three months from now and all we've done is send out save-the-date cards."

"I'm sorry. I'll look for a tux tomorrow." He sounded contrite, but Doreen was still suspicious. She'd heard it all before. *Is he having cold feet?*

Doreen shook off the irrational fear and handed Alonzo the estimated wedding budget. "I've contacted companies and put together this estimate for our wedding. It includes the church, hall, catering, decorations, everything."

Alonzo took the sheet from her. His reaction came more quickly than she'd anticipated. "Why does it cost so much?"

"Because it does." Doreen shifted on the sofa to face him. "Are you ready to elope?"

Alonzo scowled as he gave back the sheet. "I admit it's a lot of money, but I can afford it."

"Is there anything you'd like to add—"

"No. That's plenty." Alonzo rubbed the back of his neck. "But I do have one request."

"What is it?"

"I'd like to make our wedding different from yours and Paul's."

Doreen nodded. Her voice was gentle. "I understand. Do you have any ideas?"

"No."

That's not especially helpful. "We don't have a lot of time, Alonzo."

"I know."

"I'd welcome any and all suggestions you might have."

"All right."

"Because if you don't have any suggestions for the wedding you wanted to have in three months, then I'm going to suggest that we postpone it."

"I want you to move in with me."

Doreen frowned. She hadn't been expecting that. Where had it come from? "I meant suggestions for our wedding."

"I'm talking about after our wedding."

Was this about Paul again?

Doreen's gaze drifted around the family room. Its fluffy mauve and white sofa, matching love seat and chair, its maple wood coffee table and hardwood trim. There were memories here, memories that fresh paint and new furniture couldn't pack away.

"I understand why you don't want to start our life in the home I shared with Paul." Doreen held Alonzo's troubled gaze. "If the situation were reversed, I wouldn't want to live in the home you'd created with your deceased spouse, either. But if we move into your home, we're going to have to redecorate. Your color scheme is too depressing."

The twinkle returned to Alonzo's eyes. "Deal."

"Good. Then could we return to our wedding plans, please?"

"I don't want to postpone our wedding." His expression sobered.

"Alonzo, June twentieth is almost three months away." Doreen gestured toward the wedding budget she'd returned to the coffee table. "Do you see the list of things we still have to do?"

"*Mi amor,* we'll get it done."

"You're not going to get around me with your sexy Spanish endearments." Doreen rose to her feet. "You haven't even rented your tux."

Alonzo stood, too. "I'll do that tomorrow."

"You've been saying that for weeks."

He took her hands in his warm, strong, rough ones. "I promise. We'll even get the rings."

Doreen's mad was righteous and justified. She didn't want to let go of it. But the warmth of his body, the touch of his skin, his soap-and-shaving-cream scent battered against the stone facade of her temper.

She deepened her scowl. "If you don't get your tuxedo and the rings tomorrow, I'm postponing the wedding."

"Deal."

Alonzo lowered his lips to hers. Doreen slid her arms up his shoulders. Her mad disintegrated beneath the passion of his kiss. Beyond their wedding plans and where they'd live after, this is what they were protecting. Alonzo deepened their kiss. Her body responded. She wouldn't let anyone or anything come between them.

After church Sunday morning, Doreen enjoyed a cup of chai tea with her son in her kitchen. She considered the man Ean had become as he sat on the other side of the circular honey wood table. He looked so much more relaxed than he'd been when he'd first returned home almost two years ago. He'd been tense and out of sorts when he'd left his law firm in New York. Coming home to Trinity Falls had been good for him; so had Megan McCloud.

"When are you going to make me a grandmother?" Doreen battled back laughter as Ean nearly choked on his tea.

"Don't you think Megan and I should get married first?" Ean answered between coughs.

"That would be my preference." Doreen masked her excitement with a thoughtful tone. Ean obviously had been thinking of a future with Megan. *Yes!* "So when are you going to propose?"

"Mom, how about we get through one family wedding at a time?"

That seemed fair.

Doreen lowered her mug onto the table. Her pulse was jumping. Her nerves were on edge. As much as she dreaded making her announcement, she couldn't put off the reason she'd asked Ean to stop by.

She gripped the warm, white porcelain mug between her palms and breathed in. "Speaking of what comes after marriage, Alonzo and I have been talking about where we'll live once we're married."

"What have you decided?" A cautious look entered Ean's eyes. *He knew.*

Doreen was swamped with guilt. Her gaze swept the kitchen. She loved this room with its natural light, cheery yellow walls, and bright white trim. She treasured the memories it kept, not just those of raising her family but of welcoming friends. Doreen's lips curved in a soft smile. It had been in this room that Alonzo made his first romantic overture to her.

She tucked those images aside. "Alonzo and I have agreed to move into his house. I'm going to put our home on the market."

"That's sensible. Our house is paid off. The profit from the sale would all go to you." Ean's gaze roamed the room as though seeking his own memories. *What did he find?*

Yes, their decision made sense, but Doreen could feel Ean's disappointment. "I'll split the money from the sale with you. That's what your father would've wanted."

"Keep it." Ean shook his head. "Thanks for the offer, but Megan and I are doing well. You're the one who's been taking care of the house."

"But—"

"Or, if you can't think of anything better to do with it, invest it for your grandchild's law school education." Ean rose from the table, taking his mug with him. He paused beside Doreen, kissed the top of her head, and collected her mug as well. He carried both to the sink.

"Don't tease me about grandchildren." Doreen picked up his cue to lighten the mood. She turned on her chair to keep Ean in sight.

"Spoilsport." Ean leaned his hips against the kitchen counter.

Doreen tossed him a grin. "Thank you for understanding our decision to sell the house."

"I'm sure it wasn't an easy one." Ean shoved his hands into the front pockets of his tan Dockers.

"No, it wasn't."

"There are a lot of memories in this house."

Doreen nodded in the general direction of the front door. "This is the house you grew up in. Your father and I carried you through that door."

Ean frowned. "You both did?"

"Yes, I carried you through first. Then passed you back to your father and he carried you through." She blushed as Ean's eyebrows rose. "Wait until you have my first grandchild—then you'll understand."

"Maybe." Ean returned to the kitchen table. "Some of my favorite memories are of Dad and me helping you with the Thanksgiving baking."

Doreen grinned as the images moved across her mind. "The Fever Family Thanksgiving Bake-offs."

The night before Thanksgiving, they'd gather in the kitchen. Christmas music would blare from the speakers so loudly, they had to shout to hear each other. They'd dance around the kitchen. Paul and Ean would give her ingredients while she mixed the batters. Their antics were so distracting that the baking actually took longer. But it had been worth it.

"You and Alonzo will create memories in your new home." Ean stretched out his legs and crossed them at the ankles.

"That's the plan."

"Then what's wrong?" Ean knew her too well.

"Something has been bothering Alonzo for months, but he won't tell me what it is. I've asked him several times. He always says he's tired. I'm at my wit's end."

"Do you want me to ask him?"

"No, thank you." Doreen shook her head. "We need

to work out our problems ourselves. I just wish I knew what his was."

"When did you first notice something was wrong?"

Doreen set her right elbow on the table and cupped her chin in her palm. "Shortly after we started planning our wedding."

"I thought he was in a rush to get married."

"He says he still is."

"But you don't believe him." Ean sounded like the lawyer he was.

Doreen shrugged off her discomfort. "I had to threaten him with postponing the wedding to get him to order a tux."

"It's a good sign that he chose to order the tux rather than postpone the wedding."

"Is it?" Doreen met his gaze.

"What do you mean?"

Doreen bit her lips. Saying the words would give the fear power. "What if he's decided that it was a mistake to propose to me? What if he really *doesn't* want to marry me?"

"Mom, that's ridiculous."

Is it? "I'm open to other suggestions."

She was at her wit's end. She'd given Alonzo plenty of opportunities to share what was on his mind. She'd even asked him directly if he was having second thoughts. If he didn't confide to her the reason for his distant behavior, she was considering making the unilateral decision to postpone their wedding—if she could get her heart to agree.

* * *

"I'm going to need help coordinating the play." Vaughn Brooks followed Darius to one of the few available tables in Books & Bakery's café Tuesday.

It was lunchtime and the place was packed. Employees from local businesses, and students, staff, and faculty from Trinity Falls University were looking to console their sorrows over the start of a new week with Doreen's famous Trinity Falls Fudge Walnut Brownies.

"I had a feeling you might." Darius spoke over his shoulder as he closed in on the table for two. "A production that ambitious is more than a one-man show."

"I gave it my best shot." Vaughn lowered himself onto a chair at the small, white, rectangular table. He was glad Darius had snagged the spot before anyone else had claimed it. "There's a lot to do: scheduling, auditions, costumes, props."

"Not to mention promoting the performance and managing the ticket orders." Darius bit into his turkey-and-cheddar-on-wheat sandwich.

"I was thinking of asking Peyton again. She turned me down the first time." Vaughn scooped his spoon through his chicken-and-wild-rice soup.

"Why?" Darius paused with his iced tea halfway to his mouth.

"She said she didn't have experience with theater performances. But she did a great job with the fund-raising event for the Guiding Light Community Center."

Vaughn studied Darius for his reaction to his request. This past fall, *The Trinity Falls Monitor*'s managing editor had thought Vaughn and Peyton were dating. In truth, Vaughn was one of several Trinity Falls residents who were matchmaking Darius and Trinity Falls University's newest faculty member. Now that Darius and Peyton were the latest happy couple in their little town, did the newspaper man harbor any lingering resentments toward him?

Darius sipped his drink. "You're right. Peyton did a great job on the charity dance. The entire fund-raising committee worked really hard and raised a lot of money for the center."

Vaughn appreciated Darius's generous words since he was one of the members of the fund-raising committee. "Do you think I could convince her to help with the play?"

"Under different circumstances, probably. But as you know, TFU hasn't replaced Ken Hartford yet." Darius mentioned the recently retired head of the Department of History. "That means all of the history professors are carrying extra courses and advising additional students. Her plate's pretty full right now."

"I hadn't thought about that." Vaughn looked down at his bowl of soup and his half chicken-and-pepper-jack-cheese-on-wheat sandwich. He wanted to produce this musical. But to do it well, he needed help; someone who was meticulous, well organized, who could multitask and manage difficult people. Someone like Peyton, but with an edge.

"I know someone who could help you." Darius's words were like lifelines thrown to a drowning man.

"Who?" Hope sprang anew.

"Benita Hawkins."

Time slowed to a crawl. Vaughn's blood roared in his ears. His pulse pounded in his throat. In their past, the idea of working with Benita had filled him with excitement.

Now there was dread mixed with enthusiasm. He'd thought he'd see her again last Friday. Ms. Helen and Benita had been on TFU's campus that morning. But Ms. Helen had stopped by his office alone. Obviously, Benita was avoiding him. Even if he could see himself working with her, would she want anything to do with him?

"That wouldn't be a good idea." Vaughn made himself swallow more soup.

"Why not? Benita has experience managing performers and performances. She's meticulous, organized, and can handle challenging personalities. You've seen her in action."

Vaughn looked away. "I know. We've worked together before."

"And the two of you make a good team. Ask her to help with your play." Darius finished his sandwich and started on his soup.

"I don't think she'd agree." Vaughn sensed Darius's dark eyes boring into his forehead as though the journalist was trying to read his mind.

"Because you're no longer hooking up with her?"

The stinging burn of a flush traveled under Vaughn's skin. He shook his head in disgust. "How many other people know?"

"This is Trinity Falls. It's easier to count who doesn't know."

Vaughn looked around the Books & Bakery café. He and Benita had grown up in this town, alongside a lot of friends and neighbors who were still here. Their past was well known. He hadn't realized their present had been equally well observed.

"We've broken up for good this time." Vaughn returned to his soup.

"Sorry to hear that." Darius didn't sound as though he believed Vaughn.

"So am I."

He wasn't going to explain to his childhood friend his reasons for breaking up with Benita. He could trust Darius to keep his confidence. He just wasn't comfortable telling the other man that he was tired of being Benita's sexual toy; he wanted more.

Darius finished off his soup. "You made a great team in high school."

"This isn't high school." Volunteering on high school plays and musicals is what sparked their relationship. "How anxious would you be to work with an ex-girlfriend?"

"I'd hate it. But we aren't talking about me. Producing this musical has been your dream."

"I'll find someone else to help me."

"Our usual go-to people are tapped out. Peyton's carrying an extra course load. Doreen's planning her wedding and has her mayoral duties. Megan has extra work with the café. Ramona's in Philadelphia."

A pulse beat in Vaughn's temple as Darius counted off all the people who couldn't help him. "What about you?"

Darius gave Vaughn a dubious look. "I'm not your usual go-to person. Jackson's back at the paper and still remodeling the cabins, and Ean's useless."

Darius had a point. Still . . . "Benita and I can't work together, not so soon after breaking up."

"It'll be awkward at first. But by opening night, you'll either be over her or engaged."

Vaughn doubted he'd ever get over Benita Hawkins. Working with her on his musical wasn't a matter of a few awkward moments. It was about losing his heart again and again every minute he was with her. Was his dream worth that kind of torture?

CHAPTER 6

The knock on his open door at the end of Tuesday asked for Vaughn's attention. He lifted his head and found Dr. Olivia Stark framed in his threshold. He stood.

The biology professor crossed hesitantly into his office. "Am I interrupting?"

"No, come in." Vaughn gestured toward his laptop. "I'm just wrapping up for the day."

Olivia was neat and professional in her dark blue coatdress. The professor's appearance was the opposite of Benita in almost every way. She was tall and lithe. Benita was petite with slender curves. Olivia's brown hair was a sleek, bone-straight bob. Benita's hair was a thick chestnut mass that fell in unruly waves to her shoulders. Olivia's voice was as clear as a church bell. Benita's smoky tones shared naughty secrets.

"How was your day?" Olivia drifted onto one of the blue guest chairs in front of his desk.

Vaughn cut off thoughts of Benita and sat. "My classes went well. Thanks. How were yours?"

They'd spent hours together this past winter working

on the community center's fund-raising committee. He'd thought their shared experiences had gotten them past the nice-weather-we're-having conversations. What had caused them to suddenly regress?

"They were fun." Olivia's face lit up with her smile.

"That's great." He'd never considered that biology classes could be fun.

"I was wondering . . ." Olivia paused. Her gaze slid away.

"What is it?" Vaughn grew uneasy. What was on her mind?

Olivia crossed her long legs and folded her hands on her lap. "I enjoyed working with you on the fund-raising committee. It was work. But with you, it was fun work. Do you know what I mean?"

Why is she so nervous? Vaughn offered her what he hoped was a calming smile. "I'm glad one of us knew what we were supposed to do. If it wasn't for you, we never would've been able to pull it off."

"Maybe we could have lunch sometime. Together." Her brown eyes wavered. "The two of us."

She wasn't asking him as a friend. Her deepening blush and white-knuckled grip told him that. Vaughn shifted on his chair. No one had ever asked him out before. He searched for gentle words to explain he wasn't interested in a relationship—then his mind screeched to a halt.

Why not?

He didn't have to consider Benita. They'd broken up and he didn't harbor any hope of a reconciliation. The realization once again struck him like a blade through his chest. He'd loved her so hard for so long. When would this heartache end? Possibly never.

Vaughn breathed through the pain. "I'd like that."

Clouds cleared from Olivia's heart-shaped face. She gave him a smile brilliant with relief, excitement, and joy. It was humbling.

"Are you free Thursday?" Olivia rose. "I don't have any afternoon classes."

Vaughn stood as well. "Thursday works for me." *Why do I feel like a cheater?*

"Maybe we can go someplace off campus. My treat."

"You don't have to pay."

"I'll pay because I asked you. You can pay next time, if you ask me." With that, she turned and disappeared through his door.

Benita called him old fashioned. Some habits—standing when a woman entered a room, holding the door, and paying for your date—died hard.

Vaughn lowered himself onto his chair and stared at his computer. But he was too distracted to concentrate. The e-mail on his monitor was a blur. Superimposed on the unfocused words were Benita's wide hazel gaze and full, parted lips. *Dammit!* Vaughn scrubbed his eyes with the heels of his hands. He wasn't cheating on her. They'd broken up. He was free to see other people now.

And so is she.

Dammit!

Benita caught a movement in her peripheral vision Wednesday morning. Ms. Helen was on the move. The modest heels of her cream pumps were silent as they carried her across her living room's thick emerald carpet. Her great-aunt's butter yellow skirt suit skimmed her thin figure. Its hem ended just past her knees. Her matching hat served as a decoration rather than a purpose.

Benita tuned back to her cellular phone and her client's latest complaints against her recording company. "Electra, let me get started on the items you've already given me. Once the label has shown good faith in resolving those, we'll give them the rest."

But Electra Day, her chart-topping, pop-singing-sensation client, continued to list her label's latest sins and transgressions. Benita listened, growing increasingly impatient. Her bronze Movado wristwatch showed it wasn't quite nine o'clock in the morning in Trinity Falls. Benita clenched her teeth. From Los Angeles, Electra had called to enumerate her grievances well before six A.M. But Electra wasn't an early riser. This meant the singer hadn't been to bed yet. She was tired and not making much sense. Later, she might not even remember this call.

Benita only half listened to her client. She was more interested in the belongings her great-aunt was sorting. Ms. Helen dropped some items into her purse. Others, she packed into a tote bag.

What is she up to?

Benita marked the time again. Enough was enough. Electra had two minutes to wrap up her diatribe before Benita cut off the sleepy young woman. She wanted to serve her client's interests, but she was anxious to learn where her great-aunt was going.

Time's up.

"Electra, I've got to go. Get some sleep. I'll e-mail you once I've heard back from Silas. Bye." Benita closed her cell phone and turned to her great-aunt. "You look beautiful. Where are you going?"

"To Guiding Light." Ms. Helen hoisted her tote bag and purse onto her shoulder.

"I'll drive you."

"I'd rather you didn't. You smell like you just ran five miles." Ms. Helen gave her a pained look, taking in her running shoes, pants, and shirt.

Benita wasn't offended. She *had* just run five miles, from her great-aunt's house, through nearby Freedom Park, and back. She was growing chilled as her body cooled in her sopping wet clothes.

"It'll take me fifteen minutes to shower and dress."

"Are you going to the center?" Ms. Helen frowned in confusion.

"No, but it wouldn't be any trouble for me to drive you there."

"But it would be inconvenient for me to wait for you to get cleaned up. You'll make me late for my appointment."

"Call whoever you're meeting to let them know you're going to be late."

"I'm not going to do that." Ms. Helen looked scandalized. "Why do you want to drive me to the community center anyway?"

Benita wrapped her arms around her waist. She was starting to shiver from the chill. "It's not safe for you to drive."

Ms. Helen's eyebrows leaped in surprise. "Why not?"

"Aunt Helen, you're older now. Your reflexes aren't as good as they used to be. It's safer for me to drive you, not just for you but for other drivers on the road."

Ms. Helen gave her a blank look. "So you're saying you *should* drive me?"

"That's right."

"How would I get home?"

"I'll pick you up." Benita's enthusiasm for her plan was growing. "Just call me whenever you're ready to leave. I don't have any appointments today. I'm at your disposal."

"Really?" Ms. Helen nodded. "So I should wait while you clean up and get dressed now. Then I should wait again—like a sack of potatoes—for you to come and collect me."

It was faint, but Benita didn't miss the note of irritation in her great-aunt's voice. "I don't mean to offend you, Aunt Helen. I'm concerned for your safety."

"And the other drivers on the road." Ms. Helen crossed her arms. "Benita, when you're not here, do you think I sit in the house all day, wallowing in my dotage?"

"No, I—"

"That was a rhetorical question." The older lady cocked her head. "I've achieved an age in which I can go wherever I want to go, whenever I want to go. And I don't need you to take me there." Ms. Helen spun on her modest heels and strode to the door.

"Aunt Helen—"

"I won't be home for lunch, Benny." Her great-aunt called over her shoulder. "So don't wait for me."

Chilled on the inside and outside, Benita watched Ms. Helen walk out the front door.

How can I convince the stubborn woman that I'm not trying to cramp her lifestyle? I'm trying to keep her safe.

It would be a lot easier if her great-aunt weren't always flitting around. Benita mounted the staircase on her way to take a shower and clean up.

She'd supposedly retired fifteen years ago. But Aunt Helen has more meetings, appointments, and

working lunches than most top-level recording company
executives I know.

At loose ends about three hours later, Benita wandered
into Books & Bakery in search of great company and a
good lunch. It was barely noon on a Wednesday, yet the
café was packed. Impressive.

She made her way to the counter. The line was long
but moved briskly. Within minutes, hers was the next
order up.

"Benita, it's nice to see you." Doreen's brown eyes
twinkled with welcome. She looked happy but tired.
"What can I get for you?"

Benita checked the soup of the day. "I'd love some
chili."

Doreen reviewed the details of Benita's order: cup or
bowl, apple or fruit cup, drink? She handed Benita
her change, then assured her she'd hear her name
when her meal was ready.

Without an available table in sight, Benita chose a
bar stool at the counter. She hung her tote bag on the
back of her seat and settled in to people watch. An
older man and an older woman Benita didn't recognize
darted in and out of the kitchen, taking turns present-
ing lunch orders to customers as their names were called.
Benita received her bowl of chili, apple, and lemonade
minutes later.

"Hi, Benita." The cheerful greeting from Megan came
just after Benita's first spoonful of chili.

"Whatever you're paying Doreen for this masterpiece
isn't enough." Her taste buds were doing the Macarena.

"I know." Megan leaned her right hip against the

counter. "But I'm hoping my taking her son off her hands makes up for the shortfall."

Benita paused with her spoon halfway to her mouth. "Is there another wedding on the horizon?"

Megan shook her head. "We're taking things slowly."

They chatted for a while about mutual acquaintances, changes in the town, and books they'd loved and would recommend. Benita had forgotten how much she enjoyed talking with neighbors about the everyday things: friends, family, and well-loved books. It was so much easier than posturing with friendly rivals, trying to one-up each other with who you knew, where you've been seen, and how much you've earned. The late-night socializing and catty backstabbing took their toll physically, emotionally, and spiritually.

"Another lunchtime stampede in the books." Doreen circled the counter to take the bar stool beside Benita. The café crowd settled down as diners dug into their fresh and healthy meals.

"Waiting in line, I felt like I was watching a standing ovation for your food." Benita spooned up more chili.

Doreen's eyes widened with surprise. "Well, thank you for the compliment."

"How are you handling being mayor and managing the café?" Benita kept her tone light to mask her concern for her friend.

Doreen looked at least ten years younger than the age Benita believed her to be. Her friend's warm chocolate features were smooth and flawless with the barest hint of makeup. But she seemed so tired. There were clouds in her brown eyes, and tension bracketed her bowed lips.

Doreen rubbed her forehead. "It's not easy, but Megan's

taken on some of my bakery responsibilities. She's also hired a couple of people to help."

Benita sipped her lemonade. "The man and woman I saw earlier?"

"They're husband and wife." Megan glanced toward the kitchen door. "They're retired restaurant workers who were looking for part-time work. They were an answer to a prayer."

"They're wonderful." Doreen lifted her hand to cover a yawn. "Michelle still works with us. But during the school year, we only schedule her for Saturdays and school breaks."

Benita vaguely recalled the high school junior whose hair dyes kept track of holidays: blue for Independence Day, red for Valentine's Day, green for Christmas, and so on.

"You have a lot on your plate, between this successful café and being mayor." Benita finished her chili and lemonade. She bit into her apple.

"I'm also planning my wedding." Doreen should have sounded happy, but all Benita heard was fatigue.

"Aunt Helen told me." Benita smiled despite her concern. "I'm sure you and Alonzo will be very happy. How are your plans coming?"

"Slowly." Doreen's sigh hinted at frustration. "I have a to-do list, but I'm not completing the tasks as quickly as I'd like. Alonzo doesn't want to postpone the wedding. But today's April eighth. We have less than three months."

"Let me see your list." Benita took another bite of her apple.

Doreen slipped off the stool and disappeared into the

kitchen. She returned with a three-ring binder that she handed to Benita.

Benita opened the binder and found the to-do list on the first page. "This is very detailed."

Doreen returned to her bar stool. "I'm sure we'll get through everything. But right now, it seems so daunting."

"I'm sure it does." Benita finished off her apple, then dropped the binder into her tote bag.

Doreen looked from the tote bag to Benita. "What are you doing?"

"Just consider me your wedding planner." Benita shifted on the stool to face Doreen. "I'll coordinate these items and any I think you might have missed. I'll see you and Alonzo at your place this evening around six so you can give me additional instructions."

Doreen looked from Benita to Megan and back. "But—"

"There are no buts." Benita held up one hand, palm out. "Do you want to get things done or do you just want to gripe about them?"

Doreen fluttered her free hand. "I want to get things done but—"

"Then leave it to me. I'll see you and Alonzo at six." Benita slipped off the bar stool. She sensed her friend's struggle as she tried to come up with a viable argument against Benita's help.

Finally, the bakery manager gave in. "All right."

Megan gaped. "Why didn't that work for me when I offered to help with your wedding plans?"

Benita shrugged. "You're not used to unreasonably stubborn personalities. My family's full of them: people who have to do things themselves, who have to do things their way. I don't have time to reason with unreasonable people. Sometimes things just have to get done." She turned back to Doreen. "No offense intended. I'll see you and Alonzo later."

She walked toward Books & Bakery's exit, pausing to peruse the shelves of books. It was so easy for her to manage other people's lives. It always had been. Why was it such a challenge to take control of her own?

CHAPTER 7

"Why is Leonard George sitting on your front steps?" Ms. Helen stood in her doorway behind Doreen Wednesday afternoon as they stared at the Fever home across the street.

"I was wondering the same thing." Doreen returned Leonard's stare from Ms. Helen's porch.

"Do you want me to go with you to kick him off?"

Doreen smiled at the tone of Ms. Helen's voice. Her friend sounded like she was looking for excitement. "Thank you, but that's not necessary, Ms. Helen. I can handle this."

"Well, be sure you tell me about it when you do your rounds tomorrow afternoon."

Doreen turned to face her neighbor. "I keep telling you, Ms. Helen, I'm not on rounds. I like visiting with you, especially on my way home. It's a nice way to end my day."

"And I keep telling you that you and the rest of my Watchers aren't fooling me." Ms. Helen turned to go inside. "I'll see you tomorrow."

With that, the retired chemistry professor crossed her threshold and locked her door. Doreen turned back to the street. Leonard sat on her bottom step, waiting for her. *I might as well get this over with.*

Doreen climbed down Ms. Helen's front stairs and crossed the street. "What are you doing here?"

Leonard rose to his feet. "It's been a long time, Dorie. Don't I at least get a hello?"

Doreen stopped a little more than an arm's length from her ex-lover. "What do you want?"

"Could we talk inside?" Leonard jerked his head toward her house behind him.

"No."

"Why not?"

"I don't have anything to say to you. And if you aren't going to talk out here, then we have nothing to say to each other." Doreen started to walk past him.

Leonard shifted to block her path. "I want you back."

Is he kidding?

His eyes scanned her face as though searching for a weakness. He must have thought she'd lost her mind.

"How does Yvette feel about that?" Doreen settled farther into her coat. It was the second week of April. Although the childhood poem presaged that April would come in "like a lamb," it felt a lot like the lion of March.

"We broke up." Leonard didn't sound too torn up about it.

"Well, good for her." Doreen started to circle Leonard to climb her stairs.

Leonard grabbed her left arm and raised her hand to see her fingers. He studied her two-carat Monarch diamond engagement ring with disgust. "I'd heard that the sheriff had proposed. I think condolences are in order. I'd like to rip that ring from your finger and throw it into the street."

Doreen fisted her hand and yanked it from his grip. "You've said what you came to say. Now leave. I don't want to see you again." She tried to step around him a third time.

Again, Leonard blocked her way. "I wish we'd never broken up."

"Step aside, Leo."

"I miss you, Dorie."

"I won't ask you again."

"Tell me what went wrong between us."

Wide eyed, Doreen stared at him. "*You're* what went wrong between us. You wanted me to stay home and take care of you. I have other plans for my future and Alonzo supports them."

"I wanted to share my life with you."

Doreen shook her head. "But you didn't want to share mine."

"What do you mean?" He looked confused.

"You gave me an ultimatum, remember?" Doreen settled her hands on her hips. "Be the person you wanted me to be or you'd find someone else. When I didn't fall in line, you started dating Yvette."

"Why did you have to run for mayor?" Leonard pressed his hand to his chest. "I wanted you to be my wife."

"With you, it's either-or. With Alonzo, I can have it all." Doreen walked past Leonard and mounted her steps.

"This isn't over between us, Dorie."

Doreen waved her left hand over her shoulder, showing

him her engagement ring as she continued up the stairs.
"Yes, it is."

Benita sat back on the fluffy pink armchair Wednesday evening and considered Doreen and Alonzo, seated beside each other on the matching overstuffed sofa. "April Fool's Day was last Wednesday. Is this some sort of belated joke?"

The couple exchanged a look, silent communication that reminded Benita of her and Vaughn.

"What do you mean?" Doreen asked.

Benita blinked and Vaughn's handsome features faded from her vision. She was back in Doreen's family room. "You've just told me you haven't reserved a church, caterer, or ballroom. You haven't created a guest list or identified groomsmen or bridesmaids. What *have* you done to plan your wedding?"

Alonzo gestured toward his fiancée. "Doreen bought her dress and I reserved my tuxedo."

Are they kidding?

"That's a relief. At least you won't be naked." Benita glanced at the wedding task list she'd taken from Doreen earlier that day. She'd affixed it to the clipboard on her lap.

Doreen folded her arms. "We can take care of this ourselves. We don't need your help, especially if you're going to criticize us."

"My criticisms are designed to bring home the urgency of your situation." Benita balanced the clipboard on her lap. "Today is April eighth. You want to get married June twentieth. Who chose that date?"

"I did." Alonzo squirmed under Benita's regard.

Benita froze. With sudden clarity, she understood why the sheriff had asked for a wedding date that was so close to his January first proposal. He wasn't waiting a day longer than necessary to make a public commitment to the woman who'd held his heart for more than forty years.

Is there a similarity between Alonzo and Doreen's love story and my relationship with Vaughn?

Benita struggled past the uneasy feeling that question gave her. "Luckily, in Trinity Falls, we don't have to book wedding locations and services as far in advance as we would in L.A." She drummed her fingertips against the clipboard. "However, Trinity Falls has fewer venues and vendors. We can't take these things for granted."

Doreen glanced at Alonzo, then back to Benita. "You're right."

"No more fun and games." Benita stilled her fingers and gave her friends a stern look. "I'm going to knock off this list. When I call for your input or information, you're going to give me an answer yesterday. Understood?"

"Yes, ma'am." Alonzo gave her a chastened look that she didn't buy for a minute.

"Before I get started, do you have any ideas or preferences for your ceremony?" Benita turned to a blank page on her clipboard.

"We want the ceremony to be different from Doreen's first wedding." Alonzo sat straighter on the sofa.

"In what way?" Benita made a note of their preference.

"We don't know." Alonzo exchanged a look with Doreen.

Benita considered the sheriff. He'd remained a bachelor, unwilling to wed as long as Doreen was in his heart.

Will that be me in another twenty or thirty years?

Not if I can convince Vaughn to move with me to L.A.

Benita returned her attention to the wedding task list. "I have a couple of ideas."

"What?" Doreen and Alonzo asked in unison.

Benita smiled. "Let me check with the locations first. I don't want to get your hopes up if the ideas don't pan out."

She asked a battery of questions to get a better sense of the type of wedding Doreen and Alonzo envisioned. Thankfully, they both wanted a small, traditional ceremony. Neither had guests coming from out of town, which meant Benita didn't have to reserve lodging at the local inn or at Harmony Cabins. She also was able to talk them out of serving just cake and punch.

"This is Trinity Falls, people," Benita reminded them. "If you don't want your guests to speak ill of you even months after your second wedding anniversary, you should at least offer a buffet."

Alonzo gave a crooked smile. "Good point."

Doreen took Alonzo's hand. "You're right. No skimping on the food."

Benita stared at Doreen's fingers entwined with Alonzo's. In her mind, she saw her hand in Vaughn's. She even felt his rough, warm palm against her skin. The memory stole her breath. She missed him like crazy. She'd die if she had to wait as long as Alonzo had before claiming her happily-ever-after. She had to convince the stubborn composer to relocate to L.A. with her. *I just have to.*

Benita rose from Doreen's cushy armchair. "I'll get started on the list. Thanks for meeting with me."

"Thank you!" Doreen laughed. "You're doing us a big favor."

Alonzo helped Doreen to her feet. "I know we haven't given you a lot of time. If you're able to pull this off by June twentieth, you're a miracle worker."

"I have no doubt I'll be able to pull it off. But you're both going to hate me before it's over." Benita tucked the clipboard under her arm and tugged her purse strap onto her shoulder. "Besides, I'm on vacation."

"Some vacation, planning someone else's wedding." Alonzo stepped back so Doreen could lead them to the front door.

"We should pay you." Doreen gave Benita a stricken look. "I should have thought of that sooner."

"Don't you dare." Benita held up one hand. "This is my wedding gift to you."

"It's too much." Doreen turned to Alonzo.

"Doreen's right," he agreed.

"Then you can repay the favor when my wedding day comes." Benita continued on to Doreen's front door.

"Is there something you want to share with us?" Doreen gave her a bright, inquisitive smile.

"I hope to have something soon." First she had to convince one very sexy music professor that his heart was with her in California.

Benita strode across the Oval on Trinity Falls University's campus Thursday afternoon. It was April and everything shouted spring: the blossoms opening on the stately sequoia trees, the scent of freshly cut grass wafting over the lawns, the puffy, pure white clouds drifting across the bright blue sky. It was as idyllic as any Walt Disney animated movie scene. Then what was behind the feeling of tension blanketing the campus?

She followed the path to Vaughn's office. In the distance several students stopped beside Wishing Lake, the campus's contained pond, and tossed something into its waters. Benita smiled. Finals were five weeks away. That must be the source of the tension she sensed. How many of the students pitching pennies into the pond wished they'd done a better job of keeping up with their course work? Poor things. Hopefully, they will have learned their lesson by next semester.

Benita mounted the main staircase in Freeman Hall, the academic building named after one of the university's beloved art professors and benefactors. Vaughn's office was on the second floor.

"Benita?"

She looked up, pressing herself against the wall to avoid several students rushing down the steps. "Hi, Peyton."

The petite history professor was barely visible in the crowd of teenagers and young adults, many of whom towered over her. "This is a surprise. What are you doing here?"

"I'm hoping Vaughn is free for lunch." Benita led Peyton down the stairs and out of the path of stampeding students.

Peyton looked over her shoulder at the staircase as though saying Vaughn's name would conjure him. "I hope you have a nice time." She glanced at her purple

Timex. "I'm actually meeting Darius for lunch at Books and Bakery."

Behind her smile, the history professor's eyes expressed concern that triggered Benita's unease. She shook off the sensation. "Maybe we'll see you there."

Benita mounted the stairs again. Outside Vaughn's office, she scanned his bulletin board. He'd posted his office hours, upcoming classes, quotes about the value of music and music education, and a poster announcing the upcoming audition for his musical, *Mystic Park.*

Why hadn't he told me he was ready to perform it?

Vaughn's office door opened. Benita's smile of greeting froze as she watched a tall, gorgeous woman in conservative beige clothing precede Vaughn from the room.

Who is she—and why is Vaughn's right hand riding the small of her back?

"Benny." Vaughn froze when he noticed Benita in the hallway. "What are you doing here?"

He was the second person to ask her that and she was starting to understand why.

Benita lifted her gaze from Vaughn's hand, which had disappeared behind the stranger's bony back. Her gaze was starved for Vaughn. She devoured his appearance: broad shoulders wrapped in a black cotton shirt, powerful legs and slim hips in steel gray slacks.

"I was hoping we could have lunch." Her heart was in her throat. *Tell me we can have lunch.*

"I already have plans." His words were acid to her soul. Vaughn gestured between Benita and the woman at his side. "Benita Hawkins, Doctor Olivia Stark."

The pain burned deeper when Vaughn stepped closer to the other woman. How long had they been seeing each other? Had he been dating her this whole time?

Has he left me for her?

Benita pushed past the hurt—and yes, fear—to offer the other woman her hand. "How do you do?" *And why are you with my boyfriend?*

"Nice to meet you." Olivia's eyes were curious. Her long, thin fingers were cool to the touch.

Benita released the professor's hand and met Vaughn's gaze. His cocoa eyes were guarded and distant, as though they hadn't known each other since high school and hadn't loved each other since college.

Why is he doing this and how can I make him stop?

"I'm helping Doreen and Alonzo plan their wedding." Benita fisted her hands in her pockets. "I wanted to ask if you could provide the music."

That sounded both casual and plausible. Not bad for a spur-of-the-moment, face-saving ploy.

Vaughn nodded. "I can do that."

"Thank you." Benita struggled to keep her smile in place. "We should get together to discuss the music selections."

"Sure, you, me, Alonzo, and Doreen." Vaughn checked his watch. "I'll call you later. Olivia and I need to go."

Benita glanced at the other woman. She seemed to be everything Benita wasn't: tall, thin, poised. Perfect.

Is this the type of woman Vaughn really wants to marry? That couldn't be true. Why would he have spent the past eighteen years with me?

Benita swallowed back a scream of pain and denial. "All right. I'll ask Doreen and Alonzo for a time to get together." With one final, heroic effort, she offered a smile to the couple. "Enjoy your lunch."

"Thanks." Vaughn was already turning away. His

large, talented hand still braced the small of Olivia's
skinny back.

Benita watched them disappear down the hall. She'd
lost him. He was moving on with someone else. Vaughn
was never going to join her in L.A. She would never
have her happily-ever-after. Was it time for her to move
on as well?

Alonzo studied the shadows in Pearl Lake. They
lightened as Saturday's dawn stretched across the cool
blue sky. The birdsong grew louder. The sun grew
warmer. The air was fresh, crisp, and moist with morning dew. But his fishing rod remained still. It was as
though the fish sensed his troubled thoughts.

"Who goes fishing with a beach chair?" Jackson
grumbled beside him as he recast his line.

Alonzo glanced down at his companion. The cabin
resort owner sat cross-legged on a wide, faded blanket
beneath the large maple tree. Their backpacks, stuffed
with supplies, lay behind him on the blanket.

"People in their sixties who'd like to be comfortable
while fishing with a friend." The cork grip of Alonzo's
graphite rod was familiar in his hands.

Jackson's smile was quick and easy. There was a time
when his smiles were nonexistent. That was before
Audra. "How's your wedding planning?"

"Great now that Benita's taken it over." Alonzo
chuckled. "Thanks very much for letting us have our
wedding at Harmony Cabins."

"No problem." Jackson took a long drink from his
water bottle. It was the biggest water bottle Alonzo had
ever seen.

"Benita's also sent out the invitations; set up the gift registry; booked the photographer, videographer, and caterer; and ordered the roses."

"Sounds like your June wedding is on track. Congratulations."

"Thanks." Alonzo's gaze lifted from his fishing rod's aluminum reel to the whimsical ash wood bridge that stretched across Pearl Lake. The closer they got to his wedding, the more he feared something would happen to turn his dream into a nightmare, like Doreen finding out about his past.

"So if your wedding plans are going well and you've announced your retirement, what's weighing on your mind?" Jackson recast his nylon line.

Alonzo had known Jackson would sense his turmoil. Was that the reason he'd asked the younger man to go fishing with him?

"I've been in love with Doreen since college." He took a long drink of the water in his normal-sized bottle.

"A long time."

Alonzo's gaze dropped to his fishing rod. The fish were still avoiding him. "When I returned to Trinity Falls two years ago, I realized she'd changed."

"How?" Jackson obviously hadn't expected Alonzo's words.

"As a young woman, Doreen had been warm, friendly, caring—a bright light in the community."

"She's still all of those things." Jackson scowled, ready to defend his friend.

"No." Alonzo shook his head. "As a mature woman, Doreen is committed, compassionate, complex. Her bright light has become a supernova."

Jackson seemed to relax. "Doreen is an impressive person."

"And my feelings for her are even stronger now than when I first fell in love with her." Alonzo paused. "I never would've thought that was possible."

"How is that a bad thing?" Jackson's frown returned.

Alonzo shifted on his beach chair. He was a lawman, not a poet. He struggled to find the words to express his fears and concerns about the woman who would soon be his wife. "I'm not good enough for her."

The silence was long and brittle before Jackson spoke. "Seriously?"

"She's built things, created things. What have I brought to the community?"

"Law and order."

"She can point to things a lot more tangible than that, like the laptops in the elementary school computer lab." Alonzo was proud of all of Doreen's accomplishments. But they were sometimes daunting to someone who hadn't achieved as much.

Jackson uncrossed his legs and stretched them toward the lake. "*Doreen* thinks you're good enough for her."

"The man she thinks she knows is good enough for her." Alonzo so badly wanted to be that man.

"Have you spoken with Doreen?"

Alonzo hesitated. "I'm afraid of what she might say."

"You have to talk with her." Jackson's broad shoulders rose and fell with his deep sigh. "Audra taught me the importance of speaking from the heart. It's hard. It's scary. Believe me, I know. But it's worth it. If you don't make the effort, the people you love won't know how you feel or how to help you."

Jackson spoke from experience. Three years ago, the rental cabin owner had been emotionally devastated by the death of his young daughter. Jackson had shut out the town and exiled himself to the cabins. He was like Beast in the French fairy tale *Beauty and the Beast*. Then, like Beauty, Audra arrived at the then-isolated Harmony Cabins. She helped Jackson heal his broken heart and returned him to civilization.

"That's sound advice." But Alonzo still feared the risk was too great.

"Remember Doreen loves you."

But if she learned the truth about him, would he lose her love?

CHAPTER 8

Late Saturday morning, Benita climbed out of her Audi and let her senses drink in the peace and beauty of Harmony Cabins. Pink and white blossoms dotted the nearby trees, ringing the cabin's lawn and bordering the path. A faint breeze, carrying the promise of spring, teased her hair and rustled through the branches. A river rushed in the distance. She set her hands on the hips of her dark blue jeans and drew a deep breath of the fresh, fragrant air. No wonder Audra and Jackson continued to live at the cabins even after Audra had helped him reconnect with the Trinity Falls community. It was lovely here.

Benita dropped her arms. She crunched her way across the path from the attached garage to the front door of Audra and Jackson's cabin.

Audra met her on the porch. "I know you're a workaholic, but meeting on a Saturday to discuss my new contract offer is a bit much even for you."

Benita mounted the steps. "I didn't have anything better to do."

"Maybe I did." Audra crossed her arms.

"Don't worry. I won't keep you long." Benita stopped in front of her songwriting client. "You and Jackson can crawl back into bed within the hour."

Just then Jackson walked through the open front door carrying a tool box and one of the biggest water bottles she'd ever seen. "Thanks."

Benita fought a sudden, hot blush. "Hi, Jack."

"Benita." He turned to Audra, his lips still twitching with humor. "I'll see you within the hour."

Audra grinned around his kiss. "Promise?" She watched her lover descend the stairs and disappear down the path.

"Sorry." Benita shoved her hands into her front pockets.

"It's who you are, Benita." Audra led her into the cabin.

"Cabin" seemed an understatement for the large two-story structure. The decor was a near-perfect blend of stark masculine simplicity and complex feminine touches. The honey wood walls were decorated with original art-work. Benita recognized several of her great-aunt's pieces. The matching wood mantel above the stone fire-place balanced scented candles, knickknacks, and photos of both Jackson's and Audra's families.

The crimson throw pillows on the dark plaid sofa and armchair coordinated with the curtains that framed the windows and the area rug that spanned the flooring. The large flat-screen television set reminded her that the pro-fessional basketball were around the corner.

"Why are you really here?" Audra gestured Benita to the sofa and lowered herself onto the armchair.

"I told you, to discuss your contract." Benita pulled the throw pillow onto her lap.

Audra arched a disbelieving eyebrow. "The contract

language is the same as it's always been. They've offered me more money, though, which is a pleasant surprise."

"You're a multi-Grammy-winning artist. You command more money."

Audra gave her an amused smile. "It also helps to have a bully for a business manager."

"I'll take that as a compliment."

"It was meant as one." Audra crossed her legs, leaning toward Benita. "Are you going to tell me what's on your mind? Or are we still pretending you want to discuss my contract?"

Benita hesitated. "Vaughn's dating someone else."

Audra's amused expression sobered into concern. "I'd heard the two of you had broken up."

"I see you're solidly planted among the grapevine." Benita scowled. "Let's see how you feel about it when it's your private life making the rounds."

"I knew you'd be upset that I heard the gossip about your breakup." Audra settled back on her armchair. "That's the reason I didn't call to ask how you were doing. But how are you doing?"

Benita shrugged, looking away. "I'd asked Vaughn to move to L.A. with me. Again."

"Vaughn doesn't strike me as someone who'd ever leave Trinity Falls. He loves it here. It's his home."

"He won't even give L.A. a chance." Benita stood to pace the spacious living room. "He's a brilliant musician. You've heard his work."

"Yes, I have. He's very talented."

"And what is he doing with it?" Benita threw up her arms. "Wasting it in this obscure town in that unknown university."

"He's teaching the next generation of composers,

musicians, and music teachers." Audra's tone had grown cool. "Or are you unaware of the benefits of music education? It's linked to better reading, writing, and math skills, and to developing critical thinking, something you could use right about now."

Benita gave Audra a considering look. "He could teach in L.A."

"He wants to teach here."

"He wants to do more than teach." Benita paced toward the fireplace. "He's written a musical."

"I know." There was a smile in Audra's voice. "He asked for my input on the songs."

He didn't ask for my input.

Benita ignored the sting that felt like rejection. She turned to her friend and client. "What did you think?"

Audra spread her arms. "I loved all of his pieces. I wish I'd written them, especially 'Forever Love.'"

Benita's heart swelled as though Audra's praise was directed at her. "I'm very proud of him." An understatement. "But how much exposure will his work receive, being played in little Trinity Falls? Where's he going to perform it, the university?"

"This town is his home. He loves it here."

"Jack loves Trinity Falls, too." Benita waved her arm toward the front door. "His family founded this town. But he was willing to leave it for you."

"Don't compare Jack and Vaughn." Audra raised both hands. "It's not fair. They're two different people."

Benita set her hands on her hips. "I just want to understand how he could claim to love me but not want to leave Trinity Falls for me."

"The same way you say you're in love with Vaughn but won't return to Trinity Falls, which is your home."

Benita glared at Audra before pacing away. "Whose side are you on?"

"You're talking to the wrong person." Audra was irritatingly reasonable. "I left Los Angeles for Trinity Falls, remember?"

"How could I forget that my only real friend in L.A. left me?" Benita crossed her arms as she directed her scowl at the fireplace.

"If Vaughn won't relocate to Los Angeles for you, he's never going to move."

"You have a point, but where does that leave me?" Benita was suddenly exhausted.

"Move back to Trinity Falls."

Benita turned on Audra. "How can you say that?"

"I'm your friend and I want what's best for you. You belong in Trinity Falls."

"I've built a successful career in L.A."

"But you're not happy there. Admit it. Here, you tell people what to do and they listen to you. You don't get that kind of deference in Los Angeles."

"Not everyone here takes my advice." Ms. Helen was a notable exception. Vaughn was another. Benita rubbed her index finger over her bottom lip. "You're wrong. I can be happy in L.A. And now that Vaughn's with someone else, what's the point of my returning to Trinity Falls. There's nothing for me here."

"Benita—"

She held out her hand to stop whatever it was Audra was about to say. She spoke after a calming breath. "I'll tell the recording company you've accepted the new contract. Let me know when you've sent it back to them."

Benita managed to leave the cabin and climb into her

car without having a major breakdown. She slapped the tears from her eyes before driving back to Ms. Helen's house. It had been a terrible mistake to come to Trinity Falls for the university's ceremony in her great-aunt's honor. Ms. Helen didn't want the ceremony and Vaughn had broken up with her. Benita swallowed the lump in her throat. She couldn't wait to return to L.A. and shake this town's dust off her shoes.

Vaughn stood on Ms. Helen's porch late Monday afternoon. He was debating his next move. Was it a good idea to ask Benita to help him with his musical? Probably not. Working on a project with his ex-lover was probably the stupidest thing he could do. But he needed her help. Vaughn pressed his right index finger into Ms. Helen's doorbell before he could make another mental round of this circular argument.

About a minute later, the door swung wide. Benita's smile didn't reach her hazel eyes. "Come in. Doreen's here. We're all in the kitchen."

Why wasn't she surprised to see him? Vaughn entered Ms. Helen's home. He glanced at the peephole on the door, which offered one possibility; she'd been prepared to see him. But he was as nervous as the night he'd picked her up for their first date. That had been an experience. Her father had all but drug tested him.

"Actually, Benita, I'm just leaving." Doreen's voice preceded her appearance in the foyer by seconds. She was bright and cheerful in a powder blue ankle-length skirt and lemon yellow blouse.

"Welcome, Vaughn. We can use another Watcher." Ms. Helen walked beside Doreen. Her snow white hair was contained in a thick braid that hung past her shoulders. She'd paired green yoga pants with a loose gold blouse. Purple socks protected her feet.

Vaughn frowned from Benita to Ms. Helen as he stepped farther into the room. He caught Benita's cinnamon and vanilla scent. "Who are the Watchers?"

"Ms. Helen, why do you call us that?" Doreen gave her neighbor a chastising look. "We're not spies. We just like to visit with you."

"Who wouldn't want to stop by for tea and snacks?" Benita crossed to the other side of the room. Vaughn wondered whether she was putting distance between them.

Ms. Helen didn't seem convinced. "Are you here for tea, Vaughn?"

"No, thank you, ma'am." Vaughn still didn't understand what he'd missed. "I wanted to pay my respects to you. But I'm here to speak with Benita."

Benita's eyes widened with surprise. "About what?"

"Could we talk in private?" Vaughn slipped his hands into the front pockets of his dark gray slacks.

"I should leave." Doreen hugged Ms. Helen. She adjusted her purse on her shoulder, then bid Benita and Vaughn a good afternoon before disappearing through the front door.

"I'll leave the two of you to the foyer." Ms. Helen gestured toward the pale brown faux leather love seat. "Vaughn, are you sure I can't interest you in some chai tea?"

"I'm fine, Ms. Helen. But thank you for the offer."

"Then I'll leave you two alone." Ms. Helen started across the living room. "I'll be reading in my bedroom, if you need me."

"Thanks, Aunt Helen." Benita pointed toward a vent

beneath the ceiling. "From her bedroom, she can hear everything that happens here."

Vaughn shook his head with a chuckle. "Thanks for the warning."

He couldn't keep his eyes from enjoying the sight of Benita in her flowing red blouse and figure-hugging black pants. She had such long legs for such a short woman. He remembered the feel of them wrapped around his waist. Vaughn swallowed a groan.

Will I ever stop wanting her?

"How've you been?" He nearly winced at his lame question.

"Fine, and you?" She hadn't moved from her spot across the room.

"Fine." Vaughn shrugged off his tweed blazer and hooked it onto the black metal coatrack in the corner. The act brought him closer to her.

Benita moved away from him again, this time to sit on the far corner of the love seat. "What do you want to talk with me about?"

Vaughn lowered himself onto the love seat's opposite corner. "I need your help."

"With what?"

Vaughn leaned forward, placing his forearms on his thighs. "Do you remember the musical I've been working on?"

"Mystic Park." Benita crossed her long legs. "You had a flier about it on your bulletin board."

"I've received a grant to produce it."

"That's fantastic!" Benita's face lit up like a star on a Christmas tree. A wide grin curved her luscious lips. She threw herself against him.

Her arms twined around his neck. In reflex, Vaughn's

arms wrapped around her waist. Her body was warm and soft in his arms. Her fragrance surrounded him, bringing memories of the distant and not-so-distant past. Images of other days and nights when he'd held her. He remembered the touch of her, the taste of her. His body burned.

"Thank you." Vaughn set Benita aside and stood with his back to her. It hurt like ripping out his heart and throwing it into the street.

"I'm glad you decided to share your music. It's about time."

The rustling sound behind him indicated Benita was straightening her clothes. He gritted his teeth and drew a deep calming breath.

"You've been nagging me to do that for years." Vaughn dragged his hand over his clean-shaven head. Could he risk looking at her now? His body still throbbed from their embrace, brief and spontaneous as it was.

"I've never nagged, Vaughn." There was laughter in her tone. "How can I help you?"

He hesitated, then turned to face her. "Would you be willing to stay a while longer in Trinity Falls?"

Benita seemed very still. "Since I've agreed to plan Doreen and Alonzo's wedding, I'll be here until at least June twenty-first, the day after their wedding."

Why am I so nervous? What's the worst that could happen?

Benita could say no. That would crush him.

"I need help managing the production's various tasks, things like the audition and rehearsals, the promotion, props and costumes."

Benita regarded him in silence for a beat. "You want me to be your girl Friday?"

Vaughn had a premonition of danger. "You'd be more than that—like a production manager."

Benita stood, glancing toward the vent near the ceiling. She kept her voice low. "You want me to help you manage your play while you're dating Doctor Stark?"

"What does one have to do with the other?" The minute the words were out of his mouth, Vaughn wanted them back.

Benita gave him a stony stare. "Let's think this through. You want me to help you with your play like a *friend*, while you're *romancing* someone else."

Vaughn spread his arms. "Benny, we broke up."

"Then why are you here?"

Vaughn rubbed a hand over his head. He rose from the love seat. "I really don't know." He collected his jacket from the coatrack. "Sorry to have wasted your time."

He let himself out of Ms. Helen's home without looking back. Vaughn was more disappointed than he had a right to be. He'd known Benita wouldn't work with him on the play. Darius's idea had been a good one. It just couldn't work.

And now Vaughn had to start from scratch, teaching his body to forget her again.

"What did Vaughn want?" Ms. Helen wandered into the kitchen maybe seven minutes later. That hadn't taken her long.

Benita had finished straightening the kitchen—there hadn't been much to do—and she'd decided to make biscuits to go with their dinner of chicken and green beans.

"You couldn't hear us through the vent in your room?"

Benita used a fork to crush butter into a mixture of flour and salt.

"Don't take your frustration out on me." Ms. Helen pulled out a chair from under the kitchen table and sat.

Benita met her great-aunt's gaze from over her left shoulder. "I'm sorry."

"I'm not surprised that you won't help him with his musical." Ms. Helen's voice was devoid of embarrassment.

Benita sighed with resignation. Her great-aunt was a law unto herself. She spun the mixing bowl to continue crushing the butter into the flour and salt. "Can you believe his nerve?"

Ms. Helen made a noncommittal hum.

Benita released her fork. She turned to the refrigerator and selected an egg, then grabbed a mug from a cupboard. "He dumped me because I won't move back to Trinity Falls. Then, in the blink of an eye, he starts dating this woman who's gorgeous and obviously brilliant. Too smart for him. And I feel sorry for her when she realizes it."

"Vaughn's a very smart man."

Benita snorted. She broke the egg into a cup, beat it, then poured it into her mixing bowl. She cradled the bowl as she combined the ingredients. "If he's so smart, what made him think I'd help him with his play?"

"Before you were lovers, you were friends. Maybe he hopes you could be friends again."

Benita cleaned off a section of the counter on which to knead the biscuit dough. She swallowed back emotion and blinked back tears. "Well, he was wrong."

Benita didn't want to be Vaughn's friend. She wanted to be his lover, his wife, with all the ups and downs, and pain and pleasure that entailed. She wanted to take their relationship to its next, logical step: moving to L.A. together. But he'd said no. No to leaving Trinity Falls, and no to a future with her.

Ms. Helen continued her musings. "If it's not friendship you're after, helping him with his play gives you a perfect cover to try to get him back."

Benita stopped kneading the dough and considered her great-aunt's words. She turned to the older woman. "You're brilliant."

"I'll remind you that you said that."

Benita took in Ms. Helen's self-satisfied expression. Theirs was a discussion for another day. For now, Benita needed to speak with a man about a play.

∽CHAPTER 9∽

After dinner, Benita drove to Vaughn's apartment. She parked in the visitor section and walked across the lot.

The evening was still and quiet. Couples, families, and a handful of solitary residents strolled the streets for postdinner exercise. In L.A., car stereos often shattered the peace as vehicles sped past her condo. Here, the night held whispered conversations, greetings to neighbors, and bursts of laughter.

Benita rang the doorbell of Vaughn's first-floor apartment. She felt a moment's tension. What if he wasn't alone? Would he invite Olivia Stark to his home for dinner? Maybe he wasn't even here. He could be having dinner with Dr. Stark at her place. Benita gasped at the sudden sharp pain to her heart.

After what seemed an eternity, Vaughn opened his door.

"I've changed my mind." She blurted the announcement. "I'll help you with your play."

Vaughn's eyes widened with surprise, then narrowed with suspicion. "What made you change your mind?"

Benita hadn't expected that question. She stalled for time. "If we're going to discuss this, may I come in?"

"Actually, I apologize." Vaughn stepped back to let Benita into his home. "It doesn't matter why you changed your mind. I'm just glad you decided to help me."

She was off the hook. "You're welcome."

"I'm donating the proceeds from the musical to the Guiding Light Community Center." Vaughn closed and locked the door.

Benita regarded her longtime lover with new eyes as she followed him to his living room. He was using his lifelong dream to help the community. Could he be any more wonderful? "What made you decide to do that?"

"I told you I was on the center's fund-raising committee. Olivia and I were in charge of the registration database." Vaughn gestured toward his navy blue sofa and waited for her to sit.

Another stab of jealousy. Benita sat before her knees gave out under the pain. "I remember you telling me about the committee. I also read about the fund-raiser in the online edition of the *Monitor*."

Benita had been proud of Vaughn's participation in the project. But that pride was now tempered by the knowledge that he'd worked closely with the woman he was now romancing.

Urgh, the thought of the two of them together is enough to make me run screaming out of his apartment. Benita cleared her mind of everything but Vaughn's play.

"I enjoyed the experience." Vaughn leaned back onto the sofa's opposite corner. "We raised a lot of money, but it wasn't enough."

"With organizations like the center, one fund-raiser is never enough." Benita angled her body toward Vaughn. "It needs constant donations."

"I'm hoping this play will help. The grant I got will allow me to do that."

"What have you done so far to prepare for the play?" Benita crossed her legs. Vaughn's eyes followed the movement. She was glad she'd changed out of her slacks and into the floral midcalf skirt. He'd always had a fondness for her legs.

"I posted an announcement that the audition was coming."

"I saw it on your bulletin board." Benita frowned. "It didn't have a schedule."

"I don't know when I'll have time to hold them, but I wanted people to know they were coming."

Benita raised her eyebrows. "That doesn't actually do any good unless people know when they're coming. When do you want the production to open?"

"June thirteenth."

Benita sat straighter on the sofa. Disbelief sent her thoughts into chaos. "Why June thirteenth? Today's already April thirteenth."

"I want to perform the play before people leave Trinity Falls for their summer vacation."

"But that gives you only two months."

"Classes are over May eighth and grades are due May fifteenth." Vaughn spread his hands. "I'll have the rest of that time to concentrate completely on the play."

"Oh, great, four whole weeks." Benita stood to pace Vaughn's living room. "What is going on with the people in this town? Why does everyone think they can plan events overnight?" She threw up her arms and spun to face him. "Did someone get a time machine and not tell me about it?"

"I want as many people as possible to attend the play."

"No one considers what goes into planning an event. This is like Doreen and Alonzo choosing their wedding date without thinking about what goes into planning the wedding." Benita paced past his flat screen television.

Her movements were jerky with irritation as she turned away from his ebony stereo system, which stood beside a tower of compact discs. She walked toward his dual front windows, framed with navy blue drapes. She'd been with Vaughn when he'd bought those drapes. She'd encouraged him to buy them but not the sofa or its matching armchair.

"I need a date that's convenient for the community." Vaughn spread his arms. "What good is a fund-raiser if no one comes to it?"

Benita threw her arms in the air again. "These things take time to plan and prepare if you want to do them well."

Vaughn rose. He cut off her path back to his stereo and massive collection of music. Benita came to an abrupt halt in the face of his broad chest tightly wrapped in a gunmetal gray T-shirt. She used to love the way he looked in that T-shirt. But now that their relationship was hands-off, she was tempted to burn it.

Vaughn gave her his persuasive smile, the one he'd been using on her since high school. "And just like Alonzo and Doreen, I have complete confidence in your ability to help me pull this off."

Benita barely heard him. The thought of another person touching that well-muscled chest or tasting those finely molded lips made her want to bare her claws.

She spun on her heels and strode back to the sofa. She dropped onto its stingy cushions—seriously, Vaughn should have left the furniture choices to her—and crossed her legs.

"*Mystic Park* is based on Caribbean folklore. Is that right?" Benita adjusted her skirt over her knee. Vaughn's attention to her calves eased some of her irritation.

"That's right." Vaughn joined her on the couch, careful to keep his distance. Was he afraid she was going to bite? "It's a romance about a mortal man whose love for a water fairy brings the wrath of a powerful water nymph."

"I remember." Benita had been fascinated by the myths Vaughn's West Indian parents had told him as a child. She'd been thrilled when he'd decided to base his musical on some of these stories. Over the years, she'd begun to despair of his ever doing anything with his talent and hard work. But now that he was finally putting together his performance, they wouldn't be celebrating as a couple. Instead she was just a friend. For now.

"Thank you for encouraging me to finish the play." Vaughn's eyes were as solemn as his words.

"I'm looking forward to reading it." Benita stood. "We should get together tomorrow to start scheduling the audition and rehearsal dates. We also need to discuss the promotion."

"I can't get together Tuesday night." Vaughn rose with her. "I have other plans. Why don't we meet Wednesday?"

Other plans? Did he have a date with Olivia Stark? Benita fisted her hands even as she forced a casual shrug. "If you think it can wait that long."

"It'll have to." Vaughn's direct gaze sent her a message: *We're not together anymore.*

Her smile conveyed her response: *We're not done yet.*

Doreen's shoulder muscles relaxed a little bit more as she completed another item from her wedding planning tasks, the invitation list. However, seated beside her on the sofa, Alonzo seemed even more uptight.

Was he regretting his proposal?

"You're inviting Nessa to your wedding?" Benita's question didn't make sense at first.

Doreen looked at Benita who sat on a nearby matching armchair. It was Tuesday evening. Benita had requested this meeting with Doreen and Alonzo in Doreen's home to review the status of their wedding plans. They only had nine weeks left.

"Don't look at me." Alonzo lifted his hands in surrender.

Benita held Doreen's gaze. "Aunt Helen said, as council president, Nessa's been giving you a hard time."

"I'm not inviting her as council president." Doreen shrugged. "I'm inviting her as a neighbor."

"Is that a good idea?" Benita looked dubious. "Nessa hasn't been very neighborly toward you for the past almost year-and-a-half, ever since you launched your mayoral campaign."

"That's what I told her." Alonzo rested his arm on the back of the sofa behind Doreen's head.

She looked at her fiancé. His coffee-colored eyes ensnared her. *How could he look at me with such warmth and admiration if he was having second thoughts about our wedding?* "And as I told you, I can't invite everyone on the council except her."

"Then don't invite anyone on the council." Alonzo shrugged. "They aren't your friends."

Doreen shook her head even as Alonzo spoke. "I wouldn't feel right excluding them."

Benita lifted her hand. "Are you sure you're comfortable with your decision?"

"Yes, I am." Doreen nodded.

Alonzo grunted. "Then I hope she has the decency to decline the invitation."

So do I. Doreen looked to Benita. "The invitations look great. Between the three of us, we could have them addressed and in the mail tomorrow."

"Make that the four of us." Benita struggled with a grin. "Aunt Helen wants to help."

Doreen chuckled. "The more the merrier."

"We appreciate the help," Alonzo agreed.

They discussed their menu and upcoming meeting with the caterer, the rehearsal dinner schedule, and the music selection for their reception.

Doreen shook her head in amazement. "Benita, I can't believe how much you've accomplished so quickly."

"It's been fun." Benita closed the wedding planner notebook, then stood, gathering her belongings.

Doreen rose as well. "We can't thank you enough."

"You've done so much to help us." Alonzo stood.

Together, Doreen and Alonzo escorted Benita to the front door, then wished her a good evening.

Doreen watched Alonzo secure the locks on the door. "She's been amazing."

"I'm uncomfortable with her not taking any money." Alonzo turned from the door. "She's done so much work."

"I've been thinking of getting her a gift." Doreen took a deep breath. "Thanks to her we'll have our June twentieth wedding."

"Yes, we will." Alonzo smiled as he stepped away from the door. His smile didn't reach his eyes.

"Are you happy about that?" Doreen fell into step beside him as they walked back to the living room.

"Of course." To his credit, Alonzo seemed surprised by her question.

"You don't seem happy, Alonzo."

He frowned but didn't return her gaze. "I'm just—"

"Tired." Doreen repeated the excuse he'd been giving her for weeks.

He looked at her in surprise. "It was—"

"A long day." She heard the rising irritation in her voice. He must have heard it also.

"I'm sorry. I don't know what to say."

"The truth. That's all I'm asking for, Alonzo. Tell me what's wrong."

"Nothing."

"That's not true." Doreen stopped in front of the sofa but didn't sit. "I can see it in your eyes. I can sense it around you. Why won't you talk with me?"

"I *am* talking with you."

"But you're not telling me anything." Doreen wrapped her arms around her torso. "You're starting to scare me. What's so bad that you won't tell me?"

Alonzo held her upper arms in his strong, gentle hands. "I love you, Doreen. Is that enough?"

Doreen backed out of his embrace. "If you loved me,

you'd share with me whatever's troubling you. But you're not doing that, so you tell me if it's enough."

She turned on her heels and left the room. She didn't want to look at him while he continued to lie to her. What was she supposed to believe?

"Hi, Doctor Brooks, Doctor Stark. How are you?" The young hostess at Trinity Falls Cuisine, Kelsey, was a junior at TFU. She was well known and well respected on campus. The honors student seemed uncomfortable in her skinny black pants, starched white shirt, and narrow black tie.

"Fine, thank you," Vaughn replied, aware that his appearance at the restaurant with Olivia Stark would be all over campus by tonight. He could hear it now, "Do you know that Doctor Brooks and Doctor Stark are *dating*?"

"Hi, Kelsey. I'm fine, thanks." Olivia's pleased smile brightened her beautiful features. She gave the young woman a hug. "How are you?"

"I'm good." Kelsey returned her professor's embrace, then stepped back. Her dark eyes were full of questions as they flash between Vaughn and Olivia. "Are you two here for dinner?"

"Yes, thank you." Vaughn followed Kelsey and Olivia farther into the restaurant.

He'd been to Trinity Falls Cuisine three times since the restaurant had opened two years ago. Each time he'd been with Benita. Although he and Benita had ended their relationship, walking in here with another woman still felt wrong. Vaughn shrugged his shoulders to ease his sense of guilt. It didn't work.

The restaurant was heavy with the scent of tangy spices and rich sauces. As Vaughn followed Kelsey and Olivia to their seats, he observed the beige-and-gray stone walls with their dark wood trim. The restaurant's lighting was low, creating a romantic ambience. Despite the dim lights, he recognized a few of the diners—neighbors, community leaders, other faculty and staff from the university. They exchanged nods of greeting. Vaughn gritted his teeth. How will the campus interpret their date?

Kelsey stopped beside a booth in a quiet section of the restaurant. "Carl will be your server. Enjoy your evening."

She handed them each a menu. Vaughn and Olivia thanked her, then she disappeared.

Vaughn opened his menu. "Carl plays clarinet in my concert band."

Olivia glanced at him. "He's in my general biology class."

The menu provided tempting descriptions of the restaurant's offerings, including roasted chicken, wood-fired steak, rosemary salmon, and baked lemon tilapia. When he'd come here with Benita, he'd ordered the chicken or the salmon. Benita had ordered either the steak or tilapia. They would give each other samples of their meal. What would Olivia order?

Carl appeared out of nowhere. The sophomore had been born and raised in Trinity Falls. "Hey, Docs. Welcome to TF Cuisine. It's good to see you here."

"Hi, Carl. How are you?" Olivia's warmth for her students was undeniable.

"I'm fine, Doctor Stark. Thanks." He waved his order pad back and forth between them. "How are you guys?"

Vaughn chuckled at the sophomore's energy. "I'm fine, Carl. Thanks."

"Hey, Doctor Brooks, will the concert band be performing for your musical?" The clarinet player bounced on his toes.

Vaughn nodded. "Those band members who are interested in participating are welcomed to perform."

"Hey, cool." He waved his order pad again. "What can I get you guys to drink?"

Vaughn asked for iced tea with lemon. Olivia requested ice water with lemon.

As Carl vanished to get their beverages, Vaughn turned his attention to his date.

Olivia's clingy black minidress made her look cool and classy. Her long, shapely legs looked even longer in three-inch black stilettos that brought her closer to his height. Light cosmetics highlighted her cheekbones and added smoky accents to her dark eyes. She was undeniably beautiful, brilliant, and interesting. But just like during their lunch date last week, Vaughn didn't feel anything beyond a surface attraction. There was none of the curiosity, enthusiasm, or heat he experienced every time he sat in the same room with Benita. Maybe he needed to give them more time.

They chatted about their week, their students, and the restaurant while they waited for Carl to return. The young server brought their drinks, then took their order. They both requested the chicken. Why did that disappoint him?

Olivia sipped her water. "What did you think of the movie?"

He'd been dreading her question. She'd picked the romantic comedy although he'd insisted on paying. "It was entertaining."

Olivia laughed. "You hated it."

Vaughn shifted in his seat, embarrassed to be caught even in a social lie. "'Hate' is too strong of a term."

"All right." Olivia inclined her head. "Why did you dislike it so intensely?"

"Humor is very subjective." Vaughn offered a sheepish grin.

Her eyes widened. "You didn't think the dance sequence was funny?"

Vaughn shook his head. "No."

"What about when the hero met the heroine's friends?"

"No."

"That cooking scene was hilarious."

"No, it wasn't."

Olivia's shoulders shook with laughter. "Come on. There must have been one scene in that movie that you liked."

Vaughn pretended to consider her question. "The editors did a great job with the end credits."

"Oh, that's unkind." She laughed even harder. She had a great laugh. "What kind of movies do you enjoy?"

"Action adventure. Doesn't everyone?" Vaughn was relieved that Olivia was taking his criticism of her movie choice so well. Benita often tried to bully him into agreeing with her. He didn't always share her opinion of a film. But then she would never suggest they spend money on a romantic comedy, thank goodness.

Olivia arched a sculpted eyebrow. "Name one of your favorite movies."

"Battle L.A."

"The movie in which aliens invade earth? That's not even realistic."

Vaughn drank his iced tea. "It's just as realistic as that attractive heroine falling for the pudgy hero."

Olivia pressed a hand against her chest. "Oh, unkind."

Their banter was momentarily interrupted when Carl delivered their dinner. Then they returned to their movie critiques. The topic carried them through the meal and the return drive to Olivia's home. It was a cozy cottage-like house on the northwest side of town, not far from the university. Vaughn parked his Honda Accord in Olivia's driveway, then walked with her to her front door.

Olivia pulled her house keys from her purse. "Thank you for tonight. I had a lovely time."

"So did I. Thank you."

Olivia unlocked her door, then turned back to Vaughn. There was expectation in her brown eyes. But all Vaughn could think about was Benita.

Vaughn closed the gap between them and took her upper arms in his hands. He lowered his head and pressed his lips to her cheek.

"Good night." Vaughn sensed her disappointment before he saw it in her eyes.

"Good night." Her smile was forced.

Vaughn waited until she entered her house, then listened until he heard her turn the lock in her door. He dragged his right hand over his clean-shaven head as he returned to his sedan.

Benita! Dammit! She'd taken up residence in his heart,

in his head, and she wouldn't leave. It was as though she'd been in there so long she'd invoked eminent domain. Vaughn pressed the security button on his key chain to unlock his car, then yanked open the driver's side door. He threw himself onto the seat and squeezed the steering wheel.

He was attracted to Olivia. He'd had a great time with her tonight, despite the romantic comedy. So why didn't he kiss her on her lips? *Because I'm still under Benita's spell. What do I have to do to break it?*

∽⊘ CHAPTER 10 ⊘∽

"Why would you invite Nessa?" Megan asked the question for the second time.

Doreen gave Benita a long-suffering look as the three of them gathered in the kitchen at Books & Bakery Wednesday afternoon. The entertainment business manager didn't appear to notice as she finished her third cup of coffee.

"As I explained to Benita and Alonzo last night, it would be awkward not to invite the members of the Trinity Falls Town Council to my wedding." Doreen slid the sourdough rolls she intended to serve with lunch into the industrial oven.

"Alonzo doesn't seem to have a problem with that." Benita sipped her caffeine.

"*He* doesn't have to work with them." Doreen turned to the honey wood island toward the front of the kitchen to create the batter for her Trinity Falls Fudge Walnut Brownies.

Megan rose from the tiny circular matching table and crossed to the bakery manager. "Doreen, don't you remember what happened during your Thanksgiving Dessert Open House last year?"

"What happened?" Benita looked from Megan to Doreen and back.

"Your great-aunt closed the door in Nessa's face." Doreen struggled to appear exasperated by the account. But the truth was, she was still grateful for Ms. Helen's assistance. She also would have paid good money to have seen Nessa's face when the door had shut on her.

"Oh, no." Benita covered her mouth with her right hand. Her voice struck a chord between horror and humor.

"Ms. Helen was only trying to help." Megan rushed to reassure Benita. "I just wish we knew why Nessa's so antagonistic toward you."

"So do I." Doreen sighed. Talking about the town council president always put her in a bad mood.

"You don't know?" Benita crossed to the dishwasher and loaded her coffee cup.

"Do you?" Doreen turned to the younger woman.

"It's not a big mystery." Benita shrugged. "According to my mother, Nessa's resented you since high school."

"What?" Doreen was stunned. "Why?"

Megan crossed her arms and leaned a hip against the kitchen island. "What has Doreen ever done to hurt Nessa?"

Benita returned to her seat at the tiny table. "Why do teenaged girls usually resent each other? Because of teenaged boys. Apparently, all the boys in high school liked Doreen. But Doreen ended up marrying a very popular college student named Paul Fever. This made the mean girls—Nessa, my mother, a couple of others— green with jealousy. My mother eventually got over her envy when she met my father in college. But Nessa's story still hasn't had a happily-ever-after."

"Is that the reason she's been smearing Doreen all over town?" Megan sounded incredulous. "Because Nessa couldn't get a date in high school?"

"That's ridiculous." Doreen stirred her brownie batter. "We're all adults. We don't need men to define us."

"That's easier to believe when you've had healthy, loving relationships." Benita's voice grew pensive. "From what my mother's said, Nessa hasn't had those."

"Nessa's marriage was rocky." Megan leaned a slim hip against the kitchen island. "Then her husband left her for a younger woman."

"According to Aunt Helen, his mistress was a happier woman," Benita said.

The conversation halted as Doreen put the brownie batter into the mixer to whip. Instead of giving her greater clarity, Benita's theory of Nessa's hostility toward her only added to Doreen's confusion. The mixer's hum droned on. The smell of baking dough blossomed in the kitchen. Meanwhile questions continued to stack up in Doreen's mind.

She turned off the mixer. "Your mother's theory may explain high school, but we're older now, much older. Why would Nessa still resent me?"

"My mother thinks it's because you're so well liked and well respected in Trinity Falls." Benita shrugged.

Doreen frowned. "How does your mother know about Nessa's attitude toward me?"

"Aunt Helen tells us *everything* that happens in town," Benita said. "And I read the *Monitor* online. Nessa's resentment was pretty clear in some of her quotes during your mayoral campaign."

Megan paced the kitchen again. "I don't want Nessa to cause a scene at your wedding."

"Neither do I." Doreen poured the brownie batter into a baking pan. "I don't want any trouble from Leo, either."

"Leo?" Megan's eyebrows knitted. "You broke up with him almost a year ago."

Doreen set the brownie pan into the industrial refrigerator to wait for the bread to finish baking. "He came to see me a while ago. He said he wants me back."

Both women gaped at her. Megan recovered first. "When was this?"

Doreen thought that over. "A week ago, April eighth."

Benita's eyes grew even wider. "And you're only telling us this now? What did Alonzo say?"

Doreen hesitated. "I haven't told Alonzo yet."

Benita looked first to Megan, then Doreen. "Why not?"

Doreen shrugged off a sense of guilt. "He's still in a strange mood. He won't tell me what's causing it, but I'm afraid the fact that Leo came to my house will send him right over the edge."

"What if Leo confronts Alonzo himself?" Megan returned to her seat at the tiny table.

Doreen shook her head. "I don't think he'll do that. Leo isn't that brave."

"But what if he does?" Benita asked. "You should warn Alonzo that Leo came to see you. You don't want him to be caught off guard."

Doreen still hesitated. "What if telling him about Leo makes Alonzo's mood even worse?"

Benita leaned forward on her chair. "Knowing Leo is back may be the catalyst Alonzo needs to finally tell you what's bothering him."

Doreen's tension eased. "I hadn't considered that."

On the surface, Benita's idea sounded like a good one. Would it work? Doreen was desperate enough to give it a try. Things with Alonzo had to return to normal—the sooner, the better.

Benita had dressed carefully Wednesday afternoon for her meeting with Vaughn. She didn't want to look too good. But she didn't want to look too casual, either. Especially not the day after Vaughn's Big Date with Dr. Olivia Stark. She'd been aware of the furtive looks from Trinity Falls residents. Their expressions shouted, "Does Benita know Vaughn is dating someone else?!?" She hated those looks even more than the hasty whispers.

Seated on Vaughn's sofa in his living room, she offered him a smile as he handed her a tall glass of iced tea. "Thank you."

"You're welcome." He settled onto the armchair catty-corner to the couch.

"What have you done so far toward your musical's production?" *And why are you sitting so far away from me?*

"I placed a classified ad in the *Monitor*, announcing the audition date." Vaughn opened a manila folder and pulled out a sheet of paper. "The ad will run in tomorrow's and Sunday's papers."

"Good, the Thursday issue carries the *Weekend Calendar*. Both editions get a lot of reader attention." Benita made a note of the ad on her writing tablet. "When are the auditions?"

"I'm only offering one. It's on April twenty-second."

She checked the calendar on her cherry red cellular phone. "That's next Wednesday."

"Will that date work for you?"

"As long as you're holding it after my office hours. My clients know they can contact me between noon and eight eastern standard time."

"Is that your subtle way of telling me I should have asked you about the date before I placed the ad?" Vaughn's sexy grin, framed by his well-groomed goatee, made her want to crawl onto his lap and purr like a cat.

She fought the impulse. "Was I being subtle?"

"It was subtle for you." Vaughn balanced his right ankle on his left knee. He placed his manila folder on his inside right thigh.

"April twenty-second works fine." Benita waved a dismissive hand. Her gaze strayed to his thigh. "How many actors will we need?"

"There're three main characters—the farmer, the water fairy, and the water nymph—and five minor characters." The excitement in Vaughn's voice was contagious.

Benita's hand flew across the sheet of paper as she made notes. "We should get understudies."

Vaughn shook his head. "We won't need any. There's only one performance."

Benita looked up from her writing tablet. "Suppose someone isn't able to make the performance."

"Then they shouldn't audition for the play." His voice was firm. "We can't have no-shows the day of the performance."

"You have a point." Benita wasn't comfortable with Vaughn's decision. Life happens. But it was his musical, so they'd follow his rules. "We'll have to make the commitment clear to the cast. If they accept a role, they have to appear for the play. What about stagehands?"

For the next hour, they reviewed their needs for the

musical. Vaughn had invited musicians from his concert band to participate in the performance. Most students were available. For additional musicians, he'd reached out to local high schools and nearby universities.

Vaughn shared with Benita his itemized budget for prop materials. "I had to put this together for the grant application. I'm going to ask Jack, Darius, and Ean if they'll help build a few of the set pieces."

"Check with Alonzo as well." Benita made a note in her binder. "He's helped Aunt Helen with some carpentry around her house."

They reviewed their advertising, printing, and costume needs. And of course, they'd need ushers.

Vaughn sighed. "It's a generous grant. It goes a long way toward covering the costs of the production. But it doesn't cover everything. And I want to raise as much money as possible for the center."

"We're going to have to get additional investors."

"I've saved some money for this project." Vaughn tapped his pen against his folder, drawing Benita's attention back to his muscled thigh.

She swallowed a groan and ripped her gaze from his long limb. "I know you have, but the cost of the playbills alone is a lot."

"We could cut out some of the advertising." He sounded hopeful.

"Then how would you promote the musical?"

"We could ask some of the businesses to carry fliers about it. They did that for the center's dance fund-raiser."

"Printing fliers costs money, too." Benita hated to burst his bubble. "We'll ask our friends for donations for the production. You're not the only person who wants to support the center."

"All right." Vaughn's agreement was reluctant, but at least he agreed.

"Good. I'll take care of that." Benita made a note on her to-do list.

"And all of the musical's proceeds will go to the center."

"What you're doing is a beautiful gesture." And in keeping with her knowledge of the man she'd grown up with. Vaughn Brooks had always had a generous heart.

"I've spoken with Ms. Helen and the center's director. They've given me permission to perform the musical in the center's activity room."

"Wonderful. The event will allow us to showcase the center and bring its needs to the community's attention."

"Exactly." Vaughn's smile invited her to share his excitement.

Benita caught her breath again. It was time to go. "Well, is there anything else we need to cover?"

"I think that's it." Vaughn closed his folder.

"Then I'll see you next Wednesday for the audition." Benita stood. "Don't schedule any dates for those days."

Her face flamed. Why had she said that? Had she lost her mind? Benita ducked her head and feigned an absorption in collecting her purse and tote bag.

"I won't." Vaughn's reply was soft. She felt him stand.

"I'm sorry." Benita threw her notes and other belongings into her tote. "I don't know what made me say that."

"It's all right."

Of course it was all right—*for him.* He was the one dating again. No one had asked *her* out. And she didn't want anyone else to ask her out.

Benita jerked her purse and tote bag onto her shoulder and rushed toward the door. "See you Wednesday."

"Benita."

She didn't stop. Her plan of seduction hadn't worked as well as she'd envisioned. Next time, she couldn't allow past memories to make her fall apart. Her goal was too important. *I want Vaughn back.*

CHAPTER 11

"I've heard you're producing a musical." Nessa lowered herself onto one of the two guest chairs in Vaughn's faculty office Thursday.

Vaughn watched the Trinity Falls Town Council president as she glanced around his office. Her expression was disapproving. Why? There was nothing wrong with his cozy home-away-from-home. His space was clean and well organized. Four oak bookcases were packed with textbooks and nonfiction literature. Two black metal file cabinets balanced a coffeepot, filters, and grounds. A black minifridge was tucked into a corner. But based on the look on Nessa's face, one would think he'd strewn his underwear all over the room.

Why is Nessa here and why do I feel as though I'm under attack?

"Somehow I don't think you're here to congratulate me." The best defense was a strong offense. He'd learned that lesson playing youth football.

"I'm afraid not." Nessa's smile turned cold as she held his gaze. "I took an early lunch to meet with you because this matter is too important to wait."

"And too important for a phone call?"

"Yes." Nessa crossed her right leg over her left, adjusting the crease in her dull brown slacks. Her cream blouse was buttoned to her neck. She'd tucked a small strand of fake pearls under her collar. "I've heard you plan to perform the play at the community center."

"That's right." Vaughn sat back on his chair, balancing his right ankle on his left knee. "I spoke with Ron yesterday. He's going to let us use the activity room June thirteenth."

Ronald Kendall had been the Guiding Light Community Center's director since Vaughn and his brothers had been in elementary school almost thirty years ago. He must be in his early seventies by now.

"Ron Kendall does not have the authority to permit your use of the center." Nessa's officious tone made Vaughn want to ask her to leave.

"If the center's director doesn't have that authority, who does?"

Nessa's smile broadened. "The Trinity Falls Town Council, of course."

Vaughn's sense of foreboding heightened. "How do I petition the council for approval?"

"I can save you the trouble." Nessa folded her hands on her thigh. "The council cannot sanction the use of the town's community center for your musical."

"Why not?" What was Nessa's game?

"I've heard your performance includes paranormal elements."

"That's right." Vaughn kept his expression blank, but his unease grew.

Who were Nessa's sources? He'd only discussed his work with a handful of people, and very briefly. Whoever had given Nessa her intel had armed her with more details than he remembered sharing.

"As a public facility that provides services to the community at large, the center cannot be seen to condone such hedonistic messages. It would offend Christians."

"Seriously?" He sounded like his students. But he couldn't help it. Nessa had caught him completely off guard.

"Oh, I'm very serious."

"Nessa, I'm a Christian and I'm not offended."

"Then I would remind you of the scriptures. Galatians specifically references witchcraft."

Nessa probably had never read any of J. K. Rowling's Harry Potter books. A pity.

"Very good." Vaughn inclined his head. "I always go back to Matthew and the caution against judging others."

Nessa flushed a bright red under Vaughn's direct gaze. "Even the title of your play, *Mystic Park*, evokes images of evil."

Vaughn stared at the council president. She must be joking. "The play isn't evil. It's a romance."

"Isn't it based on Caribbean culture?"

"Caribbean lore and folktales."

Nessa frowned. "There are a lot of strange religions in that culture."

"You shouldn't automatically fear what you don't understand." Vaughn forced himself not to be offended on his family's behalf. But it was a struggle. "Does Ron know you've decided the center can't host the play?"

"There's no need for me to consult with Ron on my decision."

"What about professional courtesy?"

Nessa practically vibrated with displeasure. "The fact of the matter is that the center is supported largely by tax money from the town, making it a public concern."

How would Benita handle this? He glanced at his phone. If only he could call her to ask.

"Shouldn't the entire council decide whether my musical offends the public sentiment?" Vaughn was coming to the end of his patience.

"That's not necessary." Nessa gathered her purse as though signaling the meeting was coming to an end. "The council cannot give even a hint of supporting alternative religions."

"You're making this change the week before the audition. It's scheduled to be held next Wednesday at the community center. I've already bought the ads." Vaughn tried to reason with her one last time.

Nessa stood. "I can't imagine that good people would want to be involved in your production."

"A couple of council members are on the schedule." Vaughn rose from his seat. Manners had been too firmly instilled in the Brooks household to allow his grievance with Nessa to get in the way.

Surprise flashed across Nessa's thin features. "Then

I would advise you to get in touch with these people and tell them the audition has been moved."

"To where? And what about the walk-ins?"

"I'm sure you'll figure something out." Nessa shrugged. "Thanks for your time, Vaughn. Enjoy the rest of your day."

The edge of satisfaction in Nessa's tone and her expression should have sent Vaughn over the edge. Instead he shook his head with a smile, then sank back onto his black padded executive chair. He'd known producing his musical wouldn't be easy: the costs, the myriad tasks involved outside of the production, the personalities. But he had one positive—Benita's involvement. She'd help him keep his head on straight so he could deal with obstacles like the one Nessa had just planted in his path.

Vaughn's hand hovered over his telephone receiver. And what would he do when he couldn't lean on her any longer? He shrugged off the muscle-numbing dread and dialed Benita's cell phone number. She answered on the second ring.

Vaughn chose to forego the traditional greeting. "We've suffered our first setback with *Mystic Park*."

"What is it?" Her no-nonsense reply eased Vaughn's tension.

"Nessa said we can't perform in the community center." Vaughn summarized his meeting with the town council president.

"Nessa has gone off her rails." Benita's tone was incredulous. "This isn't a decision she can make by herself."

"Should we talk to the other council members?" Vaughn imagined Benita in Ms. Helen's home. Which room was she in? Was she sitting or standing? What was she wearing?

"There's no time." Her sigh stretched down the phone line. "We need to go to Plan B."

Vaughn drew a blank. "I don't have a Plan B."

"I do. Find out if we can have the musical in TFU's auditorium."

Vaughn swallowed his disappointment. "I wanted to perform the play in the community center."

"So did I." Benita's understanding went a long way toward helping Vaughn get over his disappointment. "But if you're serious about getting the musical on stage in eight weeks, we don't have time to fight Nessa and persuade the council members."

"You're right."

"I know." There was a smile in her voice. "Look on the bright side. The auditorium holds more people."

"I think the university president will agree to having the performance here. It'll be good exposure for us in the community." Vaughn checked his Timex. First, he needed to speak with Foster. There was a hierarchy and a process to be followed. "Foster says the president wants to strengthen TFU's ties with the town, especially with the university's sesquicentennial coming up."

"Will you be able to ask the president today?" Benita seemed anxious. So was Vaughn.

"I'll try."

"I'll be waiting for your call."

Vaughn recradled his telephone receiver. It was a relief not to have to deal with production issues on his

own. Those six words—"I'll be waiting for your call"—
made his impossible seem possible.

He and Benita had always worked together well. He
had the creative vision and she could make things happen.
Now if only he could find a creative way to make her love
him enough to stay in Trinity Falls.

Benita disconnected Vaughn's call on her cellular
phone. A glance at the display screen told her it was
about twenty minutes until noon. She strolled into the
kitchen and found Ms. Helen with her head in the refrigerator.

"Do you want to join me at Books and Bakery?"
Benita crossed her arms and rested her hip against the
counter.

Her great-aunt let the refrigerator door shut. She
gave Benita a critical once-over. "What's got your hair
on fire?"

Benita had thought she'd masked her temper. But her
great-aunt always had been able to read her like a book.
"I need to let Doreen know that Nessa's circumventing
her authority as mayor, as well as the rest of the town
council."

Ms. Helen's thin, still-dark eyebrows shot to her snow
white hairline. "Again? That woman's a piece of work."

"Are you coming with me?"

"I wouldn't miss it."

Forty minutes later—after Ms. Helen had dressed
to impress—Benita and her great-aunt settled onto
bar stools at the café counter. Benita had overruled

Ms. Helen's protestations and treated her great-aunt to a healthy and filling lunch of chicken-and-wild-rice soup and a half chicken-and-provolone-on-wheat sandwich. Benita had ordered the same thing for herself. They were halfway through their meal before Doreen was able to get away from the cash register. Benita recounted for the town's mayor the same report she'd given Ms. Helen on their drive to Books & Bakery.

"Nessa can't make that unilateral decision." Doreen's voice was tight with irritation. Her brown eyes sparked with temper.

"No, she can't." Ms. Helen lowered her soup spoon. "Ask the other council members if Nessa discussed her plan with them before she spoke with Vaughn."

"I will." The mayor's voice was clipped. "But regardless, Nessa still should have brought her concerns to my attention before acting. As mayor, I should be included in any discussions regarding the proper use of town resources."

"So should the rest of the council." Ms. Helen sipped her iced tea. "Nessa had no business acting alone."

Doreen expelled a frustrated breath. She leaned heavily on the café counter. Benita had eased some of the load from Doreen's shoulders by taking over her wedding plans. But it was obvious the mayor was still overworked and overtired.

Benita glanced past Doreen. The retired couple Megan had hired moved efficiently between the kitchen and the counter, taking new orders and serving hungry customers. But was their help enough? That was a discussion for another time.

She met Doreen's concerned gaze. "I'm not asking that you or the council overturn Nessa's decision. Vaughn and I are looking at another venue. But you need to know what Nessa did."

"I'll call her at home to discuss this tonight." Doreen crossed to the beverage cart behind the café counter and brought back the pitcher of iced tea. She refilled Ms. Helen's and Benita's glasses. "I don't know why she thought she could speak for the entire town government on her own and without consulting us."

Ms. Helen finished her sandwich. "Do you think the attack was personal against you, or was she targeting your office?"

"I don't know." Doreen returned the pitcher to the beverage cart. "Nessa knows I'm concerned about the community center. I sent an e-mail to the council members. The center needs more financial support than our tax base can give it. The January fund-raiser helped a lot. But the center's staff needs to do regular fund-raisers and community outreach."

Ms. Helen snorted. "Good luck getting Ronald Kendall to work on a fund-raiser. That man should've retired ten years ago."

"Darius told me June Cale's looking for a new job." Doreen glanced at Benita. "June is the mother of Darius's half brother, Noah."

Benita sipped her lemonade. "Aunt Helen told me about June and Noah."

"June has fund-raising experience." Doreen greeted a group of guests who returned their trays before leaving. "I'm hoping I can convince her to relocate from Sequoia to work for our community center."

Benita finished her sandwich. "I doubt she'd be able to find a better job offer in Sequoia."

"The trick will be to convince Ron to take on the added responsibility of fund-raising." Doreen cleared Benita's and Ms. Helen's dishes, adding them to a hard plastic tub behind the counter.

Ms. Helen sat back on her bar stool. "The bigger trick will be getting the residents of Trinity Falls to accept June Cale into our community. There are some people who wouldn't want her here."

Benita thought of Darius's parents, Ethel and Simon Knight, whose marriage had finally ended when Ethel realized June Cale had given Simon a son eighteen years ago that he'd never told his wife about.

Benita's eyes widened. "That could be awkward."

CHAPTER 12

Vaughn counted nearly thirty people assembled in the Trinity Falls University auditorium Wednesday night. He recognized many of his neighbors and students, and of course the university's faculty and staff. They were all waiting to audition for his musical.

His pulse pounded with a sense of accomplishment. Seated beside him, Benita glowed as she looked at the patiently waiting crowd.

"What are you thinking?" He kept his voice low.

She turned her brilliant smile on him. He blinked at its power. "You did this."

He so badly wanted to kiss her. But he couldn't do that here, in front of all of these people. And he couldn't kiss her now, not while they were supposed to be breaking up. *Could I?*

"Let's get started." Vaughn stood and raised his voice. "Thanks, everyone, for coming. I wasn't expecting such a strong turnout. Most of you know me. I'm Vaughn Brooks. I teach music here at TFU."

"*Doctor* Vaughn Brooks," Benita interrupted, speaking above him. "He's the university's music professor, concert band director, and writer/composer of the musical, *Mystic Park*."

"Are you going to do a lot of that?" Vaughn lowered his voice. He didn't want to draw attention to their disagreement.

"I'm just clarifying a few things." Benita waved a dismissive hand. "You're too modest."

Vaughn turned back to their audience scattered across the large auditorium. During the day, the sun shone through the stained glass windows carved just beneath the ceiling, making the images sparkle like jewels. But tonight, the darkness looked like velvet behind paintings. In the front of the auditorium, Vaughn and Benita stood in a concert pit that stretched between the rows of chairs and the mahogany stage.

"Let me tell you a little about the musical." Vaughn paused to collect his thoughts. "It's a romance based on the Caribbean folklore of water nymphs and water fairies. The hero is a farmer. The heroine is a water fairy. The villain is the water spirit, Mama D'Leau. She's part woman, part serpent. The five other characters are the farmer's friend, three other water fairies, and Mama D'Leau's accomplice."

"So you're looking for eight people all together?" Simon Knight called from a seat near the middle of the center section. Simon was the father of Vaughn's childhood friend Darius Knight.

"Eight main characters and a few additional people

for the chorus and crowd scenes." Vaughn spotted Simon's estranged wife, Ethel Knight, a few rows behind Simon.

Oh, boy. What bad fortune has brought these two people together for my audition? He still had bad reactions to the memory of their frequent bickering during last year's fund-raising committee meetings.

"Do all the characters have to be able to sing?" Novella Dishy, a stylist with Skin Deep Beauty Salon, sat in the back of the auditorium with other salon stylists.

"Only the eight main characters," Vaughn responded. "The additional actors don't have songs."

"Do they have lines?" Novella sounded suspicious.

"No, they don't." Vaughn shook his head.

"Well, then, I'm done." Novella stood. The older woman squeezed past Belinda Curby, the salon's owner, and Glenn Narcus, another stylist, then left the auditorium without a backward glance.

"What was she thinking?" Simon's bark of laughter broke the awkward silence. "Of course everyone would have to be able to sing. It's a *musical*."

It wasn't a good idea to agree with Simon out loud. Instead Vaughn changed the subject. "Are there other questions?"

Glenn raised his hand. "When are the performances?"

"We're doing one performance on June thirteenth," Vaughn answered.

"June thirteenth?" Belinda's voice squeaked with surprise. "Are you crazy?"

"That's only seven weeks away." Ethel added her voice to the chorus of surprise circling the room.

"It's not as bad as it sounds." Vaughn's assurance

didn't make a dent in the rising cacophony. "Wait a minute. Everybody just wait."

"Listen. Up." Benita's voice cut through the noise like a machete. "Today is Wednesday, April twenty-second. The musical is scheduled for Saturday, June thirteenth."

She rose to pace the auditorium. Her voice was stern. Her body language was determined. This was Benita Hawkins in her element, taking charge.

"Yes, the schedule is tight. But it's doable." Benita paused in front of the center section. Her hands were planted on her hips. She glared at the aspiring actors. "If you can't handle the schedule, leave now with our thanks for coming. But if you want a once-in-a-lifetime chance to star in a professionally written stage performance while serving your community, we'd love for you to stay."

Vaughn waited with increasing tension for the crowd's reaction. Had Benita been too stern? Would they all get up and leave? He never would have given his neighbors an ultimatum. He needed their help if he was to realize his dream of producing this musical. But Benita didn't have anything to lose, so she'd played the heavy, a role that fit her well.

The crowd settled down. Vaughn exhaled as he realized no one else was leaving. He gave Benita a grateful smile. She winked at him in response.

Vaughn turned back to their audience. "If there aren't other questions, we'll get started with the auditions."

* * *

More than four hours later, Vaughn and Benita said good night to the final auditioner, Virginia Carp.

Benita watched Vaughn as Ginny disappeared through the auditorium door. She didn't like his rapt expression. "I've heard Ginny's nuts."

"Who would've thought a voice that big could come from someone so petite?" The admiration in Vaughn's voice set Benita's teeth on edge.

"She may have a beautiful singing voice but her behavior's erratic." Benita angled her body toward Vaughn.

They sat side-by-side on the uncomfortable crimson-padded folding chairs in the auditorium's audience. It was late but she wasn't tired. Maybe she was running on the adrenaline of managing the night's audition. Or maybe this restless energy came from Vaughn's company. They were the only two people left in the cavernous room. Maybe the only two people left in the almost one-hundred-and-fifty-year-old building. The sense of intimacy was as thick as a mattress.

"What makes you say she's erratic?" Vaughn turned from his rapt attention of the auditorium exit through which Ginny had left.

"I don't think you want her to be involved in your production." Benita was torn between keeping her friend's secrets and warning Vaughn away from Ginny.

"You still haven't told me why not." A smile flirted around Vaughn's too-sexy-for-words lips. She'd known those lips so well for so long.

"She's the kind of person who'll key your car if she doesn't get her way." *Why won't he just listen to me and move on?*

"You're talking about Ginny keying Darius's car and

spray painting his apartment door." The smile materialized, curving his lips and brightening his eyes.

"You know about that?" Surprise lifted Benita's eyebrows.

"Trinity Falls has very few secrets." Vaughn balanced his right ankle on his left knee. "But how did *you* hear about it all the way in Los Angeles?"

"Aunt Helen told me. She was concerned for Darius."

"Ginny's reaction to Darius's breaking up with her was extreme. But this play is different." Vaughn linked his fingers together. "It's a professional commitment. It's not personal."

"Do you think someone who'd key another person's car can be professional?"

"With a voice like Ginny's, I'm willing to take the chance." Vaughn lowered his right leg and pushed himself to his feet. "It's late and I have an early class in the morning. Let's get together tomorrow night to cast the rest of the parts."

Benita uncrossed her legs and stood as well. "Ginny has a beautiful voice. But I think we can find other women in Trinity Falls with attractive singing voices."

"I don't want to hold another audition." Vaughn collected his folder and writing tablet. He packed everything into his black knapsack and threw the bag over his shoulder. "We don't have time."

Stubborn man.

"I know." Benita stuffed her paperwork into her emerald green tote bag. "But you don't want Ginny on your cast. Trust me."

"Benny, let's give Ginny a chance."

Benita fell into step beside Vaughn as they walked to

the auditorium's exit. Their footsteps echoed in the empty room. "What about Audra?"

"She didn't audition." Vaughn sounded dismissive.

"She doesn't need to. You've heard her sing dozens of times while she was rehearsing with your concert band for the town's Sesquicentennial Celebration."

"I could be wrong, but I think Audra didn't audition because she doesn't want to be in the play." Vaughn's voice was dry.

"I'll ask her. I'm sure she'll be happy to play the lead in your musical. Think of the publicity that'll give you."

"Benny, the audition is over." Vaughn came to a stop at the exit and faced her. "Don't make Audra uncomfortable by asking her to participate. I respect her decision not to be in the musical. She shouldn't have to be in every performance the town has."

"Fine." Benita sighed. "If you really want Ginny Carp as the female lead for your play, I'll accept that."

"I really do."

"You're making a mistake."

"Benny—"

"I just hope she doesn't key your car." Benita turned to lead Vaughn down the stairs to the rear parking lot.

"I appreciate your concern, but I'm sure my car will be fine."

They'd both parked in the first row of the visitors' parking lot, which was steps from the academic building's rear exit. Streetlights cut through the inky darkness, aiding their visibility and adding a cloak of security.

Benita used her security keypad to deactivate her car alarm. "Your place tomorrow night?"

Vaughn nodded. "I should be home by six."

"I'll expect dinner since you aren't paying for my services."

"Fair enough. But don't expect anything fancy."

"I know your limitations." Benita gave him a teasing smile before slipping onto her driver's seat.

She couldn't wait for tomorrow night. Operation Lure Vaughn Brooks to L.A. was in full swing.

Vaughn needed to get off TFU's campus. It was half past four o'clock on Thursday evening. Benita would be at his house by six P.M. He wanted to clean up and start dinner before she arrived. It wasn't a date. He knew that. They were getting together to review their casting choices for *Mystic Park*. But there was no reason he couldn't look nice while they were doing that.

He shut down his laptop computer and stood from his desk. The knock on his office door was unexpected. "Come in."

Olivia Stark stood in his doorway. Her fist gripped his doorknob. "Can I interest you in dinner?"

Why would having a beautiful woman invite him to dinner make him tense? Because she wanted something he couldn't give her.

"Can I have a rain check?" Vaughn found a smile. "I have a meeting."

"I understand." Olivia laughed nervously. "I'm not usually spontaneous. Actually, I'm never spontaneous. But I thought I'd try it today."

"And I would've loved to have joined you."

"But you have a meeting." Olivia's gaze wavered. "Is it just a meeting?"

"What do you mean?" But he thought he knew.

"I've been asking about you around town."

That couldn't bode well. Vaughn gestured toward his guest chair in an invitation for Olivia to make herself more comfortable. "What've you found out?"

"You recently broke up with Benita Hawkins, a woman you've been dating since high school." Olivia settled onto one of his gray cushioned chairs.

"You learned a lot." Vaughn sat. He thought he'd been prepared to hear her say that. He'd been wrong.

"It had been a long-distance relationship." Olivia watched him closely.

Vaughn was afraid to blink. "Benny and I went to separate out-of-state colleges. After college, I came back to Trinity Falls. She didn't." Vaughn forced himself not to shift on his seat.

"May I ask why you broke up?"

The question hurt, but he understood Olivia's need to ask it. They'd dated a couple of times. He'd thought he could move on, but he hadn't been able to. And she could tell. Olivia was an attractive, intelligent, charming woman who seemed to enjoy living in Trinity Falls. On the surface, she was perfect for him.

Then why am I allowing Benita to come between us?

"We want different things out of life." Vaughn worked hard to keep his voice steady.

"But you still love her." It was a statement, not a question.

"We're not together anymore."

"The two of you dated for half of your life. You don't

just wake up one day and decide you're over the other person."

"I wish it was that easy." Vaughn looked away from Olivia.

"Each time we went out, I sensed someone else was on your mind."

"I'm sorry." He'd never meant to make her feel uncomfortable or disrespected.

"So am I." Olivia stood. "I think our relationship was over before it had a chance to begin."

Vaughn rose to his feet. "Olivia—"

She raised her right hand, palm out. "Benita's a very lucky lady. I hope she comes to her senses soon."

Why can't I fall in love with Olivia? She would be perfect for me.

"I'm an idiot." Vaughn scrubbed his hands over his face.

"No, you're a man in love." Olivia turned toward the door. "Like I said, Benita's a very lucky woman."

"Thank you, Olivia."

She paused with her hand on the doorknob. "I've heard you have two brothers who look a lot like you. Any chance they'll be visiting soon?"

Vaughn smiled. "They're coming home for my play."

"I look forward to meeting them." Olivia disappeared through his office door, closing it behind her.

There was a burning sensation where his heart should have been. Vaughn drove the heel of his hand into his chest. Did Benita consider herself a lucky woman? Somehow he didn't think so.

* * *

"Thanks again for dinner. It smells delicious." Benita stole another look at Vaughn, seated across from her at his small circular ash wood table in his tiny kitchen Thursday evening.

Benita gathered a forkful of the wild rice Vaughn had made to accompany the curried chicken. She'd bought the set of dishes for him as a housewarming gift when he'd moved into his first apartment in Trinity Falls.

Vaughn was a wonderful cook. *Has he cooked for Olivia Stark yet?* Benita felt the sharp bite of jealousy.

"Thanks for your help." Vaughn seemed preoccupied as he sliced into his chicken again.

"Does Olivia know you invited me to dinner?" From where had that question come?

"Don't start, Benny." Tension bracketed Vaughn's mouth framed by his neatly shaped goatee.

Interesting. "I just asked whether she knew we were having dinner together. I'm curious."

"There's no need for you to be." Vaughn drank his iced tea.

"Is that your polite way of telling me to mind my own business?" Benita cut another piece of chicken. It had a strong, spicy flavor and melted on her tongue like well-seasoned butter.

"Yes." Vaughn paused as he ate more rice and drank more iced tea. "Olivia and I aren't dating any longer."

"Oh? What happened?" The stranglehold around Benita's throat eased. Her heart felt lighter.

"Nothing happened." Vaughn shrugged his broad

shoulders under his gray long-sleeved TFU jersey. The material flirted with the well-developed muscles across his chest. "We just aren't right for each other."

"I see." Joy washed over her.

For the remainder of the meal, they talked about their day, shared memories from their past, and discussed their plans for the rest of the week. Benita helped Vaughn clear the table and load his dishwasher. Then they made two cups of chai tea.

"OK, let's talk about casting your musical." Benita led Vaughn back to his kitchen table. She resumed her seat, crossing her legs. "I assume I can't talk you out of giving Ginny Carp the lead female role?"

"Not a chance." Vaughn's warm cocoa eyes laughed at her as he sipped his tea.

"And I can't change your mind about holding another audition?"

"No, you can't." Vaughn set his mug on the table and cupped his hands around it. "Why would you want to?"

"Producing this musical has been your dream for years. Now that you have your chance, you should give it your best shot. Instead you're rushing it."

"I'm satisfied with the people we found during yesterday's auditions." Vaughn shrugged off her suggestions.

"That's my point. You've worked too hard to settle for being 'satisfied.'" She flung her arm in a dramatic flourish. "You should be thrilled, excited, enthusiastic."

"Another day or two of auditions isn't going to make a difference. I'd rather start the rehearsals."

"Fine." It was clear she wasn't going to change his mind. *Stubborn man.* Benita studied him over the rim of her cup. His determination was sexy—except when he was being obstinate with her.

"With Ginny as the female lead—the water fairy— whom do you have in mind for the male lead—the farmer?" Vaughn referred to his notes.

"Glenn Narcus." Benita opened her project folder and scanned her summaries.

"I agree."

"Well, that's a nice change."

"Be kind, Benny."

"Whom do you want to play the villain, Mama D'Leau?" Benita ran her right index finger down the sheet of paper.

"That one's hard." Vaughn shuffled some papers. "I'm torn between Belinda Curby and Yvette Bates. What do you think?"

"Yvette Bates." Benita was decisive. "Her voice is fuller, richer. Belinda fits better in the fairy chorus."

"Good point." Vaughn looked up from his papers and captured her gaze.

Benita smiled into his eyes. Was Operation Lure Vaughn Brooks to L.A. working? "This is fun. It reminds me of working on our high school senior project to- gether."

"Yeah, it does." His voice was full of special memories, some innocent, some not quite as innocent. "Whom do you have as the villain's accomplice?"

They agreed on all of the remaining roles: Simon Knight, Darius's father, as the villain's right-hand person; and Stan Crockett as the hero's neighbor and best friend. In addition to Belinda, they agreed to cast as members of the fairy chorus Ethel Knight and Cece Roben.

The only casting on which they disagreed was Ginny Carp as the water fairy. Benita considered Vaughn in her peripheral vision. She'd pushed as hard as she dared. Vaughn was immovable. She'd have to come up with an alternate plan just in case her worst fears of Ginny flaking out on the production came true.

Vaughn gathered together his summary sheets. "It's nice to have someone to bounce off ideas about the play. Thank you."

"You're welcome." Benita packed her notes as well.

"I also owe you my thanks for defending the performance schedule to the auditioners yesterday."

Benita smiled at his wry tone. "You'd have done the same for me. We make a good team."

"We always have."

Then why are you willing to throw that all away?

Benita folded her arms on the table and leaned into it. "It's like the time in high school when you backed my campaign for senior class treasurer against one of your football teammates." The memory of his support made her feel warm inside even eighteen years later. She needed him to stand with her again now and agree to her decision for them to live in L.A. Why wouldn't he?

"I still think you should've run for president." Vaughn leaned back on his chair. He rested his right ankle on his left knee.

Benita pulled her gaze from his muscled thigh wrapped in denim. "And you'd still be wrong. I've explained this a thousand times. First, Jack was running for president. No one would've voted for me over a descendant of our town's founding family."

"I would've."

Benita ignored his interruption. "Second, the real power is with the money. Aunt Helen told me that and she was right."

"You drove Jack nuts." Vaughn chuckled.

"You guys had to justify every penny to me—for homecoming, prom, the senior class trip, everything. It was wonderful." Benita licked her lips at the memory.

"Jack wanted to impeach you." Vaughn's husky voice shook.

The comment burst her happy bubble. Vaughn had shared that insight before.

"You can't impeach a treasurer." Benita scowled. "Can you?"

"If you hadn't relented on the prom theme, we would've found out." His voice was full of laughter. She still couldn't decide if he was serious.

"Whatever happened to the football player who ran against me?"

"He works on Wall Street." Vaughn propped his elbow on the table and cradled the side of his head on his palm. The movement brought him closer to her. She could smell his soap. Her heart fluttered.

"Are you serious?" It was a struggle to concentrate on their conversation, especially since she didn't want to.

"He must have gotten Ms. Helen's speech on money and power." The warm laughter glowing in Vaughn's eyes was like a caress.

Benita's body responded to it. She didn't want to lose this man. Could she find a way to hold on to him as well as her dream of living in L.A.?

"I'm glad losing the election for high school senior class treasurer didn't distract him from his career goal." Benita stood, carrying her empty tea mug to the dishwasher. She could feel Vaughn behind her.

"He seems to have everything: a job he enjoys and a family he loves."

"His life does sound perfect." Benita turned, finding Vaughn too close. She extended her hand for his mug, placing it beside hers in the dishwasher. "And what is it that you want?"

"What I've always wanted—you." His voice was low, dark, and deep.

CHAPTER 13

Yes!

Benita didn't know how she ended up in Vaughn's arms, but it was exactly where she'd wanted to be since the last time she'd felt his embrace. He held her so tightly to him. She felt every long, hard inch of him against every welcoming part of her. *Delicious.* His touch made her body ache. Benita twined her arms around his shoulders and slipped her hands up his neck and over his clean-shaven head. His skin was warm and smooth. Electricity coursed through her.

Vaughn's mouth moved over hers, caressing her, teasing her, filling her with anticipation. Benita parted her lips to catch her breath and Vaughn swept inside. His tongue slipped past her entrance, giving her a taste of what she could have again. And she wanted it. She craved the way he made her burn. She needed the excitement of touching him, tasting him. She longed to hear her name on his lips that way. But most of all, she ached for him to know she was the only woman who

could give him what he needed. She would start by
showing him what he liked.

Benita stepped away from Vaughn, ending their kiss.
He looked at her with hot cocoa eyes. Benita braced her
hands on his shoulders and leaped, wrapping her legs
around his hips. Vaughn's eyes glowed. His hands
squeezed her hips, pulling her tighter against his torso.
The message in his eyes made Benita dampen. Her
breath caught.

She lowered her head for another kiss. But this time,
she took control. She pressed her way inside and ex-
plored. She ran her tongue over his teeth. He held her
tighter. She stroked the roof of his mouth. His body
trembled. She suckled his tongue. Vaughn groaned,
long, low, and deep in his throat. A shiver of awareness
rippled through her blood.

Vaughn turned and crossed the room. He stopped
when her back pressed against a wall. "I don't want to
drop you."

"You're stronger than that."

Vaughn groaned. "You make me weak."

His words, his touch, his taste, his scent, his everything conspired to make her head spin. She lowered her
hands to tug his jersey over his head. Vaughn helped her.
Her lips parted with awe as her gaze ate up the broad
expanse of muscled nutmeg torso. Her gaze followed
the narrowing trail of hair until it disappeared between
them. She lowered her head to kiss him again. Her fingers
played in the hair on his chest.

Vaughn tucked a hand between them. A tug at her
emerald silk blouse let her know he was freeing the row
of buttons on the front of her shirt. Benita kept kissing
him, tasting his lips, caressing his mouth, sucking his

tongue. Vaughn stepped back from the wall and stripped her blouse free. A pull at her bra and the flesh-colored lingerie followed suit, falling to the wall-to-wall cream carpet.

She was topless before him. Her perch at his waist left her bare breasts practically at mouth level. Benita's breath grew shallow. Her pulse beat harder. Her nipples pebbled, aching for Vaughn's lips.

He lifted his gaze to hers. His cocoa gaze was scalding and intense. "You've always been my fantasy."

Benita's heart melted. She offered him her breast. Vaughn drew her into his mouth. He suckled her, nipped her, rolled her on his tongue. Benita cupped the back of his head. She moaned her pleasure as her body flooded with desire.

Vaughn nudged her legs free of his waist. Together, they quickly disrobed, leaving their clothes in a pile near their feet. Benita's gaze rose from Vaughn's large, bare feet to his long, lean legs, and up to his bold erection. Her body grew hungry at the sight of its thick, proud length. Benita stroked it with her fingertips. Vaughn caught his breath. Benita lowered herself to her knees to taste him.

"Benita." Vaughn's hand cupped her shoulder. His voice held a note of caution. Was he close to the edge? So was she.

She ran her tongue over the length of him, then drew him back into her mouth. Benita cupped his hips and found a rhythm for her ministrations. She wanted him to know this is what he'd have—and more—if he moved to L.A. with her.

"Benny, wait." He sounded urgent.

Benita took him deeper, moving her tongue over him. Vaughn stepped back, his breathing ragged.

"I want to come inside you." He helped her to stand, then escorted her to the living room.

Benita watched as he tossed his sofa cushions to the floor. He came back to her, swept her from her feet, and carried her to the makeshift bed. He laid her on the cushions, then braced himself on his arms above her. "This is what I want."

Vaughn cupped her breast, kneading it and pinching her nipple as he gazed into her eyes. Benita couldn't lay still. Her legs shifted restlessly on the pile of cushions as sensation radiated from the tip of her breast to the core of her desire.

"I thought you were going to come inside me." Her voice was broken and breathless.

"I am." Vaughn lowered his head and kissed her.

He stroked his tongue across the seam of her lips at the same time that he separated her folds with his fingers. Benita shivered with surprise. He penetrated her mouth with his tongue as he pressed first one finger, then a second inside her. Benita gasped. Vaughn deepened their kiss. He picked up a rocking motion with his hand. His thumb stroked her clitoris. Benita spread her thighs, hungry for his attention. Her hips lifted to him, twisting under the sensation. And then he stopped.

"Vaughn." Benita gritted his name past her teeth. "I need you."

"I need you, too." He gave her a full-body caress with both of his hands. His palms moved over her breasts, down her torso, past her hips.

His mouth followed. Vaughn kissed her nipples, then

took her breast into his mouth. Benita's core heated again. She felt her desire pool inside her. Vaughn kissed his way down her body, lingering at her navel, her waist, her hips. His breath blew against her nest of curls. Desire flowed freely now. Vaughn dragged his fingers through her soft shield. Her lips trembled. Benita's muscles tightened with anticipation. Then he cupped her derriere and lifted her to his mouth. Benita gasped in surprise, anticipation. Joy. Vaughn kissed her intimately, deeply, over and over and over again. He licked her. He sipped her. And when he slipped his fingers inside her again, a fireworks display exploded behind her tightly closed eyelids. Blood pounded in her ears. Wave after wave of sensation rolled over her. Her body shook and tossed like a toy lifeboat at sea. Vaughn kissed her one last time, then lay her hips back down on the cushion.

Benita spread her thighs as the echoes of pleasure still pulsed inside her. They'd stopped using condoms years before. Benita was on an oral contraceptive and they were both clean. Vaughn came to her and with one long, smooth thrust joined with her. Benita's body trembled with sensation.

Vaughn's heart pounded in his chest so hard he thought it would punch its way free. Benita was driving him crazy with desire. It was more than her sultry body, the sexy way she kissed, or the seductive way she touched. It was the way she looked at him that said they were to-gether. It was the way she reached for him as though she needed him close. He held her gaze as he moved inside her. He felt her inner muscles squeezing him. He clenched his teeth as sweat broke out all over his body.

He whispered with his lips beside her ear. "None of your tricks, vixen. I want to stay inside you a little bit longer."

"Stay as long as you'd like."

Vaughn groaned. He pressed against her and rolled his hips. She wrapped her legs around him and held him close. Vaughn gathered her against him and turned onto his back.

"Ride me." Vaughn stared up at Benita as she straddled him. Her firm, curvy figure wore a sheen of perspiration. Her hazel eyes glowed with desire. Her hair was tangled around her heart-shaped face.

Benita smiled. She arched her back and set a rhythm that made his eyes cross. Vaughn cupped her breasts, letting her nipples graze his palms as they bounced in time with her movements. She rocked him, squeezed him, pressed her hips against him. Vaughn panted, straining toward completion. He felt himself slipping toward the edge. He released Benita's breasts and cupped her thighs, holding on for dear life. He heard her groans like the lyrics to a song as her body urged her to pleasure with him. Vaughn raised his hips against her, deeper, harder. His body bowed with strain. He slipped his hand between Benita's thighs and found her spot. He touched her. Benita gasped. Her body convulsed, drawing him with her over the edge, falling together and landing as one.

CHAPTER 14

"Thanks for cooking breakfast." Vaughn accepted the plate of French toast and turkey bacon Benita handed him Friday morning.

She could smell him on the shirt he'd loaned her. His scent was a mixture of soap and cedar. Her heart squeezed.

"You're welcome." Benita carried her plate to Vaughn's kitchen table and took the seat to his right. "I would've made the coffee, too."

"You do many things well, sweetheart." Vaughn gave her a teasing look. "Making coffee isn't one of them."

"Your inability to handle my high-octane java doesn't make it bad." Benita cut into her French toast. "I also appreciate the loan of your shirt."

"It looks good on you." The expression in Vaughn's eyes as they skimmed the button-down powder blue shirt reminded Benita that she wasn't wearing anything underneath.

She'd fastened only a few of the buttons. Vaughn's gaze lingered on the gap at her neckline before moving lower to where the shirt's hem fell to midthigh. Her body grew hungry for another form of sustenance.

"You don't look so bad yourself." Benita's voice was breathless. Her eyes caressed the warm cream dress shirt that stretched across Vaughn's broad shoulders and complimented his nutmeg skin. She'd bought him the brick red tie.

"The last time you made me breakfast wearing my clothes was college." Vaughn's voice was pensive. "I was living in an apartment off campus. You wore my Heritage High football jersey."

"I remember that." Benita kept her gaze on her plate as she fed herself a forkful of French toast.

"I'm still upset about losing that jersey."

"I know. I'm sorry." Benita pictured his jersey in her drawer with the rest of her night wear. She felt guilty but not enough to return it.

"It just disappeared."

"Hmmm." Benita made herself swallow another bite of French toast. They ate in silence for a while. Benita wrestled with her guilt over Vaughn's jersey.

"The same thing happened to my diary." She finally broke the silence. "I used to write in it every day. One day it was there, the next it was gone."

"That's strange."

"I think my mother took it. It disappeared while I was home from college during summer break." Benita sipped her coffee. "She denies it, but who else could it be? She knew about the diary and had access to it."

"You have a point."

"It's bad enough that she'd take my diary, but why keep it for all these years? That's just silly." Benita shrugged off her irritation. "Anyway, let's talk about something happier, like how wonderful *Mystic Park* is."

"Thank you." Pleasure warmed Vaughn's cocoa eyes.

"I know some producers who'd be happy to read it. It's right up their alley."

The pleasure faded from his expression. "I'm not interested."

Benita had anticipated that response. She knew Vaughn too well to have expected this pitch would be easy. "Why not?"

"I'm producing my play here, in Trinity Falls."

"I know, and I'm proud that you're using your work to raise money for the community center. But after the fund-raiser, you could produce *Mystic Park* in other cities and expose your work to a wider audience."

Vaughn stacked his dishes with Benita's, then rose from the table. "Benny, why do you want to show my work to this producer?"

Was he kidding? Benita followed Vaughn to his dishwasher.

"Your play is fantastic, the script as well as the music." Her words sped up with her enthusiasm. "It should be performed in front of as many audiences as possible. Why don't you want that?"

"I'm not interested in meeting with producers, pitching my work to investors, touring. I don't want any of that." Vaughn stacked the dirty dishes in his dishwasher. "All I ever wanted was to share my work with my community."

"But, Vaughn, you could do so much more with your talent." Benita spread her arms. "I don't understand why you don't want to."

Vaughn straightened from the dishwasher. "And I don't understand why what I do want isn't enough for you."

"Because it isn't." Benita spun on her bare heel and marched out of the kitchen. "You have too much talent to let it go to waste."

Vaughn followed her up the stairs and into his bedroom. "Putting my talents to use in Trinity Falls isn't a waste. This town is enough for me. It used to be enough for you, too, before you let your mother change your mind."

"My mother was right. And, if you'd ever left this town, you'd see that." Benita kept her back to Vaughn as she pulled on the clothes she'd worn yesterday.

If she faced him as she took off her clothes, she'd drag him back to bed. Sadly, it was getting late. Vaughn had to get to work and she wanted to accompany her great-aunt to another meeting with Foster.

"I've visited you in Los Angeles several times. If that's your idea of having more, you're welcome to keep all of it." Vaughn's disgruntled words carried to her from across the room.

"Is that your final decision?" Benita turned as she adjusted the hem of her T-shirt over the waistband of her capris.

"Yes, it is." Vaughn's tone and expression were stubborn.

"All right. I won't say I'm not disappointed, but I promise not to bring it up again." Benita crossed the room and led Vaughn back downstairs.

"I appreciate that." His clipped response came from behind her.

"Don't mention it." Benita waited at the foot of the

stairs. She grabbed his shirt front to pull him down for a quick kiss. "Have a good day."

"Thanks." He regarded her warily.

Benita paused in the living room just long enough to grab her purse, then followed Vaughn out of his townhome to his car. She ignored the suspicious looks he kept sending her way.

Promising not to bring it up again to Vaughn didn't prevent her from sending his script to the producer on her own. And, if the producer's interest in Vaughn's work finally convinced him to move to L.A. with her, well, that was just a bonus.

Benita pulled her spring jacket more closely around her shoulders. Outside, the weather was starting to resemble spring. Inside, Foster's TFU office in Butler Hall was an icebox this Friday morning. Was he trying to ensure that she and Ms. Helen didn't overstay their welcome? If that was the case, he shouldn't talk so much.

"And so, Doctor Gaston, TFU would consider it a great favor if you would reconsider your opposition to a small celebration in recognition of this endowed chair." Foster wrapped up his speech.

Benita was incredulous. The older man must have spoken for more than five minutes. Had her great-aunt even listened to all of that?

"You want me to let you host a celebration in my honor?" Ms. Helen summarized the university vice president's five-, six-, maybe even seven-minute speech.

"That's right." Foster nodded as though in emphasis.

"No." Ms. Helen's response was swift and short.

Benita could have told Foster his long-winded speech wasn't going to persuade her impatient great-aunt.

Foster's lips parted in shock. "Doctor Gaston—"

"Foster, let's wait until the donor arrives." Benita checked her Movado watch. "She should be here any minute now. Aunt Helen and I were early."

"She's here now." A new voice joined the conversation.

Benita turned to see an attractive older woman stride confidently into Foster's office. So this was Dr. Lana Penn, Ms. Helen's protégé. Why had Benita expected a mousy woman with much less fashion sense? The research scientist was tall and slender with great clothes and even better shoes.

Lana's thick cap of dark brown hair was layered around her diamond-shaped face. Her chocolate-colored trench coat hung open over a simple black dress. The pencil straight hemline ended at the chemist's knees. Her matching black stilettos boosted her height by about three inches. A chunky silver necklace, bracelet, and earrings brightened the dark outfit.

"Thank you for convening this meeting, Doctor Gooden." The woman stopped in front of Foster's desk and extended her hand.

Foster was already standing. He returned her greeting. "Please call me Foster."

"Thank you." Lana gave the university vice president a gracious smile before turning to Benita. "You must be Benita Hawkins. It's a pleasure to finally meet you. Doctor Gaston has told me wonderful things about you over the years."

Really? Benita blinked. The first she'd heard of Doctor Lana Penn was when Ms. Helen had mentioned the endowment in the same tone Benita used to schedule a dentist's appointment. Benita gave her great-aunt a look that assured her they'd discuss this later. Ms. Helen replied with a look that said only if she was in the mood.

Ms. Helen started to rise from her seat, but Lana approached her chair and rested a hand on her shoulder. "Please don't get up, Doctor Gaston. It's great to see you again." She bent over to give Ms. Helen a hug.

"How many times do I have to tell you to call me Ms. Helen?" Her tone was querulous, but the elder chemist returned Lana's embrace with obvious affection.

"It will take some getting used to." Lana took the extra seat to Ms. Helen's left. "So, why don't you want a formal ceremony to announce the endowed chair?"

Benita tilted her head at the research chemist's direct approach. Impressive. Ms. Helen couldn't dismiss Lana's question with another one-word answer.

"This endowment shouldn't be about me." Ms. Helen folded her hands in her lap. "Your donation will do a lot for the students and the department. Keep the focus there."

"The students are the point of this endowment." Lana shifted in her seat to face Ms. Helen. "But I want the second-year chemistry students, faculty, even staff to know you're the inspiration behind this donation and why. Faculty members who apply for the chair have to be prepared to follow your example. That's a big commitment."

Benita stilled as she heard the brilliant, accomplished, successful woman express the impact her great-aunt had had on her. It was almost overwhelming.

But Ms. Helen was shaking her head. "Don't put me in the limelight."

Benita glanced at Foster. The vice president of academic affairs looked almost hopeless. She sensed his fear that the endowment was slipping from his fingers. "Aunt Helen, you have to agree to this ceremony. I came all the way back from L.A. for it."

"I told you before you came that I didn't want a fuss. Don't you remember?" Ms. Helen sighed her exasperation. "And you say I'm going senile."

Benita's face filled with heat. "I never said you were senile."

Lana chimed in. "Of course you're not senile, Doctor Gaston. That's ridiculous. What you are is unreasonable."

"Because I don't want a party?" Ms. Helen sniffed.

"You're putting your discomfort with this tribute ahead of students' needs." Lana locked gazes with Ms. Helen. "That's not the Doctor Gaston I remember."

Benita's eyebrows rose. *Oh, Lana Penn was good.*

Foster raised a hand. His manner was urgent. "Lana, perhaps we can find a suitable compromise."

The researcher gathered her coat and purse, and rose to her feet. "I'm not compromising on this, Foster. The endowment is a considerable donation that I want to ensure is invested appropriately."

Foster lowered his hand. "I agree with your concerns, Lana—"

"The applicants for the chair have to fully appreciate the commitment required. We can't ask that of them unless we showcase Doctor Gaston's deeds." Lana turned to Ms. Helen. "I do hope you reconsider."

After Lana left his office, Foster broke the silence. "Our chemistry department could really use this funding, Doctor Gaston."

"I know." Tension vibrated from Ms. Helen in thick waves.

Benita looked from Foster to her great-aunt. "What are you going to do?"

"I don't know." Ms. Helen smoothed the thick chignon at the nape of her neck. "Lana is making me out to be some kind of patron saint of chemistry. I was far from that. I was just a teacher, doing the best I could for my students."

"What bullshit." Benita sighed.

"Benita!" Ms. Helen's sharp, dark eyes were wide with surprise.

"You were a black woman who earned a doctorate in the nineteen-sixties so she could teach chemistry at the college level." Benita willed her great-aunt to recognize her own accomplishments. "You earned a *doctorate* during Jim Crow and before women were even allowed to vote."

Ms. Helen frowned. "I know—"

"I don't think you do," Benita continued. "You were raised at a time when women were taught to be humble and modest. The meek shall inherit the earth. Well, forget that."

"Benita, have you lost your mind?" Ms. Helen's scowl darkened.

Benita spoke over her great-aunt. "This is about more than students and academic endowments. It's about celebrating your accomplishments, Doctor Gaston. You achieved them during some of the darkest days in our history and inspired our next generation to succeed. Now, what are you going to do?"

Ms. Helen sighed. "Let me think about it."

"I trust you'll make the right decision." Benita scooped up her belongings and stood. She turned to Foster. "We'll be in touch."

Foster stood and shook their hands. "Thank you both for coming. Doctor Gaston, I look forward to your decision."

Benita mentally kicked herself as she escorted her great-aunt to the parking lot. Why had it taken a stranger to put her great-aunt's accomplishments in perspective? All of these years, her aunts, uncles, and cousins had dismissed their elderly relative and her dedication to their small hometown. Benita knew the former university professor was special. Seeing her through a stranger's eyes made Benita even more determined to keep her great-aunt safe—even from herself. And that meant she had to convince Ms. Helen to move into a senior residence.

Running footsteps sounded behind her on the jogging trail in Freedom Park Saturday morning. The footfalls were barely audible above her heavy breaths. Benita shifted farther to her right, allowing the other jogger to pass on her left. But the jogger didn't pass. Instead, the presence remained steady on her left.

"Morning." Vaughn didn't even sound breathless.

At the sound of his voice, Benita stumbled over nothing. Vaughn's hand shot out, grasping her elbow to steady her. His quick reflexes still stole her breath.

"Good morning." Yes, she'd hoped she'd see him here.

She kept jogging even as she sucked in a breath to ask him a question. "Starting? Or done?"

"Starting." He released her elbow and adjusted his stride to remain beside her. "You?"

He wasn't even out of breath. Benita resented that. "Second. Lap."

"Mind if I join you?"

"No." Benita puffed her response. She didn't mind at all, though she might regret it. She and Vaughn hadn't jogged together since college and she'd had trouble keeping up with him then.

"I apologize."

"For what?" He sounded as though he knew. Either way, Benita was willing to play along.

"Upsetting you." She drew another breath. "Proud of your work. *Mystic Park* is wonderful."

"I appreciate that." His twinkling cocoa eyes and sexy smile framed by his debonair goatee melted her heart.

He was mesmerizing her. Benita knew it. The question was whether the spell was deliberate or a byproduct of his charms. Either way, Benita pulled her gaze away. She needed to stick to her plan: remind Dr. Vaughn Brooks of what the two of them had together, then make him want her back.

Benita drew a deep breath, inhaling the scents of grass and earth. The late April weather was cloudy and cool. Spring was still a distance off. There were a few other joggers and walkers on the broad dirt path with them. They were young and old, men and women. A few were out for the solitary exercise. Others ran in groups, obviously in training for something.

The streetlamps that appeared periodically along the

path were relatively new. Benita had noticed them before. Since it was well into the morning, the lamps were off. But she imagined their glow made the path feel much safer, not that crime was a concern in Trinity Falls, unlike L.A.

Benita wiped sweat from her eyes. "Haven't jogged with you since high school."

Laughter low and deep rumbled up from Vaughn's chest. "You always started so fast, trying to outrun me. Then you'd struggle to finish."

Surprised laughter caused Benita to lose her balance. Vaughn's hand shot out to steady her again.

"Thanks." Benita pressed her hand to her chest. She breathed long and slow to catch her breath.

"Are you all right?" Vaughn was still chuckling.

"You were. So mean. Wouldn't let. Me stop." It was a struggle to speak between the breath-stealing laughter and trying to keep pace with Vaughn.

"I wasn't mean. I was tough." Vaughn let his hand drop from her elbow. Benita missed his touch. "You had to finish what you started. You just needed to learn to pace yourself."

A familiar trail came into view on the left side of the path. Benita's heart leaped. "Is our tree. Still there?"

Vaughn hesitated. "Probably."

"Let's see." Still jogging, Benita prodded Vaughn toward the path with gentle nudges to his shoulder.

In the distance, birds sang their neighbors awake. Squirrels and chipmunks rustled in the undergrowth. At least, Benita hoped the sounds came only from squirrels and chipmunks. She'd rather not cross paths with rats, snakes, or skunks. *Good grief.*

They jogged deeper onto the path, past white ash,

beech, and big elm trees, and a few evergreens. It was quieter here. Traffic and pedestrian sounds were muted even more this far from the park entrance. There were fewer lamps as well. Benita slowed as they approached the thick, old oak tree on which young lovers had been carving their initials for generations.

As they came to a stop, Vaughn pressed a button to pause his stopwatch. Benita did the same. He was silent beside her as she searched the tree trunk for their initials.

"It's still there." Her voice rose with excitement as she located their carving near the middle of the trunk.

"VB + BH" was ringed by a lopsided shaky heart. It was crowded among other initials, some even more weathered.

"Did you think someone would've removed it?" Vaughn's expression was hard to read. His voice was without inflection.

"No, I'm just happy to see it." Benita studied the markings, tracing her finger over the rough bark. "Do you think we can find our way back to this time and place?"

"We're not eighteen anymore, Benny." Vaughn's voice was soft and low. "I can't live in the moment. I need to plan for my future."

Her heart absorbed the blows. It was battered, but hope kept it from breaking. She turned to him and saw an echo of her sadness in his eyes. "We can plan for our future together."

"My future is in Trinity Falls." His words opened a chasm between what she wanted, what he wanted, and the love she knew they still had for each other.

"Mine isn't."

Vaughn nodded as though he'd expected her response. "We can't have a future together if we're living in different time zones."

"There must be a way to make this work." She held her breath as his silence grew.

Vaughn crossed his arms over his chest. "The only way is for one of us to move to be with the other."

One of us. But which one?

CHAPTER 15

A friend in need is a friend indeed. Vaughn hadn't realized he'd had so many friends. He looked around the clearing at Harmony Cabins and the many friends who'd joined him this Saturday morning to build props for *Mystic Park*: Jackson, the Harmony Cabins owner and newspaper publisher; Alonzo, who was getting married in eight weeks; Darius, the recently promoted managing editor of *The Trinity Falls Monitor*; Ean, whose law practice was expanding; and Juan Garcia, Alonzo's deputy. They were all either cutting wood, hammering nails, or putting props together.

Vaughn gulped the iced tea Audra had dropped off before leaving them alone to their "noise" as she called it. "Thanks for helping me build these set pieces."

"No problem." Ean added another cut block of wood to the collection.

They were all wearing jeans and flannel shirts, as though they'd coordinated clothing. A soft, subtle breeze floated across the clearing, carrying the scents of spring blossoms, lush grass, and rich earth.

"I'm glad your ladies didn't mind you leaving them alone for the day." Vaughn positioned another four-by-four block of wood for the horse and buggy he was building for the farmer. The model was going to sit on tracks to simulate being drawn by a horse.

"I don't have a lady. I'm my own man." Juan grinned as he drove a nail into the tree prop he was building.

"That'll get old after a while." Alonzo stood back to check the tree prop he'd completed.

Vaughn needed four more just like those and a bigger one for the weeping willow to give *Mystic Park* the right atmosphere. He looked at the expensive pile of wood, cut and uncut, stacked off to the side of the clearing. "I also appreciate your donations to the play."

Ean measured off another four-by-four. "I was happy to donate when Benita told me about your project. It's for two great causes: the community center and your musical."

"Ean's right." Jackson drove another nail into the buggy. "I'm glad you're finally producing your play. The *Monitor*'s offering a complimentary full-page ad. Benita's working with us to design it."

Vaughn frowned. "She didn't tell me that."

"We're also going to run an article." Darius took a long drink of iced tea.

Vaughn was surprised and touched by his friends' generous support, the free promotion, their investments, and their time. Incredible. "Thank you very much."

Darius positioned another block of wood on the electric

saw. "I was surprised that you cast my parents in your play."

Vaughn was surprised himself. "They're good."

Darius faced him. "Growing up, I've heard them shout, yell, and scream. I've never once heard them sing."

Vaughn's heart was heavy with his friend's admission. Music had filled his childhood home, along with laughter and the occasional fights. He'd grown up with two brothers after all. "You'll hear them sing when you come to the play."

"I'm looking forward to it." Darius returned to cutting the four-by-fours.

"I'm glad Quincy and Ramona will be back in time for the musical." Ean took a long, deep drink of the iced tea.

"Ramona made the reservations." Jackson wiped sweat from his eyes with the back of his wrist.

"They're staying at Harmony Cabins?" Vaughn's brows were knitted.

"Yeah." Ean looked around at Vaughn. "As much as we love Ramona and Quincy, and they love us, we all agreed we'd choke each other if we were together in the same house for more than a weekend."

Darius chuckled. "I can believe that."

"I'm glad Quincy and Ramona are making it back for our wedding." Alonzo pour himself more iced tea. "Doreen would have been very disappointed if they weren't there."

"You would've been disappointed, too." Juan chuckled.

"True," Alonzo conceded.

Vaughn held a board in place while Jackson hammered it. "Speaking of weddings, do you think Quincy will propose while he and Ramona are at Harmony Cabins or wait until they visit his parents in Florida?"

"Quincy won't be ready to propose this summer." Darius position another four-by-four to cut.

"He'd better not wait much longer." Ean marked another board to cut. "Megan said Ramona's getting impatient."

"Is Ramona the only one getting impatient?" Darius arched an eyebrow at Ean. "You and Megan have been together for more than two and a half years now."

Ean shrugged. "Thirty months, but who's counting?"

"Is your wedding on track, Alonzo?" Jackson asked.

"Everything's great, now that Benita's in charge." Alonzo drank his iced tea. "Doreen and I are glad she insisted on planning our wedding."

Vaughn's chest swelled with pride. "Benita's always had a talent for organizing events and keeping projects on schedule."

Darius sent Vaughn a curious look. "What about your musical? How're things going with you and Benita managing the production together?"

"Things are working well." Vaughn nodded. "Benny and I are fine. Nessa gave us a hard time at first, but things worked out."

"Nessa feeds on conflict." Jackson hunkered down to adjust something on the bottom of the farmer's buggy. "She isn't happy if other people are happy. I don't understand people like that."

"Neither do I." Juan nailed together the top of the fake tree.

Alonzo crouched to lift his nearly completed tree

model into position. "She criticized Doreen and me for not being married. Once we were engaged, she criticized us for planning our wedding."

"Alonzo, you're getting married and retiring." Vaughn held a four-by-four steady for Jackson. "The rest of us should have such success planning for our futures."

Darius's expression was a mixture of curiosity and amusement. "What's in your future?"

Vaughn shrugged. "Producing my musical and buying a house for starters."

"Are you planning on settling down with a woman as well?" Juan asked.

"If the right one comes along." Vaughn avoided meeting his friends' discerning gazes.

"Are you sure she isn't here already?" Ean asked.

"When it comes to Benny, I'm not sure of anything." Thursday night, he'd thought he and Benita could try again. But after their argument Friday morning about showing some Los Angeles producer his play, he wondered if she would ever admit that Trinity Falls was home.

Alonzo glanced over his shoulder at Vaughn. "Don't wait your whole life to tell Benita how you feel. Living without love is not living at all."

Vaughn couldn't fathom how the sheriff had spent so many decades without the woman of his dreams. He wasn't anxious to find himself in the same situation.

He turned toward Jackson. "You offered to leave Trinity Falls and move to Los Angeles to be with Audra. How did you know you were willing to make that move?"

Jackson looked up from the prop wagon. "I knew I wanted to be with her. It didn't matter where."

Vaughn lifted his hammer. Jackson had a point. It shouldn't matter where he and Benita lived as long as they were together. But it wasn't that simple. Being in Los Angeles changed Benita. How could he be sure that their being together would keep that from happening?

CHAPTER 16

"Thanks for stopping by, Sheriff." Benita escorted Alonzo from Ms. Helen's kitchen to her front door late Monday morning.

"It's my pleasure." Alonzo paused to collect his jacket and campaign hat from the coatrack.

Ms. Helen grunted. "I'm surprised you're all still checking on me with Benita here. It's been more than a month."

Alonzo tossed the elderly woman a teasing grin. "Then we must be coming by for your company."

"That's hard to believe," Benita quipped.

Alonzo chuckled. "Have a nice day, ladies."

"You do the same, Sheriff." Benita held the door open for Alonzo, then locked it behind him.

Ms. Helen sniffed. "For your information, I've been told that I'm excellent company."

Benita followed her great-aunt back into the kitchen. "The people who've told you that must be hard of hearing or immune to your sharp tongue."

"Probably both."

Benita grinned. She leaned against the kitchen counter and watched her great-aunt rinse the three teacups before loading them into the dishwasher. "Aunt Helen, have you given any more thought to moving into a senior living residence?"

"Why would I do that when I'm perfectly happy where I am?"

Why did her great-aunt have to make this so difficult? "You're getting older now. You shouldn't be on your own. Suppose something happened to you?"

"There are people around me who are looking out for me."

"Aunt Helen, Doreen's put her house on the market. She won't be across the street anymore."

"You're not very observant, are you?"

"What do you mean?"

Ms. Helen leaned back against the dishwasher and crossed her arms. "Haven't you noticed all the people who parade in and out of this house every day? What do you think they're doing?"

The front doorbell chose that moment to interrupt their conversation. Benita straightened from the counter. "Saved by the bell."

Benita marched out of the kitchen, through the dining and living rooms, and into the foyer. She checked the peephole and spied Doctor Lana Penn on her great-aunt's doorstep.

She felt a rush of relief as she pulled open the door. "Thanks for not giving up on my great-aunt."

"Doctor Gaston never gave up on me." Lana crossed the threshold.

Benita relocked the door. She watched her guest hook her jacket on Ms. Helen's coatrack before leading her into the living room. She gestured toward the thick purple sofa. "Please make yourself comfortable. Can I get you anything? We have iced tea and lemonade. I think we have some pastries from Books and Bakery."

"I'm fine. Thank you." Lana shook her head with a smile.

"Then I'll get Aunt Helen. Excuse me."

She found Ms. Helen poking around her kitchen cupboards. "What are you doing?"

"Making a grocery list." The elderly lady answered without looking around. "Who was at the door?"

"It's Lana Penn. She wants to speak with you."

Ms. Helen's sigh was long and weary. She closed the cupboard and turned to Benita. "I've been expecting her."

So have I. Benita followed her great-aunt back into the living room. Lana stood to greet her mentor.

Ms. Helen accepted Lana's hand. "So what do you have to say to me today that you haven't already said?" She sat primly on the sofa beside her former student, her hands folded on her lap.

Lana smiled, apparently unoffended by Ms. Helen's crankiness. "I'd hoped I wouldn't have to say anything. That I'd arrive and find that you've come to your senses."

Benita grinned. She liked this woman. "I'm afraid the years have only made my great-aunt even more ornery."

"Don't apologize for me." Ms. Helen frowned at Benita.

"Aunt Helen, I wouldn't dream of it." Benita crossed the living room to settle onto the matching purple armchair.

Ms. Helen eyed her suspiciously. "Don't you have clients to check on?"

"Not at this time." Benita leaned against the chair's

high back. "I'm waiting for a few of them to return my calls."

Lana shifted toward the edge of the sofa, smoothing the hem of her pleated navy skirt over her knees. "Doctor Gaston, I respect that you're uncomfortable being the focus of the endowed chair celebration. However, it's not my intent to make this a flamboyant event."

"Help me to understand why there has to be an event." Ms. Helen sounded like an educator, looking to make a connection with a stubborn student.

Lana dropped her gaze. She was quiet and still as though collecting her thoughts. "I was a freshman, the first in my family to go to college. But I wasn't convinced a degree could do anything for me. Then a black woman walked into my chemistry one-oh-two class and introduced herself as *Doctor* Helen Gaston."

That must have been almost twenty years ago, five years before her great-aunt had retired. Benita tried to imagine what that scene must have played like. Aunt Helen, an accomplished, highly intelligent woman in a position of authority, and Lana, a young woman in an unfamiliar environment without any role models.

"Someone like Aunt Helen must have been an alien concept for you." Benita hadn't realized she'd voiced those thoughts until both women looked at her. Ms. Helen seemed pensive. Lana looked surprised.

"Yes, she was." Lana turned back to Ms. Helen. "Seeing you made me realize there were a lot more options for me than I'd realized."

"When I was a student in the fifties, there weren't many black women studying for doctorates in the sciences." A ghost of a smile curved Ms. Helen's lips. "They didn't even keep records of us until the late seventies. I'm proud to know there are a lot more now."

"You were a trailblazer, Aunt Helen." That realization had never crystalized in Benita's mind before. How could someone play such a large role in your life without your knowing the impact they've had on others?

"I don't know about that," Ms. Helen demurred. "But I do know Trinity Falls gave me the opportunity to share my love of chemistry with others."

Benita stilled. "Trinity Falls has a way of helping a lot of people realize their dreams, even the ones they didn't know they had."

Audra had left Los Angeles to make a life here in Trinity Falls. She seemed happier, and the songs she wrote were even stronger. Ean had left New York and returned home, where he opened a law practice to serve his community. And according to her great-aunt, Dr. Peyton Harris had found her true self here. For being a small town, Trinity Falls had a big impact on a lot of lives.

"You did more than share your love of chemistry." Lana's statement pulled Benita from her revelations. "There were fifteen students in that chem one-oh-two class. Most of us are now practicing medicine, teaching chemistry, or doing research."

"I know." There was quiet pride in Ms. Helen's voice. "The others have been successful, too: bankers, advertisers. One of your former classmates is now a chef on a cruise line. He's always trying to get me to take a trip."

Benita sat up straighter on her chair. "Aunt Helen, that's an incredible testament to your work. Why haven't you ever told us?"

"It never occurred to me." Ms. Helen shrugged.

"I'm happy if I helped to spark an interest. But their accomplishments—research, teaching, banking, advertising, medicine, cooking—that's all on them."

"You're too modest to agree to this event in your honor, but Darius told me you're planning on writing your memoir." Benita crossed her legs as she set her trap. "Isn't that contradictory?"

Ms. Helen shook her head. "The purpose of my memoir is to encourage women not to let others' perceptions stand in the way of achieving their dreams."

"And that's what this event is meant to do as well." Benita smiled as she boxed her great-aunt into a corner. "Isn't that right, Lana?"

"Yes, it is." Lana returned her smile. "So how about it, Doctor Gaston? Will you allow us to use you as the example of the qualifications required for the endowed chemistry chair, the chair named in your honor?"

Ms. Helen's thin shoulders rose and fell on a sigh. "All right. I'll allow it."

Lana's smile was radiant as she leaned forward to embrace her mentor.

Benita was filled with gratitude, pride, and so many other emotions she couldn't even begin to identify. This little town had opened up its doors and opportunities to so many. Was Vaughn right? Had she allowed her parents' dissatisfaction with Trinity Falls to blind her to what her hometown really had to offer?

Vaughn smothered a sigh of disgust. Four months ago, when Peyton and Darius had cochaired the community center's fund-raising committee, they'd made the group project look easy. He studied the expressions of the eight would-be actors seated in front of him in the Trinity Falls University auditorium Wednesday night. It was their first rehearsal. The read-through had gone well. They'd discussed the costumes and props, then all hell had broken loose when Vaughn had reviewed the rehearsal schedule.

"I don't understand why we can't have extra time." Ethel Knight, one of the musical's three supporting water fairies, crossed her right leg over her left and tapped the air with her right foot to a frantic rhythm only she could hear. "It's your play."

Vaughn opened his mouth to respond but was interrupted by Glenn Narcus, the performance's male lead. "This schedule is too stressful."

"Glenn and Ethel are right." Simon Knight raised his voice to be heard above the low rumbling of agreements. "Why can't the play open later in the summer or even in the fall?"

Vaughn raised his hands in an effort to get his cast's attention. "We discussed the timing of the musical before the audition last week. The fact that we have an ambitious schedule isn't news."

"But why does it have to be so ambitious?" CeCe Roben, another supporting water fairy, asked.

Vaughn addressed her directly. "We don't want to go too deep into the summer because people start taking vacations between Independence Day and Labor Day weekend."

"Well, I'm thinking about going on vacation over Memorial weekend." Virginia Carp, the musical's heroine, shrugged her narrow shoulders.

"Why didn't you tell us that when we asked you to be the female lead?" Seated on the stage beside Vaughn,

Benita had been silent until now. But when she spoke up, her question had been confrontational in contrast to Vaughn's more diplomatic tone.

Ginny shrugged again. "I didn't think about it then."

"You should have." Benita hopped off the stage and approached the audience seats where their actors had gathered. "This is the schedule, people. We have fourteen rehearsal dates on Wednesdays and Thursdays from now until the performance June thirteenth. That means we have another rehearsal tomorrow. And we'll be depending on you to also practice your lines, songs, and dance steps on your own."

"Suppose we can't make a rehearsal date?" Belinda Curby, the third supporting water fairy, asked.

Benita turned toward the beauty salon owner. "This is the schedule you committed to when we invited you to join this project. Tell us now if you can't keep your commitment so we can replace you."

Vaughn stiffened. What if the entire cast walked? If he had to hold more auditions, his already ambitious schedule would go right down the toilet. Did Benita know what she was doing?

Benita looked around the group. "We want you for this musical. That's why we cast you. But if you've changed your mind about this commitment, there are other people who auditioned who can replace you. Just tell us now."

Yvette Bates, the mermaid villain Mama D'Leau, raised her hand. "I can make the rehearsals and the performance."

Benita nodded. "Thank you, Yvette."

Stan, the hero's buddy, shifted in his seat. "I'm good."

After a quick frown at Stan seated beside her, CeCe

spoke up. "I can keep the schedule, too. I didn't think there'd be any harm in asking if there was wiggle room."

Benita arched a brow. "The time to ask about the schedule came before you accepted the role."

CeCe looked chagrined. "Sorry."

The rest of the group also agreed to make every rehearsal and the performance.

"Thanks, everyone." Benita looked at their female lead. "And, Ginny, in the future, please remember the rehearsals start promptly at six o'clock. You were almost half an hour late today. That can't happen."

Ginny blew out a breath as she rose to her feet. "I thought this was going to be fun."

Benita arched a brow. "It can be. But first and foremost, this is a professional performance. Everyone needs to be ready and on time."

Watching Benita in action, Vaughn realized again this was the reason Darius had suggested he ask Benita to help. She had a talent for handling difficult personalities. This left Vaughn to concentrate on just the performance. He wanted to do a fist bump in the air.

"It's late." Vaughn slid off the stage. "Let's wrap this up. Remember to bring your measurements to rehearsal tomorrow."

Tension drained from Benita's shoulders as the actors filed out of the auditorium. Their voices drifted back but she couldn't make out the words. That was probably for the best. Benita grimaced. She doubted they were saying anything good about her.

"Thank you." Those two words, coming from Vaughn's warm baritone, drained what remained of her tension.

She smiled at him. "I keep telling you we make a great team."

"I know you don't like being the disciplinarian." Vaughn leaned against the stage. "Although you're good at it."

"We can't have *you* yelling at the actors." Benita crossed to the audience seats and settled onto one. "You won't build loyalty that way."

"You're right."

"People have always liked you, though." Her lips curved into a smile. "They were more wary of me."

"And you never gave a damn." Vaughn jerked his chin toward the auditorium doors through which their cast had left. "Who do you think will back out?"

"No one." Benita stood, collecting her jacket and purse. "Are you ready to go?"

"What about Ginny?" Vaughn straightened from the stage. He grabbed his coat from one of the folding audience chairs. "She's going on vacation."

"She's *thinking* of taking a vacation." Benita fell into step beside Vaughn as they left the auditorium. It felt good to have his tall, lean body beside her. "Ginny tested us and failed."

"CeCe's not comfortable with the schedule."

"She's dating Stan." Benita attempted to shrug into her jacket.

"So?" Vaughn reached behind Benita to assist her with her coat. Benita wanted to linger over the moment. His body was warm behind her. His soap and cedar scent wrapped around her.

What was his question? "Stan's not worried about the

schedule." She led Vaughn down the narrow staircase from the second floor to the main lobby. "He'll reassure CeCe that the schedule's feasible. Don't worry, Vaughn. You won't have to suffer through another round of auditions."

"I hope you're right." Vaughn slipped into his jacket with an all-too-brief shrug of his muscles.

By this time, they were outside. It was well after nine P.M. The campus was almost eerily silent. Benita walked beside Vaughn to the university parking lot across the street. They followed the lampposts that weaved around the campus Oval, cutting a path through the inky darkness.

Benita inhaled the late spring breeze, crisp and sweet. "Are you ready for Opal's interview tomorrow?"

Opal Gutierrez was the newest reporter with *The Trinity Falls Monitor*. Darius was her boss. He'd assigned Opal to interview Benita and Vaughn about the musical.

"Why do I have to be interviewed?" Vaughn's question was querulous.

"Do you want people to actually attend the musical?"

"Of course I do." Vaughn gave her a look. Even in the shadows, she could see the glint of annoyance in his dark eyes.

"Then unless you want to go knocking door to door, I'd suggest you do the newspaper interview."

Vaughn's scowl deepened. "Why don't *you* do the interview?"

Benita chuckled. "It's not my play."

"You've read the script."

"You wrote it. You're the best person to discuss it." Benita paused at the curb, looking left, then right before crossing the street. "But I'll be there with you."

Vaughn was silent for several steps. Benita could feel his mind turning over plots and ideas.

"Why do we have to do the interview if we're running an ad?" Vaughn asked.

"Do I need to give you a quick lesson in public relations and promotion?"

Vaughn grunted. "No."

"You'll be fine." Benita kept her gaze on the parking lot coming into view ahead of them. "I still think you should let me send your script to the producer I know in L.A."

"I'm sure you do, but that's not going to happen, Benny."

"Why not, Vaughn?" She barely kept the exasperation from her tone. "It's a great script. The music is strong. The lyrics are beautiful. Why don't you want it to reach a wider audience?"

Vaughn was silent for several long seconds. "I told you, I'm not interested in flying all over the country, setting up performances."

"Other people could do that for you."

"I'm a teacher." Vaughn stopped and captured her gaze. "That's who I am and what I do. I'm not interested in becoming a playwright or a director. I just want to teach. Can you understand that?"

No, not really. But she knew he loved teaching and that he was good at it.

Benita's sigh lifted her shoulders. "So you don't want me to send it to the producer?"

Vaughn shook his head slowly. "No, I really don't."

Uh, oh. Too late. "All right."

Vaughn smiled. "I appreciate your respecting my wishes." He turned to continue on to the parking lot.

With a heavy heart, Benita fell into step beside him. She'd already sent a copy of Vaughn's script to a theater producer, asking him to contact her as soon as he'd had a chance to read it. She didn't feel good about doing this behind Vaughn's back. But she felt certain she was doing the right thing in making this opportunity for him. She swallowed yet another sigh. This was a classic case of doing what needed to be done and asking for forgiveness later. She hoped he'd be in the mood to grant it.

CHAPTER 17

Benita considered Opal Gutierrez as *The Trinity Falls Monitor* reporter flirted openly with Vaughn in his office Thursday afternoon. Opal had curled up on the other gray guest chair in front of Vaughn's desk. Wasn't this supposed to be a newspaper interview? It seemed more like a speed dating session. The younger woman was entirely focused on Vaughn. Opal hadn't even glanced Benita's way since she'd arrived.

Does she even realize I'm here?

Benita checked her Movado wristwatch. It was almost a quarter after four o'clock in the afternoon. The reporter had been flirting with Vaughn steadily for almost fifteen minutes.

Benita unclenched her teeth. "I suppose we should start the interview."

"Of course." Opal laughed lightly as she bent forward to rummage through her tote bag. The emerald bodice of her figure-hugging dress fell away from her cleavage.

Benita shot a look at Vaughn to see if he'd noticed. Luckily for him, he hadn't. Instead, he caught her eye, sending her a questioning look. Benita shook her head and made an effort to relax. It was the last day of April. It would help her nerves some if the weather actually warmed up. She was used to Southern California climes. These chilly days were making her tense.

Opal reached forward and set an audio recorder on Vaughn's desk. "I don't like using these things, but Darius insists I record my interviews. And, well, he's my boss."

"I think it's a good idea." Benita came to Darius's defense. "You can have more of a conversation this way."

"It's a little intimidating for the person being interviewed, though." Vaughn regarded the recorder with discomfort. "It's unnerving to know that your every word is being recorded."

Opal pressed her right hand to her bosom. "That's what I said to Darius."

Why was Vaughn agreeing with the reporter? Benita wanted to pinch him. Really hard.

"Isn't that better than being misquoted?" Benita tried for a smile. Did it look as insincere as it felt? "Let's get started. We don't want to take too much more of your time, Opal."

Opal blinked and looked at Benita as though finally registering that she was in the room. Benita set her teeth.

The newspaper reporter pressed a couple of buttons on the recorder, then settled back on her chair. "The title of your musical is *Mystic Park*. What's it about?"

Benita considered Opal as she reclined in the chair beside her. Her long legs were crossed. Her hands were folded on her lap. She looked more like she was on a coffee break than interviewing someone for a serious article. Why should that bother her? Benita shrugged off her irritation. Opal could sit in Vaughn's office wearing a bikini as long as she wrote a decent article, promoting his musical. She looked at the other woman again. On second thought, nix the bikini. More like a turtleneck sweater and Mom jeans regardless of the temperature.

"*Mystic Park* is based on Caribbean folklore." Vaughn seemed comfortable with that question, much to Benita's relief. "A farmer falls in love with a water fairy, but a jealous water nymph is determined to keep them apart."

Opal hummed noncommittally. "On which island does the story take place?"

Why wasn't Opal taking notes? The reporter had activated a recorder. But Benita was certain Darius would still take notes, regardless of the recorder. Why wasn't Opal?

"Stories of the water nymph are most popular on Trinidad." Vaughn became more relaxed as he talked about his play. "The water nymph is known as Mama D'Leau. She's part woman, part anaconda."

"Sounds scary." Opal pretended to shiver.

Benita lowered her head and rolled her eyes. "Mama D'Leau is considered the protector of the rivers and waters."

"She punishes men who hurt the environment, especially the waters." Vaughn straightened in his chair. It was as though he'd forgotten that he was supposed to be irritated about the newspaper interview.

Benita hoped his good mood continued when the newspaper's photographer arrived to take his picture for the article. He looked very handsome. His bronze shirt made his nutmeg skin look warmer, richer. The material stretched across his broad I-can-rock-your-world shoulders.

"Why did you want to do a story featuring Caribbean folklore?" Opal asked.

"My parents were from Trinidad. They're both dead now." There was love and a touch of heartache in Vaughn's voice. "But they told my brothers and me some of these stories."

Benita had great memories of Vaughn's parents. There was a lot of love and laughter in the Brooks household, with Vaughn's parents, Jerome and Geneviève; his older brother, Benjamin; Vaughn; and his younger brother, Zachariah.

Vaughn's mother had been as beautiful as a silver screen movie star and his father was sinfully handsome. The Brooks brothers took after their parents in looks. When Benita had been in high school, all the young women in Trinity Falls felt they owed a debt of gratitude to Mr. and Mrs. Brooks for bringing such handsome young men into their community.

"As a talent manager for famous celebrities, what did you think of the auditions?" Opal's question for Benita brought her back to the present.

"There's a lot of natural talent in Trinity Falls. I was very impressed. I'm confident *Mystic Park* is going to be a great performance. And that it will raise a lot of money for the Guiding Light Community Center." Benita glanced at Vaughn. The musical would be the realization of one of his fondest dreams and it wouldn't be a disappointment. She'd make sure of that.

The interview lasted several long minutes more. Benita grudgingly gave Opal due credit. The reporter asked good questions, including a few about the Guiding Light Community Center and how the performance would benefit it. Still, Benita wasn't disappointed when the leggy reporter packed up her recorder and left.

"What was that about?" Vaughn turned from his closed office door after wishing Opal a pleasant evening.

Benita didn't pretend not to understand Vaughn's question. "She was flirting with you—"

"No, she wasn't."

"—and you didn't stop her."

Vaughn regarded her in silence for several tense seconds. "Benny, what are we doing? You act as though all we have is a hookup, but you talk as though we have a serious, committed relationship. Which one is it?"

"I've asked you to move to L.A. with me."

"You're not happy in Los Angeles. Why don't you come home?"

Benita spread her arms, palms up. "I've told you. L.A. has so much more to offer than Trinity Falls, for both of us."

"Then why aren't you happy there?" Vaughn stepped closer, shrinking the distance between them.

"I'd be happier if you were with me." Benita held Vaughn's gaze, willing him to change his mind and join her in the Golden State.

"Suppose I move to Los Angeles and you're still unhappy?"

"We wouldn't be." She spread her arms again. "L.A. has everything: concerts, performances, museums, palm trees."

"The only thing Los Angeles has that I want is you. And we both belong here."

"You're wrong." Benita's patience snapped. She circled Vaughn and stomped toward his closed office door. "I belong in L.A."

"And I belong here." Vaughn turned to face her. "Where does that leave us?"

The fact Benita couldn't answer that question only made her angrier. She yanked open Vaughn's door but didn't trust herself to close it.

Stubborn man! Why couldn't he see that she was right? Los Angeles was where they both needed to be. Everything would be fine, as long as they were together. What did she need to do to convince him of that?

Benita knocked on Darius Knight's office door Friday afternoon, the first day of May. The newspaper reporter turned managing editor looked up from his computer monitor. Benita took that as an invitation to enter.

"You've come up in the world." She surveyed his office, taking in the myriad reference tombs on his over-crowded three-foot-by-two-foot mahogany bookcase, the announcements and production schedules pinned to his bulletin board, and the knickknacks and tchotchkes positioned on his desk and file cabinets.

"That's what Ramona said when she heard about my promotion." Darius swiveled his chair to face her.

"Ramona's never liked me." Benita lowered herself onto one of the two gray guest chairs facing Darius's desk. The chunky tweed-upholstered seats were probably older than she was.

"Ramona doesn't like a lot of people." Darius shrugged. "She barely tolerates me. But my investigative reporter senses tell me you're not here to discuss Ramona."

"Your instincts are right." Benita tried a diplomatic approach. "I wasn't happy with the way Opal interviewed Vaughn and me yesterday."

"What happened?" Darius's face and voice were devoid of inflection.

"She spent the entire time flirting with Vaughn." The memory of the gorgeous newspaper reporter fawning all over her boyfriend took a toll on her diplomacy.

"Vaughn left a message on my voice mail this morning." Darius glanced toward his phone. "He sounded happy. Thanked me again for the publicity. Never said anything about Opal being unprofessional."

"That's because he doesn't think Opal was flirting."

From the thick black executive chair on the other side of his desk, Darius returned Benita's regard in silence. She recognized that look in his eyes from high school. It was unsettling the way it made her think he could read her mind.

"I've read Opal's article." Darius broke his silence. "It's good. Her best piece yet."

"I'm sure she's a good writer. But you need to talk with her about her interviewing style. She's not just representing herself. She's representing your paper."

"Are you sure she was flirting?" It was as though Darius hadn't heard her.

"She absolutely was."

"Or are you jealous?"

Benita stiffened. "Of Opal?"

"She's an attractive and younger woman."

"I'm not jealous." And if she said it often enough, she just might believe it.

"Women seem to find Vaughn attractive." He shrugged. "I think it's the goatee."

Was Darius deliberately testing my temper? "Vaughn is an intelligent, successful, handsome man."

"Does that worry you?"

"Should it?" Benita crossed her arms and legs. It was getting harder to keep her composure as Darius picked at her as though testing a scabbed wound.

"You live almost two thousand miles away." Darius shrugged again. The gesture seemed intended to mask how closely he was watching her. "You make it back to Trinity Falls how often—three or four times a year for a day or two?"

Benita cast her gaze around Darius's office, buying time while she breathed in her calm. The room was clean and well organized. But there was a chill in the air. The room even smelled cold.

She wrapped her arms more tightly around her torso to stay warm. "I'm just here to offer constructive criticism on one of your reporters. How did I become the focal point of this conversation?"

"Lucky, I guess." Darius gestured toward her. "If you're that insecure about your relationship with Vaughn, why don't you move back to Trinity Falls?"

Benita stilled. How had Darius known she was feeling insecure in her long-distance relationship with Vaughn? She hadn't realized it herself until Vaughn had broken up with her. Still, she wasn't ready to give up her dreams. She could have a high-powered career and a happy personal life.

Benita uncrossed her legs and leaned forward on her seat. "Why do *I* have to move back to Trinity Falls? Instead ask Vaughn why *he* doesn't move to L.A."

"I know the reason Vaughn won't move to Los Angeles." Darius sounded as though he held the answer to the secret of the universe.

"What is it?" Benita held her breath.

"Trinity Falls is home."

That old argument. Benita dropped back against her seat. "L.A. could become his home. It's become mine."

Darius shook his head. "No, it hasn't. And, if you were honest with yourself, you'd realize that."

She couldn't hold Darius's gaze. Everyone kept telling her that. Worse, she was beginning to fear that everyone was right.

⚈⚈ CHAPTER 18 ⚈⚈

Vaughn couldn't take his eyes off Benita Friday evening during Trinity Falls University's gala in Ms. Helen's honor. She was a vision in a modest cream A-line dress. The hem came to just above her knees, showing off her shapely calves. He took a long drink from his glass of lemonade. His gaze tracked her as she escorted Ms. Helen into the university's President's Dining Room.

Darius nudged him with his elbow. "Are you going to stand there staring at Benita all night or are you going to greet our guest of honor before her crowd of admirers gets larger?"

"Lead the way." Greeting Ms. Helen would also get him closer to Benita.

Peyton poked Darius's arm. The history professor's voice was dry. "Why don't *I* lead the way since you gentlemen are more interested in debating."

The trio paused behind a small group of faculty, staff, administrators, and board members that claimed Ms. Helen's attention. Vaughn shifted his stance to watch

Benita while he waited. Her hair hung in loose waves that floated just past her slender shoulders. An easy smile lit her hazel eyes. Its warmth cast a spell on him, making him feel as though they were the only people in the room.

Darius stepped forward. His movement broke Vaughn's trance. He could finally see Ms. Helen, standing beside Benita.

"Ms. Helen, you're beautiful." Darius took the emerita professor's hand and leaned over to kiss her cheek.

The diminutive lady glowed in her ankle-length black evening gown. The dress was accented with a chunky silver necklace and matching dangling earrings. Her snow white hair, swept into her customary thick chignon, was a dramatic contrast to her outfit. Her makeup was minimal.

Ms. Helen slipped her hand from Darius's hold. Her dark eyes twinkled up at him. "Save your flowery compliments for your age-appropriate girlfriend."

Darius wrapped his left arm around Peyton's waist. "Your words wound me, Ms. Helen. Besides, Peyton knows you hold a special place in my heart."

"Give it a rest, Romeo." Peyton patted his chest, then offered Ms. Helen her hand. "Congratulations, Ms. Helen. This recognition is very well deserved."

"Thank you, dear." Ms. Helen beamed at Peyton with affection.

Vaughn took their guest of honor's hand. "Ms. Helen, it's always been an honor to know you."

Ms. Helen's smile faded and a blush rose into her pale gold cheeks. "The honor has been mine, Vaughn."

The elderly professor stepped forward to hug him. She was small and slight in his arms. He bent lower to return her embrace. Her fragile hand patted his back twice before she stepped back.

"Well." Ms. Helen waved her hand to encompass Vaughn, Darius, and Peyton. "After this welcome, I don't think the rest of the ceremony is necessary. Benita can just take me home now."

"Nice try, Aunt Helen." Benita's laughter wobbled a bit. "But the guest of honor has to stay until the end."

"That's right," Peyton added. "We have a lot more in store for you, Ms. Helen."

"It's Doctor Gaston tonight." A new voice joined the group. Lana Penn, the donor of the Doctor Helen Gaston Endowed Chemistry Chair, joined their circle with Foster. She stood between Vaughn and Ms. Helen. "Good evening. I'm glad everyone could make it."

"Lana, I was Ms. Helen before I was Doctor Gaston." Ms. Helen squeezed the other chemist's forearm. "I don't need a special title to keep track of my accomplishments. The people who care about me—like you and the others you see here—are the only reminders I need."

The simple words hit Vaughn in his heart. Benita gave her great-aunt's hand a gentle squeeze. What did she think about Ms. Helen's words? Did they give her any insight into how people felt about the town and their neighbors?

Foster gestured toward the tables. "We should take our seats. The university's president will make his speech soon."

Vaughn glanced toward the front table where the president sat with several members of the board of trustees. "Hopefully, he won't be as long-winded as he was during Ken's retirement dinner."

"Be nice, Vaughn." Foster led the group to Ms. Helen's table. He held her chair.

Benita sat to the left of her great-aunt. Vaughn found himself sitting beside her. Lana sat on Ms. Helen's other side with Foster beside her. Darius sat on Vaughn's right with Peyton beside him. Conversation paused as other dinner guests greeted Ms. Helen and Lana, and offered Ms. Helen their congratulations.

The parade of well-wishers ended when the university president took the podium. As he spoke, servers quietly distributed small salads to each attendee. Fifteen minutes later, the president's speech mercifully came to an end.

Foster turned to Ms. Helen. "Would you say grace?"

Vaughn and the six other people at the table bowed their heads as Ms. Helen gave thanks for the food and the friendships, and asked for God's blessing on the university community.

"In addition to the classroom, Doctor Gaston also has had an impact on the Trinity Falls community." Foster addressed his comment to Lana. "She was the driving force behind the Guiding Light Community Center."

"The center turned forty years old in January." Ms. Helen's smile was both pleased and proud.

Lana forked up more salad. "One of the things I enjoyed about TFU was the sense of a close-knit campus community as well as its connection to the town."

"I agree." Foster sipped his ice water. "I was proud to have three of our faculty members serve on the fundraising committee for the center's fortieth birthday celebration, including Doctor Harris and Doctor Brooks." He gestured from Peyton to Vaughn.

"It was an honor." Peyton looked from Foster to Ms. Helen.

"Peyton and Darius provided great leadership to the fund-raising committee." Vaughn felt Benita's eyes on him.

Darius refilled his glass with iced water from the pitcher on the table. "I was glad to help the center. Growing up, I spent a lot of hours there."

"So did I." Vaughn accepted the water pitcher from Darius. He filled his glass as well as Benita's. Benita then filled Ms. Helen's.

Foster started his salad. "Vaughn, how is your play coming?"

Vaughn swallowed a mouthful of salad. "Rehearsals are going well. I'm glad Benita's been able to help."

"This isn't much of a vacation for you." Lana sipped her water. "Between assisting with this event and helping Vaughn with his play, when are you finding time to relax?"

Benita glanced at Vaughn before responding. "These three months are more of a working vacation. I'm still managing my clients."

"And she's helping to plan a friend's wedding." Ms. Helen waved a fork toward Benita. "She's never been able to relax, even as a child."

Vaughn could attest to that. Even in high school, one student group hadn't been enough. She'd joined several of them. However, whenever they were together, she would give him her total attention. Why was she so different in Los Angeles?

"I must get that from you." Benita squeezed her great-aunt's arm. Her love for the older woman was in her voice.

Ms. Helen patted Benita's hand. "Doreen—the friend

whose wedding Benita is helping to plan—is putting her house on the market."

The announcement caught Vaughn's attention. He was looking for a house. "That must have been a hard decision. She's lived in that house for decades."

"But she and Alonzo are starting a new life together." Peyton finished her salad. "They're moving into Alonzo's house."

"I'm going to ask her about it. I wonder what she's listing it for." Vaughn considered the timing of Doreen's decision to be divine providence.

The servers returned to clear away the salad plates and distribute the main course. Vaughn drew his dinner plate to him. Tonight's menu consisted of orange chicken, wild rice, and green beans. Steam rose from his plate. The scent of the well-seasoned chicken reminded him that he'd skipped lunch.

Benita looked at him in surprise. "Are you house hunting?"

"It's a nice house." Vaughn looked into Benita's eyes. "It'll probably sell quickly once she lists it."

Her bright brown eyes dimmed as she lowered her gaze. *Yes, Benita, I'm staying in Trinity Falls and I want you to stay with me.*

Foster sliced into his chicken. "Speaking of Doreen and Alonzo's wedding, I assume Quincy and Ramona are planning to attend?"

"They'll be here next Monday." Darius scooped a forkful of rice. "They're staying at Harmony Cabins."

Foster nodded as he chewed his food. "His contract with the University of Pennsylvania is up in June. I was hoping to lure him back to TFU."

"I can understand the appeal of a larger university."

Lana sipped her iced water. "But Trinity Falls is a special place. And the university offers faculty a lot more flexibility than a larger institution would."

"I left Trinity Falls." Benita turned to Vaughn. "And both of Vaughn's brothers left Trinity Falls."

He understood what she was doing. Benita was staging a public protest with her subtle digs. Vaughn remained calm and returned fire. "Ben and Zach are returning to Trinity Falls later this year."

Benita blinked at him. "You didn't tell me that."

"I just did." Vaughn returned to his dinner.

"I'm from New York." Peyton broke the short silence. "Moving to Trinity Falls is one of the best decisions I've ever made. Audra Lane, who moved here from Los Angeles, feels the same way."

Darius caught Peyton's gaze. "I'm glad you made the decision."

Envy pricked Vaughn as he watched the other couple exchange a loving look. He glanced at Benita from the corner of his eye. Audra was one of Benita's celebrity clients. Born and raised in Los Angeles, the songwriter said she'd moved to Trinity Falls because it felt more like home. How could he convince Benita that Trinity Falls was home for both of them?

CHAPTER 19

Early Saturday morning, Benita curled up on the love seat in Ms. Helen's foyer and sipped her chai tea. She contemplated her great-aunt as the older lady sat on a straight-back oak chair positioned before her front windows, providing Ms. Helen a comfortable spot from which to survey her neighborhood.

No matter how early Benita woke up, she found Ms. Helen awake and dressed before her. This morning, her great-aunt wore the fashionable cherry red cotton lounge suit Benita had bought her for Christmas.

"What's on your mind, Benita?" Ms. Helen's quiet question brought their companionable silence to an end.

"My vacation's halfway over." She was stalling for time. "I'm driving back to L.A. June twenty-first, the Sunday after Doreen and Alonzo's wedding."

"I still don't understand why you chose to drive all that way." Ms. Helen sipped her tea.

"I wanted my car with me. But I appreciate your worrying about me and it was more convenient to pack it up.

I worry about you, too." That was a smooth transition to the conversation she had in mind.

"You want to talk about that old-age home again, don't you?" Apparently, Ms. Helen saw through her.

"It's not an old-age home, Aunt Helen."

Her great-aunt shifted on her seat to face Benita. "One of the reasons I love living in Trinity Falls is that everyone counts. Everyone contributes."

"I suppose you're right." What was behind the abrupt change of subject?

"When Megan McCloud took a leap of faith and diversified her family's bookstore, she created new jobs for the community."

"That's true." Benita liked the new Books & Bakery even more than the old bookstore, but she'd never considered the impact the store's changes had on the community.

"When Ramona McCloud returned from New York and ran for mayor, she repaired the damage the previous mayor's mismanagement had caused the community. Now we're starting to thrive again."

"I remember that." It had taken a lot of courage and strength of character to stand up to the establishment and turn the town in a new direction.

"Darius Knight convinced Stan Crockett to enter an Alcoholics Anonymous program. Now Stan's a healthy, contributing member of the community. He even volunteered on the fund-raising committee for the community center."

"That's wonderful." What was her great-aunt's point?

"As you heard last night, I'm also a contributing member of this community." Ms. Helen's voice cooled.

"And I won't be driven from my home until I'm no longer able to contribute."

Benita swallowed a sigh. "Aunt Helen, you live alone. There's no one here to go to for help if, God forbid, something happened to you."

Ms. Helen cradled her mug of tea in her left hand and gestured toward her window with her right. "Haven't you noticed the parade of people who stop by every day?"

"I've noticed you have a few regular guests."

"You're not very observant, are you?"

"What do you—"

"I call them my Watchers. They stop by every day." Ms. Helen lifted her fingers to count off her team. "Megan and Ean stop by at the end of their morning run around six. Alonzo drops in around noon on his way to lunch at Books and Bakery. Doreen checks in after work around four. Darius has the last shift at six. The others—Vaughn, Peyton, and Jackson and Audra, Ramona and Quincy when they were here—aren't as predictable."

"I hadn't realized they were checking on you." Benita stared at the four fingers Ms. Helen held aloft, each representing the shifts her Watchers covered, a twelve-hour service.

"They are. I've asked them to stop, but they've ignored me."

"I'm glad. But Aunt Helen, suppose they forget or get out of the habit of checking on you? Doreen is moving. Will she still stop by at four?"

Ms. Helen smiled. "You don't know Doreen."

"But wouldn't you feel more comfortable living in a residence in which there are nurses to check on you regularly and who are there if you need medical attention?"

"No, I wouldn't." Ms. Helen stood. "I'd rather be here, in my own home."

Benita watched her great-aunt walk into the kitchen. Was she wrong to push so hard for her great-aunt to move into a senior residence? She might as well ask herself whether she was wrong to love the elderly lady.

But Ms. Helen had inherited more than her fair share of the stubborn gene for which their family was well known. It was already May second. Benita was running out of time. How was she going to convince Ms. Helen that she was right about her great-aunt moving into a senior residence?

The peaceful goodwill Doreen always felt after church services was fading fast this afternoon. She slid another sideways look toward Alonzo as he sat beside her on his living room sofa. "Thank you for helping me move my belongings into your house."

"*Our* house," he corrected. "Of course I'm going to help my fiancée move in with me. What kind of man would I be if I didn't?"

He's still not looking at me. Why? Have I become Medusa?

"I'm not questioning the kind of man you are." Doreen shifted on the sofa to face him. "I just wanted to thank you. I don't want you to think I'm taking you for granted."

"Thanks aren't necessary."

"I get that." *Perhaps someone should have gone to church with me this morning. It might have helped to prevent the weird mood he was in.* "You seem on edge. Is everything all right?"

Alonzo still avoided eye contact as he stood and crossed the room. "I'm fine. Just tired."

"You've been tired a lot lately. Should I take you to the doctor?" *Or is your fatigue a convenient excuse to keep you from telling me what's on your mind?*

"I'll be fine." Alonzo dragged a hand over his still-dark hair.

"All right." Doreen rose to her feet as well. She studied Alonzo's broad shoulders. Even from across the room, she could tell they were stiff under his brick red jersey. "The realtor said my house would show better with the furniture in it. But we should decide now what pieces of mine we'll keep and what we'll donate to charity."

Alonzo turned back to face the room—not her. "Whatever you want to do is fine."

Doreen scanned the living room. Alonzo's modest furnishings were a strong contrast to her warm and welcoming decor. His dark brown recliner, sofa, and area rug were practical but lacked the warmth of her pink and white fun furniture patterns. It would be so easy to make the executive decision to pack up his belongings and deliver them to a nonprofit organization. But her moving in and making unilateral decisions wasn't the way she'd envisioned starting their life together.

Doreen gestured toward the furniture surrounding them. "So I can just replace everything in here, including that oversized flat-screen TV, with my stuff?"

"That's fine." Alonzo's tone was dismissive.

Doreen's patience slipped another notch. "Is that really the sum total of the effort you're going to put into building a home together? 'Whatever you want to do is fine'?"

She had his attention now. "They're just things, Doreen. I'm not emotionally attached to them."

"I haven't sensed a great deal of emotion from you at all these past few weeks." Doreen crossed her arms as she regarded her soon-to-be husband. "This is just another task to you, another day to you."

Alonzo's coffee-colored eyes grew wary. "What should it be?"

"I'm giving up my house in preparation of sharing my life with you." She jerked her chin toward his staircase. "You helped move my suitcases into your bedroom as though you were welcoming a roommate."

Alonzo pulled his long fingers through his thick hair again. "What should I have done?"

What should it be? What should I have done? Wasn't this day special to him in any way at all?

Doreen spread her arms. "I wasn't expecting Harry Belafonte to serenade us. But I think I deserve to be treated like something more than a check mark on your to-do list."

"I don't mean to treat you that way." Alonzo's expression was stricken. "Do you want me to take you to lunch?"

"We've been together for ten months. We're about to get married. I shouldn't have to tell you what to do to make this day special." Doreen blamed him for her ridiculous behavior.

"I don't know what you want from me, Doreen."

"I just want you to talk to me, Alonzo. Tell me what's bothering you."

"Nothing." The look in his eyes told her he was lying.

Doreen stepped back. The back of her calves came into contact with his sofa. The plump cushions were soft against her slacks. She held Alonzo's gaze despite the pain in her heart. It was less than seven weeks before their wedding and they'd never been farther apart. What was she supposed to do?

"Are you sure there's nothing wrong? There's nothing you need to discuss with me?" Fear kept her from asking the direct question: *Do you still want to marry me?*

"I'm sure."

"All right." Doreen walked past him toward his staircase.

"Do you want me to take you to lunch?" Alonzo's ridiculous question followed her as she mounted his stairs.

"No, thank you. I'm just going to unpack." Doreen never paused.

She kept her chin up as she climbed to the top floor. At the landing, she turned right to enter the master bedroom. Doreen closed the door behind her. She leaned against the solid wood and let the tears flow. Her engagement was a disaster. This whole thing—moving in together, getting married—was beginning to feel like a mistake. But she couldn't fix it alone and Alonzo wouldn't even try.

What should she do?

CHAPTER 20

Quincy parked his Buick in front of the garage of one of the Harmony Cabins rental properties. His muscles were stiff as he climbed from his driver's seat after the six-hour trip from his new home in Philadelphia. He circled the trunk in time to help Ramona from the car.

"Thank you." She gave him a pained smile.

"Maybe next time, we should stop and stretch during the trip."

Ramona chuckled as she shut her car door. "You said you were in a hurry."

"I'm paying for it now." Quincy glanced up as he heard the cabin door open.

"You're here." Audra hurried down the porch steps with Jackson beside her.

She stopped in front of Quincy's car and hugged first Ramona, then Quincy. The joy on their friends' faces glowed like neon Welcome Home signs. Emotion swelled in Quincy's heart.

Quincy embraced the little songwriter before greeting Jackson with a one-armed man hug. He stepped back to get a good look at his childhood friend and owner of Harmony Cabins. "I'm glad to see you're still shaving."

Jackson rubbed the side of his face with a rueful smile. "I don't know why I missed you, Q. We missed both of you."

"It's good to see you, too." Quincy's words were an understatement.

It was the second Monday of May. The sky was a cloudless cerulean blue. The weather was perfect. Quincy's gaze devoured their surroundings, the lush carpet of grass rimmed by maple trees and wildflowers. He filled his lungs with a deep breath. Instead of the big city stench of smog and garbage, he reveled in the scents of freshly cut grass, moist earth, and the nearby Pearl River.

Ramona wagged a chiding finger at their host. "Now you know how we felt when you exiled yourself to these cabins for two years."

Jackson started toward Quincy's trunk. "I'll help you with the bags."

"We both will." Audra trailed Jackson.

"I'd appreciate it." Quincy unlocked his trunk. "Ramona still hasn't embraced the concept of packing light."

"We're going to be vacationing for two months." Ramona opened the rear car doors to pull suitcases from the backseat.

With the six suitcases distributed among the four of them, Quincy followed Audra, Ramona, and Jackson to the cabin. He mounted the steps to the wraparound porch and waited while Jackson nudged open the door. The rental cabins owner obviously hadn't felt a need to lock the door while he waited for his guests.

"Thanks for letting us stay here." Quincy deposited

his suitcases beside the others in the great room. "We appreciate your generosity, but we want to pay for the rental cabin."

Jackson shook his head. "If you feel that strongly about it, give the money to the elementary school. They could use some supplies."

"Done." Quincy relaxed. He'd anticipated an argument. He should have known Jackson would have a quick solution—and one that benefited the community. That sense of community was one of the things he'd missed about his hometown.

"I don't think the front office phone has stopped ringing." Audra's champagne eyes were wide with amazement. "So many people have called to find out when you're arriving."

"I was tempted to rip the phone from the wall." Jackson's grumble was halfhearted. He linked his fingers with Audra's, then led everyone back onto the porch.

Audra laughed. "It's a good thing you're staying for six weeks. Something tells me you'll need every day of that time to catch up with the people who want to see you."

"We were coming for Doreen and Alonzo's wedding." Quincy slipped his hands into the front pockets of his khakis. "We're glad Vaughn's play is scheduled for the weekend before."

Quincy scanned his surroundings. A modest lawn lay like a rich green carpet between the cabin and a lush spread of evergreen and poplar trees. In the distance, sunlight danced on Pearl Lake like diamonds on blue velvet. The area was quiet, isolated, peaceful. The tension of being in Philadelphia these past nine months eased from his shoulders. He was home. Could he convince Ramona that she was home, too?

"We're excited about Vaughn's play." Ramona rubbed Quincy's back in an almost absent gesture of affection. Her warmth seeped through his cotton short-sleeved shirt.

"After Doreen and Alonzo's wedding June twentieth, we're leaving to spend two weeks in Tampa with my family." Quincy breathed in Ramona's scent, powder and roses.

Ramona's smile seemed forced. "Yay."

Quincy squeezed Ramona's waist. "We're going to have a great time."

Ramona looked from Jackson to Audra. "Quincy's mother doesn't like me."

"She doesn't know you well yet, honey." Quincy planted a quick kiss on Ramona's forehead. "She'll love you once she gets to know you."

"I can empathize, Ramona." Jackson released Audra's hand and drew her closer to his side. "Audra's parents are visiting later in the summer."

"And you'll impress my mother, the voracious reader, by introducing her to the owner of Books and Bakery." Audra smiled up at him. "And you'll win over my father, the workaholic, by taking him fishing, which he hasn't done in decades."

"You see?" Ramona waved a hand in Jackson's direction. "You have a plan. But after the Wedding of the Century, I'll be counting the days until Quincy and I return to Philadelphia and reclaim our lives."

Quincy tensed. How would Ramona react if they didn't return to Philadelphia?

"You'll win them over, Ramona." Audra's assurance

recaptured Quincy's attention. "But we should let you get settled in. Let us know if there's anything you need. It's so good to have you home."

After exchanging more hugs and handshakes, and promising to see each other later, Quincy and Ramona found themselves alone again. He followed Ramona back into the cabin.

It was a cozy, welcoming floor plan. The great room's walls, floors, and ceiling were made of gleaming honey-colored wood. A granite stone fireplace dominated the room. The furniture was decidedly masculine, including the dark overstuffed sofa and fat fabric chairs. But feminine accents complimented them. Quincy gazed at the large flat-screen, cable-ready television with relief. He'd be able to track the countdown to Major League Baseball's World Series.

"The color scheme in this room is perfect." Ramona's comment drew Quincy's attention from the T.V.

Quincy hadn't noticed the color patterns. Since Ramona was an interior designer, he wasn't surprised that she had. His gaze touched lightly on the brown leather sofa and brown fabric chair, then lifted to the green curtains in the windows around the room. The delicate doilies were swirls of red, yellow, and orange.

He turned to Ramona and frowned. "What are you doing?"

"Trying to improve the chi in this great room." Ramona paused with her hands on the sofa and met Quincy's gaze over her shoulder. "The furnishings are too close together. It impedes the flow of energy."

Quincy realized she was referring to feng shui. He still didn't understand it, though.

"Let me help you." Quincy positioned himself on the

other side of the sofa. He allowed her to direct him in making the necessary chi adjustments. "It's good to be back."

"Yes, it is." Ramona straightened from the sofa and stepped back. "That's better."

Quincy kept his eyes on Ramona as she evaluated the rest of the room. So beautiful! His heart sighed every time he looked at her. An oversized yellow linen top complimented her café au lait skin and made her wide ebony eyes appear even more exotic. Her long dancer's legs in her black yoga pants made his mouth water. Her canvas shoes were almost the same color as her top. And long, silver earrings spied through thick, shoulder-length raven hair that featured in his fantasies.

He'd had an almost paralyzing crush on Ramona all through high school. But Quincy had been invisible to the homecoming queen. Her high school heartthrob had been Ean Fever, captain of the football team—and one of Quincy's best friends. Ean had been larger than life. In contrast, Quincy had been in the shadows. However, Ean and Ramona's relationship had ended shortly after Ean had graduated from law school and taken a job at a prestigious firm in New York. Quincy was still thanking the Fates for this second chance with Ramona as well as the courage to take it. But would his doubts about his future ruin the happily-ever-after they were working toward?

Quincy pulled his gaze from the dark sweep of Ramona's hair and looked around the cabin. "I'm glad we're spending part of the summer break here with our friends."

"Me, too." Ramona settled her elegant hands on her

hips. "Maybe while we're here, I'll give Jack some tips on incorporating feng shui into the decor for all of his cabins."

"It's worth a try." Quincy couldn't picture the rental cabin owner buying into the feng shui principles on which Ramona based her interior design business.

"You don't think I'll convince him, do you?" Ramona sent Quincy a cheeky grin over her shoulder.

"It'll be a tough sell." His eyes lingered on her full lower lip.

"You'll see."

Quincy crossed to their suitcases. "We've missed a lot of events, like the endowed chair dinner in Ms. Helen's honor."

The ceremony was an occasion they would have participated in—if they'd been home. He regretted missing the evening. Had Ramona thought of it at all?

"We had events at Penn." Ramona sounded distracted. She wandered the great room, opening curtains and adjusting furniture. "We can't be two places at one time." Ramona shrugged a slim shoulder.

"No, we can't." Quincy tracked Ramona's movements. "But are we making the best choices regarding the events we do attend?"

"We don't have a choice." Ramona's eyes sought his. Hers were dark with confusion. "We're part of the University of Pennsylvania community now."

"Are we? You haven't met many people."

"I will." Ramona shrugged a shoulder as she crossed to him. She grabbed a suitcase and led them into the bedroom. "And my interior design business will pick up with time. I've only been in Philadelphia four months."

"Are you happy in Philadelphia? Do you like Penn?" Quincy hoisted two suitcases and followed Ramona. He searched for any sign she was homesick.

Ramona lowered the suitcase at the foot of the bed and faced him. "This isn't like living in New York with Ean, if that's what's been worrying you."

Quincy released the suitcases. "I didn't mean—"

"I'm not the same person I was nine years ago when Ean and I lived in New York."

"I know—"

"I'm not going to pack my things and leave. You can trust me."

Quincy held her upper arms to get her attention. "Ramona, I do trust you. I didn't mean to upset you. I'm asking these questions because I want to make sure you're happy."

"Of course I'm happy." Ramona raised her hand and cupped Quincy's cheek. "I'm with you."

Her words warmed his heart. Her touch stirred his senses. Quincy held Ramona closer to him.

He had the career of his dreams and the woman of his heart. Still, neither would be enough until they found their home. But would home be the same for both of them?

CHAPTER 21

A key turned in the lock inside Books & Bakery early Tuesday morning. Ramona straightened from the outside wall, tucking her home decorating magazine into her canvas tote bag.

"You're up early." Megan stepped back, pulling the door wide. She looked the epitome of professionalism in her bronze skirt suit and black pumps.

"I live with a university professor who insists on scheduling eight o'clock classes. My body clock is still on university time." Ramona embraced her younger cousin. "It's good to see you. I've missed you so much."

"I've missed you more." Megan hugged her tight. "It's great to have you home."

Ramona stepped back, blinking away tears—of joy, obviously. She walked with her cousin to the store's café. Their footsteps tapped lightly against the dark hardwood flooring.

"Where's Quincy?" Megan inspected the book and magazine shelves as they made their way across the store.

"He's visiting friends at the university." Ramona scanned the magazine titles.

"Hopefully, I'll see him later." Megan paused to straighten a row of periodicals.

The scents of cinnamon, cocoa, and confectioners' sugar grew stronger as they made their way to the bakery. Ramona breathed deeply, savoring the aromas. "I've missed that smell."

Megan chuckled. "I'm sure all those big city attractions helped distract you from Doreen's heavenly baking."

Megan's comment dampened Ramona's spirits a little more. "Nothing can distract me from Doreen's baking."

Arriving at the café's counter, Ramona slid onto one of the bar stools and watched while Megan continued into the kitchen. Seconds later, her cousin returned with a beaming Doreen. The bakery manager's lemon yellow apron protected her clothing from neck to knees. But Ramona spied a pink floral blouse and dark blue jeans behind the baker's armor.

"Welcome home!" The town's mayor and Books & Bakery café manager circled the counter.

The greeting brought a lump to Ramona's throat. This was home. *Why have I realized it so late?*

"It's great to see you." Ramona rose from the bar stool to exchange a long, hard embrace with Doreen. Although she suspected they wouldn't have had a close relationship if she'd actually married Doreen's son, Ean.

"What would you like for breakfast?" Doreen finally stepped back, releasing Ramona.

"How about some French toast?" Ramona returned to her bar stool.

"Coming right up." Doreen disappeared into the kitchen.

"Have you settled into the cabin?" Megan offered Ramona a white porcelain mug of coffee.

Ramona smiled her thanks. The mere anticipation of caffeine lifted her spirits. "Yes, we're very comfortable, although it needs some help with the feng shui."

While they waited for her French toast, Ramona and Megan caught up on the happenings in Trinity Falls—town events, friends, neighbors, and notorious personalities. It seemed like no time at all before Doreen reappeared. She set a plate bearing several slices of hot French toast in front of Ramona.

Ramona inhaled the fragrant steam rising from the bread. She closed her eyes in ecstasy. "Heaven. You're not going to tell me your secret ingredient, are you?"

"Never." Doreen accepted a mug of coffee from Megan. "But if you keep flattering me, I'll keep making it for you."

"Done." Ramona ate a forkful of Doreen's special French toast. Her taste buds popped and swirled in her mouth.

Megan leaned a hip against the counter. "Now that we've caught up on the latest events in town, what's new with you and Quincy?"

Ramona hesitated before slicing more French toast. She lifted her gaze to Megan's, then Doreen's, before dropping it to her plate again. "Quincy's been acting weird, more weird than usual."

"In what way?" Megan sounded concerned.

Ramona glanced blindly around the café as she struggled to put her worries into words. "He's been distant, preoccupied. Moody."

"Does it have something to do with the university?" Doreen's straight eyebrows knitted in concern.

"I don't know." Ramona shrugged her frustration.

"Why don't you just ask him?" Benita's voice came from somewhere behind Ramona.

The presence of her rival triggered all of Ramona's high school resentment. She tried to bury the eighteen-year feud as she shifted on the bar stool to face Benita. It didn't help that her former classmate was even more beautiful than she'd been when they'd attended Heritage High.

Ramona's tone cooled. "I have asked him. He says it's nothing." She returned her attention to Megan and Doreen. "I've stopped asking. I thought he'd tell me when he was ready. But it's been months."

"When did you notice his mood change?" Benita settled onto the bar stool beside her, much to Ramona's regret.

"After we came back from Ken's retirement party." Ramona sliced into her French toast. Part of her resented Benita's questions. It made it harder to ignore the other woman.

Benita inclined her head toward Megan and Doreen. "Good morning. How are you ladies?"

Doreen gave Benita the warm smile she reserved for her friends. "I'm fine, thanks, Benita. What can I get you?"

"Just coffee for now, please. I'm still easing into the morning." Benita's dimple winked into her right cheek.

Ramona scowled some more. "Has Quincy said anything to either of you? Or to Ean and Darius?"

"He's sent Ean and me a couple of e-mails." Megan

poured a mug of coffee for Benita. "He didn't mention any problems."

"He hasn't said anything to me, either." Doreen shook her head.

"Maybe it's time to ask him again." Benita sipped her coffee. "And this time, don't take 'It's nothing' for an answer. The two of you are a team. Communication is the foundation of every relationship. If your relationship is going to flourish, you have to communicate."

Benita sounded so smart and confident. She set Ramona's teeth on edge.

"I should have spoken with you weeks ago." Doreen cradled her coffee as though desperate for its warmth.

Ramona considered Doreen. "Is there trouble on your island, too?"

"Alonzo has been distant, preoccupied, and moody for months." Doreen gave Ramona a pointed look. "Sound familiar?"

"He and Quincy must be on the same prescription medication." Ramona's tone was dry with sarcasm. She loved a good mystery but not when it interfered with her personal life.

Benita's brows knitted. "Alonzo seemed fine every time we discussed your wedding plans."

"I can tell when something's on his mind." Doreen shrugged restlessly. "He's been acting strangely since I accepted his proposal."

"Maybe that's why Quincy's been moody." Ramona suspected she was grasping at straws. "Maybe he's going to propose."

"I think it's more likely that Alonzo's getting cold feet." Doreen stared into her coffee mug as though seeking answers.

A chill traveled Ramona's spine. Doreen's words echoed the fear she'd been shutting out for the past four months.

"That's not possible, Doreen." Megan's denial was confident. "Alonzo's loved you too much and for too long to have cold feet."

"Just ask him what's wrong." Benita leaned into the counter, holding Doreen's gaze. "And this time, don't allow him to be evasive."

"Well, Doreen, we have our homework." Ramona slid a glare toward Benita. The other woman was right. Darn her. "We have to ask our men why they're acting like . . . men."

What was behind Quincy's distance, his preoccupation, his moodiness? Did she have the courage to find out?

"I want to come home to Trinity Falls." Quincy stared at his sandwich, roast beef and cheddar on whole wheat.

He was seated at one of the window tables at Books & Bakery Tuesday afternoon, sharing lunch with Ean and Darius. Ramona was catching up with friends and former coworkers from the mayor's office over lunch. With her absence, he could speak freely about his thoughts on living in Philadelphia.

"Are you sure you gave Penn a fair chance?" Darius was playing devil's advocate again. Quincy hated that.

"Positive." Quincy met the newspaper man's eyes. "I prefer teaching at a small liberal arts university, much smaller. I can get to know students and faculty members who aren't in my academic division. I also can spend time with staff in different departments."

Darius lowered his glass of iced tea and lifted his hand. "You don't need to get your feathers ruffled, Q."

"Darius and I want you to come home." Ean gestured across the table to Darius before returning his attention to Quincy beside him. "But we want to make sure returning to Trinity Falls is in your best interests."

"What do you mean?" Quincy looked from one childhood friend to another.

"Don't sell yourself short." Darius's voice was somber. "Teaching at Penn, your grad school alma mater, has been a dream of yours for a very long time."

"How can you abandon that goal now that you've finally achieved it?" Ean sounded dubious.

Quincy looked from Darius to Ean and back. "I thought you guys would be happy that I want to come back."

"Are you sure you have a PhD?" Darius looked at Quincy as though he'd sprouted a second head. "Of course we want you to come home. But we don't want you to settle for less than your best."

"Trinity Falls University is a great institution." Ean nudged his empty soup bowl aside and folded his arms on the table. "But Penn has more resources, better pay, and great prestige. Do you really want to walk away from that?"

"Penn isn't home." Quincy dragged a hand over his clean-shaven head. "Foster said TFU would take me back—with full tenure."

"When did you speak with Foster?" Darius exchanged a look with Ean.

"This morning." Quincy drank his root beer.

Ean frowned. "Does Ramona know you met with him?"

"There's no need to tell her yet." Quincy took in his surroundings.

Books & Bakery's customer base had increased even more since the last time Quincy had been home. Before Megan had expanded her bookstore to include the bakery section of her operation and hired Doreen to help her, foot traffic to her store had dwindled. But now that the café had opened and she'd upgraded her special events, such as the Halloween party, her customer base had surged.

"You haven't told her you're thinking of getting your old job back?" Darius shook his head. "That's a recipe for disaster, my friend."

Quincy flushed at the rebuke in Darius's eyes. The other man was right. "I had to make sure I could get my job back first."

"You have to tell her before someone else does." Ean drank his iced tea.

Quincy frowned. "No one else knows about our meeting. How would she find out?"

"Two words: Trinity. Falls." Darius gave him a knowing look. "But this isn't about the job, is it?"

"Of course it is." Quincy looked away from Darius's intense gaze. "With Ken Hartford's retirement, there's an opening in TFU's history department. Current faculty members have taken on more courses and are advising more students. But next year, they want to hire a full-time professor."

"Everything's in place for your return." Darius shrugged. "What's holding you back?"

"Ramona." Quincy stared into his half-empty glass of root beer.

Ean frowned. "Is she happy at Penn?"

"She seems to be." Quincy looked at Ean, then allowed his gaze to slide away. "We've gone to museums, plays, and concerts. And of course the shops."

Darius settled back onto the spindly white café chair. "Does she know you're unhappy at Penn?"

"I haven't told her." Quincy shook his head. "I accepted Penn's offer because I thought Ean and Ramona were getting back together."

"I told you I hadn't returned for Ramona." Ean finished off his iced tea.

"I didn't believe you at first. And I never expected Ramona and me to be together this long." Sometimes he wondered if he was dreaming.

"Are you sure you have a PhD?"

Quincy looked up at Darius's question. "I still don't understand what you mean when you say that."

Ean leaned into the table, drawing Quincy's irritation away from Darius. "What Darius means is that it's obvious Ramona loves you."

Quincy gave Ean a pained look. "Will she love me if I want to move back to Trinity Falls?"

"Ask her." Darius shrugged.

"And how do I do that?" Quincy's heart pounded. Nerves? "'Honey, once my contract with Penn is up in June, let's move back to Trinity Falls, the town you hate because you think it's so small.'"

Darius shook his head. "Her friends are here. Megan, her only surviving relative, is here."

"Just be direct with her." Ean slapped Quincy on the shoulder. "If she knows how unhappy you are in Philadelphia, she'll return to Trinity Falls."

"At least have the conversation, Q." Darius held Quincy's gaze.

"What if she doesn't want to return?" Quincy rubbed his forehead. "What am I supposed to do then? How can I choose between the town I love and the woman I need?"

"This is a far cry from the first time we had dinner here." Quincy observed the interior of the Trinity Falls Cuisine restaurant from the comfort of their booth seating Tuesday evening. The decor was comfortingly familiar.

"Yes, it is." A satisfied smile curved Ramona's full red lips. It made Quincy hungry for something more than dinner. "You threatened to order my meal for me. Would you really have done that?"

Ramona tilted her head to the left. Her hair swung behind her left shoulder, exposing a silver and gold earring she'd recently bought at a modest jewelry store in Philadelphia.

Quincy returned his eyes to hers. "Yes, I would have. You were being obnoxious to our server."

"That would have taken a lot of guts." She shook her head in amazement.

"If you hadn't noticed, Ramona, every day with you takes guts." His smile was meant to soften his words.

An unreadable expression flashed across Ramona's classic features. Quincy tensed. *Did I say something wrong?* But then she smiled and his worries seemed unfounded.

The first time they'd had dinner at this restaurant, they'd been with Megan and Ean. Although Ramona's brusque behavior had been embarrassing to Megan and Ean, they'd allowed her to get away with it. Quincy hadn't in part because he'd recognized it for what it was: insecurity. Now that she was more secure in who she was and what she wanted, Ramona was much more fun to be around.

Quincy had recognized their server, Agnes Benchley, as a Trinity Falls University student. She remembered him as well. He enjoyed catching up with her. While they waited for Agnes to return with their drink orders, Quincy asked Ramona whom she'd seen and what she'd done their first full day back in town. She was curious about his day as well. Quincy left out his meeting with Foster Gooden. He'd wait for a persuasive opening to spring that news on her.

"Have you offered Jack any feng shui tips for furnishing his cabins?" That seemed like a safe topic for now. Besides, the image of Jackson practicing feng shui was a source of unholy amusement for Quincy. Wait until he told Darius and Ean.

"I don't have any tips, not yet. I might e-mail a list of suggestions to him so he has it in writing."

Better and better. Ean and Darius would love that.

A comfortable silence settled over the table as they studied their menus. Specialty items included herb-roasted chicken, wood-fire-grilled steak, and lemon-broiled salmon.

Agnes returned with their drinks, lemonade for Ramona and root beer for Quincy. She took their dinner orders—fresh salmon and vegetables for Ramona, wood-fired steak and potatoes for Quincy—then disappeared.

"I'm glad you suggested this date night. You've seemed preoccupied." Ramona swept her gaze up at him, then away.

"Have I?" It was a lame response, but he couldn't think of a better one.

"You know you have." Ramona held his gaze. "What's bothering you?"

"Nothing." Even worse.

Ramona reached across the table to squeeze his hand. "Don't lie to me anymore."

He was cornered. But he wasn't ready to tell her the truth. Then what could he say?

"I'm worried about you." This wasn't a lie.

"Why?" Ramona seemed taken aback.

"Are you happy in Philadelphia?" Quincy had the curious sensation that his response had disappointed Ramona.

"Why wouldn't I be?"

"I'm at work all day and you're alone in our town house."

"Don't worry about me." Ramona waved a dismissive hand. "Everything's fine. And I'm proud of what you've accomplished at Penn."

Quincy was grateful for her support of his career. But wouldn't she be proud of his accomplishments at TFU? "Aren't you bored being on your own all day?"

"Is that why you've been so moody? You think I'm bored on my own?" She gave him a dubious look.

"I don't think I've been moody." Even he could hear the defensiveness in his tone.

"You have. But you can stop worrying. My interior design business will pick up." Ramona sipped her lemonade. "Then I'll be as busy as I was here in Trinity Falls."

Quincy was doubtful. The residents of Philadelphia wouldn't be as impressed with Ramona's interior design vitae. The McCloud name didn't have as much stature outside of Trinity Falls. And her time in New York wouldn't be as persuasive to potential clients.

How could he gently break that news to Ramona? "Philadelphia isn't Trinity Falls."

"That's true." Ramona's ebony eyes twinkled at him. She'd misunderstood his meaning.

Quincy tried again. "You have family and lifelong friendships in Trinity Falls."

"I'm making friends at the fitness club I've joined in Philadelphia." Ramona reached across the table and pressed his hand again. "Really, Quincy, you don't have to worry about me."

"I want you to be happy."

"Promise me you'll stop worrying. Then I'll be happy." She squeezed his forearm this time. "I'm having a better experience in Philadelphia than I had in New York. I'm making more of an effort to fit in."

"I'm glad." Could she hear the disappointment in his voice?

"What about you?" Ramona leaned forward, her hand still on his arm. "Are you happy?"

Come clean, the voice in his head shouted. *Tell her how you feel. Explain you made a mistake.* Quincy knew he should admit that he wanted to return to Trinity Falls

University and their hometown. He needed to confess that Foster was willing—indeed anxious—to give him his old job back with full tenure.

But what if Ramona refused to leave Philadelphia? She'd just confirmed that she was happy there. What if she forced him to choose between Trinity Falls and her? What would he do? How could he choose between his heart and his soul?

Quincy smiled. "Being with you is what makes me happy."

As if on cue, Agnes appeared with their dinners and the moment was lost. The savory, seasoned fragrance of their entrées should have made his mouth water with anticipation. Instead, his stomach clenched with dread. The love in Ramona's expression should be all the reward he needed.

Then why was he so unhappy?

CHAPTER 22

"May I join you, Ramona?" Benita had spotted the other woman seated alone at a table at Books & Bakery Wednesday afternoon.

"If you must." Ramona could be so deliciously grouchy.

"Yes, I must." She set her tray of chicken-and-wild-rice soup, turkey and cheddar on wheat bread, ice water with lemon, and a Trinity Falls Fudge Walnut Brownie on the table and sat on the chair opposite her reluctant companion.

Ramona spooned up her vegetable soup. "I'd've thought you'd want to spend every waking hour with your great-aunt before returning to L.A."

Amused, Benita returned her high school classmate's skeptical stare. "I do. But apparently she doesn't want to spend her every waking moment with me. One of her civic committees is having a lunch meeting. Where's Quincy?"

"He's having lunch with friends. For these first few days, we've agreed to visit with friends and family during the day. But the evenings are for us." A smile softened

Ramona's disapproving expression. Something very much like envy pinched Benita in the gut.

"That sounds like a good plan." Benita spread a paper napkin on her lap and prepared to dig into her lunch.

"I'm glad you agree." Ramona slid aside her empty soup bowl and lifted her glass of lemonade.

Benita lowered her spoon. "Ramona, why are you always sniping at me?"

"It's residual resentment from when you ran against me for homecoming queen."

Benita gave her undeclared rival credit. Her reasoning was ridiculous, but at least she didn't deny her behavior. "Our *high school* homecoming competition?"

"That's the only one we had." Ramona responded in a singsong voice.

"That was almost two decades ago. You're still holding a grudge?"

"It seems that way."

Benita frowned. "But you won."

"Yes, but you still ran against me. And you're a big success in Los Angeles."

"You were mayor of Trinity Falls. And now you're living in Philadelphia." Benita paused as a curious expression feathered across Ramona's face. "What is it?"

"It's nothing."

"Don't say it's nothing when it's clearly something. Tell me."

Ramona blinked at her. "I've got to use those words and that delivery on Quincy."

"Be my guest, but I don't think it works on men."

"Probably not." Ramona turned her head to look around Books & Bakery.

Benita followed her gaze. It was high noon and the

café was packed. Several groups had crowded around the café tables and didn't look as though they were in a hurry to leave. The bar stools were all taken and a line stretched the length of the café. To-go bags were being packed as Doreen and the older couple she'd hired hustled to keep up with customer orders.

Benita returned her attention to Ramona. "So what's on your mind?"

"I'm not sure I'm happy in Philadelphia." Ramona shrugged. "I supposed I can tell you that. Since we aren't friends, I don't really care what you think of me."

Benita uttered a surprised laugh. "That's good, because I think you're strange."

Ramona frowned. "No, I'm not."

"Yes, you really are." Benita sipped her water. "We may never be friends, but could we at least agree to bury the past? High school was eighteen years ago."

"I suppose you're right." Ramona picked up her sandwich, avocado and provolone on whole grain.

"Thanks." Benita smiled at Ramona's grudging acceptance. "Listen, Philly's a big change after Trinity Falls."

"Mansfield is a big change after Trinity Falls."

Perhaps Ramona was right. After all, Mansfield, Ohio, boasted almost forty-seven thousand residents compared to Trinity Falls's mere fifteen hundred.

Benita continued. "Give yourself some time to adjust."

"I don't have a choice." Ramona put down her sandwich and absently traced a line through the condensation on her lemonade glass. "Quincy's happy at Penn. He says his work is challenging, although he has less of it since Penn's history division has more support staff. He advises a lot of students, which means he isn't able to get to all of them as often as he'd like."

Benita frowned. "Then what does he like about it?"

A new voice interrupted their discussion. "Benita, I'm glad I saw you sitting here."

Benita turned to greet the new arrival. "Why don't you join us, Ethel? Are you ready for tonight's rehearsal?"

"Of course." Ethel Knight took the empty seat beside Benita. "Hello, Ramona. How long will you and Quincy be in town?"

"We're staying until after Doreen and Alonzo's wedding." Ramona seemed surprised by the warm greeting.

"Good. You'll be here for Vaughn's play. *Mystic Park* is a great musical." Ethel's voice bounced with enthusiasm. "The only drawback is Simon's presence in it."

"What do you mean?" Ramona tilted her head.

"He's making a *pest* of himself." Ethel sighed with exasperation. "He calls, *pretending* he wants to talk about the play. What makes him think I *want* to talk with him about the play? I *don't*."

"How do you know he's pretending?" Benita watched the older woman methodically arrange her lunch on her tray.

"Because I didn't come down with the last *rain*." Ethel snorted. "He may *say* one or two things about the play. But then he starts hinting *hard* that he wants to come over for dinner. What makes him think I'd *want* to have dinner with him? I *don't*."

"I can see how that could be a problem." There was humor in Ramona's voice.

Benita exchanged an amused look with Ramona before returning her attention to Ethel. "Would you consider reconciling with Simon?"

"Absolutely *not*." Ethel shook her head adamantly. "He lied to me for *years*. I can tell he *wants* me back, but he could hold his breath."

Benita nodded at the confirmation. "There are other good-looking men in Trinity Falls."

"Speaking of which, I saw Quincy while I was at TFU Tuesday morning." Ethel turned back to Ramona.

Ramona frowned. "He had breakfast with former colleagues."

"I don't know about *that*." Ethel returned to her soup. "But I *do* know that it was Quincy Spates coming out of Foster Gooden's office first thing Tuesday morning."

"I believe you." Ramona's tone was pensive. "I just don't understand why Quincy never mentioned meeting with Foster."

Benita exchanged a puzzled look with Ramona. "He probably just forgot to mention it."

"Probably." Ramona nodded.

Neither of them seemed convinced. Was there trouble in paradise?

"I still can't believe Ginny missed rehearsal." Vaughn pulled his black Acura into his townhome's garage Wednesday night. He'd stewed the whole drive home from Trinity Falls University after rehearsal.

"I can." Benita unfastened her seat belt. "I hate to say I told you so."

"Do you?" Vaughn didn't want to hear how right Benita had been. He pressed the button to unlock the car doors, then unfolded himself from the driver's seat. "Don't get me wrong. I appreciate your filling in for her. And you were wonderful."

She really was. Benita was a natural actor and a gifted singer. If she wasn't busy managing other celebrities, she could have a successful career of her own.

"You know Ginny Carp has been unreliable since birth." Benita stood from the passenger seat and shut her car door. "Aunt Helen claims Ginny's mother was pregnant with Ginny for ten months. She swears that's the real reason Ginny's an only child."

Vaughn chuckled. He gave Benita a grateful look as her ridiculous story eased his tension. He offered her his hand, enjoying the feel of her much smaller one.

"We only have nine rehearsals left." He unlocked his breezeway door, stepping aside to let Benita enter first.

"The rest of the cast is making remarkable progress. They have their marks down, and they've memorized most of their dialogue and their songs."

"But Ginny's a lead actor." Vaughn followed Benita into his town house and secured his door. "Last week, she struggled through both rehearsals."

"And she really butchered the musical's signature song, 'Forever Love.'"

"Yes, she did." It had been hard to watch and listen to Ginny sing that song. "You performed it beautifully."

"We may have to spend extra time with Ginny." Benita led them into Vaughn's living room. "Which we wouldn't have to do if you hadn't let her siren's voice make you forget all her flaws."

"Jealous?" Would that jealousy convince her to stay in Trinity Falls?

"Of Ginny Carp?" Benita's expression was dubious. "She's not taking her performance seriously. I'll have a talk with her tomorrow."

She hadn't answered his question. Was that a good sign?

"I should call her. I'm the director." Vaughn's eyes moved over Benita's slender, fit figure. Looking at her distracted him from his irritation with Ginny.

Her dark hair fell in soft waves to her narrow shoulders. The thin purple material of her blouse cascaded over her full breasts and past her firm hips. Her black yoga pants clung to her long, shapely legs. After eighteen years, his body still reacted to hers with the eager anticipation of the first time.

Benita crossed to him, raising her right hand to cup the side of his face. "I play the bully in this partnership, remember?"

"I'm not going to hide behind you." Her touch wrapped around his heart, luring him to agree with her. He resisted her pull.

"As the director, you need to be liked by the cast so you can get the most from them." Her soft smile was further persuasion. "They're not doing this performance for money. They're volunteers."

She had a point. "What if Ginny continues to miss rehearsals?"

Benita's hand fell to her side. "We'll have to find an understudy for her."

"What about you?" Vaughn offered her a winning smile. "You're doing a really good job filling in for her now."

Benita shook her head. "Don't get any ideas, V."

"But, Benny—"

She held up her hand, palm out. "You know I get horrible stage fright."

He was aware of her condition. It was the reason she

managed performers instead of performing. But she had so much talent.

"You were great tonight." Vaughn drew nearer, breathing in her scent, cinnamon and vanilla.

"It was a rehearsal." Benita retreated. Her movements brought her closer to the sofa behind her. Had she realized that?

"You knew the character's lines and marks."

Tonight, Benita had embodied the character Vaughn had created in a way Ginny hadn't been able to in any of their four previous rehearsals.

"I've paid attention during the rehearsals." Her words flattered him, whether intentional or not.

"You have a beautiful singing voice." Vaughn paced forward, more from a need to be closer to her than to persuade her to agree to his proposal.

"Which conveniently disappears when the curtains rise."

"That's not true."

Benita stepped back. Her eyes widened as the back of her legs came into contact with his sofa. Vaughn grinned. He used his body to crowd her onto the cushions. She smiled up at him as he covered her body with his own.

"You were meant for this role." He touched his lips to hers. So soft. So sweet.

"Let's just hope Ginny's performed her last disappearing act." She twined her arms around his neck. "I'll speak with her tomorrow. But for tonight, it's all about you."

He was falling into her hazel brown eyes. Midnight rimmed her irises. The heat in their depth stoked a need deep inside him for this woman, only and always. She was magic, the way she made him feel. The things she made him want. In her eyes, he found his yesterday and today. What would it take to find his tomorrow?

Vaughn lowered his lips to Benita's. She was soft and sweet, responding to his touch. He stroked the seam of her mouth with his tongue, asking her to let him in, into her mouth, into her life, into her heart. Benita opened for him. His tongue slipped inside and he tasted her. Sweet and soft. Hot and wet. She moaned as he deepened their kiss, a lyric he'd never get enough of.

Benita's hands roamed his body. Gentle on his back. Feathering his jaw. Her fingers pressed into his shoulders. He broke their kiss and lifted away from her to slip the buttons free of her blouse.

"You have such pretty clothes." He smiled into her heated gaze.

"So do you." Benita tugged his shirt free of his waistband.

"But there are too many of them." Vaughn stood from the sofa and gathered Benita into his arms. He carried her up the stairs.

She twined her arms around his neck. "Sofa's not your style?"

Vaughn slid her a look. "Not with you."

He lowered her to stand beside the bed. Benita stepped out of her shoes. Her loose purple blouse hung open over a flesh-colored bra. Her black yoga pants molded her hips. Vaughn leaned in and nuzzled her neck as he tugged off her blouse. He kissed her ear and traced her jawline with his tongue as he freed her bra. The scrap of silk and lace joined their growing pile of clothes near their feet.

Vaughn felt Benita's small hands unbuttoning his shirt and tugging at his belt. She flung his dress shirt aside. He gathered her against him, loving the feel of her soft breasts on his chest. He breathed in her fragrance, cinnamon and vanilla. The scent haunted him, awake and asleep.

Vaughn stepped back to admire Benita's beauty. He cupped her breast in his palm, feeling its weight. Her skin was soft and smooth. Like a dream. He never wanted it to end. He ducked his head and captured her nipple with his lips. Benita arched against him. He suckled her. He teased her. He rolled her in his mouth. Vaughn tucked his hands into the waistband of her yoga pants and slid his palms over her hips to draw down her pants and underwear together. He kissed her breast one last time before he straightened to lift her onto the bed.

Benita rolled onto her knees. "Vaughn, take off your pants."

Naked, she came to him. Helped him unfasten his belt. Benita studied him like a work of art. Her fingertips trailed down his torso as though it was the first time she'd ever touched him. She was his past and his present. He wanted to give her such passion and pleasure. He would be the only man for her, just as she'd ruined him for any other woman.

He climbed onto the bed with her and took her into his arms. "Let me love you, Benita."

She smiled as she smoothed his goatee. "As long as you let me love you back."

Vaughn smiled as he lowered his head to kiss her. Careful to keep his full weight from her, he pressed her into the mattress. Her body moved beneath him, beckoning him. He deepened their kiss, tasting her passion. He stroked his hand over her body, feeling her urgency.

Benita's body was humming with desire. Vaughn's large palm caressed her, shaping her breast, molding her torso, tracing her hip. She couldn't stay still. She could feel her blood heating in her veins. She could sense her passion spreading from her core. She wrapped her arms around Vaughn's shoulders and lifted her body against him, showing him what she wanted.

Vaughn captured her wrists and pressed them back against the mattress. He kissed his way down her neck, over her chest to her breast. He kissed its fullness. Licked its curves. Coming closer but not quite to the nipple.

"Vaughn, let me touch you." Benita heard the need in her voice.

"You are," Vaughn whispered into her ear.

His hair-roughened leg slid between hers. Benita shivered. She arched her back, offering her breasts to him.

"Let go of my hands." She tugged against his hold.

"Why?" He traced his tongue around her nipple. Benita's legs moved restlessly.

"So I can touch you, you wicked man."

"Not yet." He drew her breast into his mouth.

Benita panted her arousal. The pulse at her core kept a steady rhythm. He sucked her breast into his mouth. He teased her nipples with his teeth. She moved against him as her body burned.

Vaughn left her breast. He licked his way down her torso to her hips. Benita felt her moisture build. Her heart raced. Her pulse thundered in her ears. She grabbed a fistful of his sheets and gripped them hard. Vaughn palmed her hips and drew her to his mouth.

Benita pressed her head back into the pillow and screamed. The pleasure was too intense. Her desire knife-edge sharp. She couldn't think. She couldn't see. She could barely breathe. Vaughn worked her against his mouth. Licking her. Stroking her. Teasing her. Sending tremors through her muscles. Benita's body quaked. Her nipples tightened painfully. Her legs trembled. Vaughn used his hands to move her. He squeezed her cheeks. He rocked her hips, pumping them until Benita took up the rhythm mindlessly. A pulse beat inside her, pitching her desire. Her core tightened. A pressure built and built and built until it broke. She gasped as her body spun free. Finally, Vaughn released her hips, laying her back down on the bed. Then he surged into her.

Her core was moist and ready, accepting him. Benita gasped again as her body flooded with pleasure. Vaughn's hips pressed into her. Benita wrapped her legs around him. Her body rose to meet his thrusts. His features were chiseled with desire. His cocoa eyes scorched her. A sheen of perspiration cloaked him. She lifted her head to kiss him. He kissed her back, hard and deep, as though he wanted to touch her soul. His heart beat against her.

Benita moaned as her desire rushed to a peak inside her. She freed her lips from Vaughn's and tried to catch her breath. Her body twisted and turned beneath him. He tucked his hands beneath her hips and pressed her tighter against him. She rocked her hips, following the motion he directed.

Vaughn moved his right hand between them. Benita felt his fingers at her folds.

"Vaughn, touch me." She whispered the plea into his ear.

"I will." Vaughn's finger slipped within her folds and pressed her spot.

Benita's body stiffened. She felt Vaughn tense above her. Their bodies rocked together until spent. Benita went limp in his arms. Exhausted, she slept.

CHAPTER 23

Ms. Helen's doorbell rang Thursday afternoon. Benita set her basket of freshly laundered clothing on the floor beside the staircase, then changed direction to answer the door. She found Vaughn on the other side.

"Did you get my message?" She stepped back, inviting him in. He looked very professorial in his tan blazer, black shirt, and brown pants. "I hadn't expected you to come over. I thought you'd call."

"I wanted to see you." He placed a brief kiss on her lips as he crossed the threshold. "Is Ms. Helen home?"

Benita's heart skipped a beat. "Vaughn, I'd rather not—"

"I want to give your great-aunt my regards. Why? What were *you* thinking?" Vaughn arched a brow, though his eyes laughed at her.

Benita rolled her eyes at him before turning to lock the front door. "She's at a breakfast meeting with a committee at her church. But I'll give her your regards. Would you like something to drink?"

"No, thank you." Vaughn hung his blazer on the onyx

coat tree in the corner before following Benita into the living room. "Your message said you'd finally heard from Ginny."

"I went to her office. She said she got my message but she'd been too busy to return it."

"Did she tell you why she missed rehearsal last night?" Vaughn settled beside her on the thick purple couch.

"She went out with her new boyfriend." Benita tried to keep the irritation from her voice. She failed. "I reminded her of the commitment she'd made to us. But she said that, since we're not paying her, we're not her priority."

Vaughn sprang from the sofa and paced across Ms. Helen's hardwood floor. "No one's getting paid. This play is a fund-raiser for the community center."

"I told her that her new guy would be turned on by her beautiful singing and sexy costume." Similar to the way Benita was getting turned on by staring at Vaughn now. Her gaze moved over his broad shoulders, paused at his firm gluts, then continued to his long legs.

"Did it work?" Vaughn turned to face her. This view was even better.

"She said she's committed to the play. But she's said that before. We need an understudy." She shook her head when Vaughn's cocoa eyes focused on her. "Not me."

"It's too late to get anyone else." Vaughn returned to the sofa. "We only have seven rehearsals left."

"Then we'll have to hope that Ginny keeps her word." Benita crossed her arms and legs.

Vaughn rubbed the back of his neck. "I do have some good news. Thanks to people like you, Jack, Ean, Darius, Alonzo, and Juan donating your time and talents, I've been able to cover expenses with the artist's grant and other donations."

"Then all of the proceeds from the ticket sales will go to the center." Benita's scowl cleared.

"We're already receiving ticket orders."

"That's wonderful news."

"Trinity Falls needs more people like you, who are willing to help in the community and who can inspire other people to volunteer, too."

"This town needs a lot of things." Benita shifted toward Vaughn. "Luckily, L.A. has those things and more."

"You never miss an opening, do you?"

"Nope."

"Los Angeles doesn't have the sense of community we have here, does it? How well do you know your neighbors?" The look in Vaughn's eyes told her he already had the answer.

"I don't spend much time with my neighbors."

When she'd tried to introduce herself to the woman in the apartment next door, her neighbor had reacted as though Benita had beamed down from outer space. Benita had no idea how someone new to L.A. went about making friends. That's why she'd decided to bring a friend—and lover—back with her to L.A.

Vaughn checked his watch. "Have you had lunch?"

"I was going to put away my laundry first." She nodded toward the staircase.

Vaughn stood, crossing toward the basket near the stairs. "I'll carry it upstairs for you."

"Thanks." Benita rose to follow him, then froze when she remembered what was in the basket. "On second thought . . ."

Vaughn straightened with the clothes basket in his hands. His attention was sewn to the Heritage High School football jersey mixed in with her other clean clothes. "You've had my jersey all these years."

Benita was mortified. She'd been caught in her lie. "Do you want it back?"

Vaughn lifted his eyes to hers. "Why did you take it?"

She couldn't hold his gaze. "I thought it would help me to not miss you as much when we went away to college."

"Did it work?"

"No." Benita chuckled without humor. "It doesn't help me in L.A., either. But I don't want to give it back."

"You don't have to." Vaughn offered a gentle smile. "But it seems to me that you'd have better luck with the real thing."

Vaughn lowered his lips to hers and gave her a wistful kiss full of dreams and yearning. He was right. There wasn't a substitute for the real man. But she needed to convince him to return to L.A. with her.

Leonard George waited for Alonzo on a seat near the Sheriff Department's front desk Friday afternoon. The sight of Doreen's ex-lover soured Alonzo's already cranky mood. What did the other man want?

"I heard you proposed to Doreen." Leonard stood.

The glare he gave Alonzo said he wished the sheriff would disappear and he didn't care how.

"We'll talk in my office." Alonzo glanced around the reception area, a fancy term for the strip of space between the front door and the bull pen.

His deputies and administrative staff were pretending not to eavesdrop. But this was Trinity Falls. Gossip was currency and his staff was looking for a big pay day. He was going to disappoint them.

Leonard didn't move. His face was a mask of hatred. His brown cheeks were flushed pink. "Is it true? Did you have the nerve to ask her to marry you?"

"If you want to talk, shut up and follow me. Otherwise, leave." Alonzo walked away. If the high school football coach wanted to talk, they could do so in private. But Alonzo wasn't giving his department a show.

Thankfully, Leonard was silent as Alonzo led him to his office. Maybe the other man realized he wouldn't have been heard above the shouted conversations, tapping keyboards, and ringing phone lines. Some members of his department stared openly as Alonzo walked past. Most made the effort to at least appear busy.

Alonzo stopped outside his office door. He considered the high school football coach's loose-fitting blue button-down shirt and navy blue pants as Leonard preceded him into his office. The other man had lost weight.

Leonard helped himself to one of the two black leather guest chairs in front of the desk. Alonzo tensed. He didn't have anything to say that would require Leonard to take a seat. And he doubted Leonard had anything to say that Alonzo wanted to hear. He checked his watch. It was four in the afternoon.

"Did you propose to Doreen?" Leonard glared up at him from over his shoulder.

"What does that have to do with you?" Alonzo shut his door, then circled the desk to take his seat.

"I care about Doreen."

That irked Alonzo. "As long as you care about her from a distance."

"I've been doing a lot of thinking about you, Alonzo, and your return to Trinity Falls." Leonard rested his right ankle on his left knee.

Alonzo wasn't fazed. He'd stared down worse situations than a jealous ex-lover. "I haven't thought about you at all."

Leonard continued as though Alonzo hadn't spoken. "I want to know what you were really doing all those years you were away from Trinity Falls and what brought you back."

Alonzo looked at his watch again. This time, he used the act to cover his unease. Leonard's demand had hit an open wound. "My bio's on the Sheriff Department's Web site."

"You're not going to answer me?"

"Why do I need to?"

Anger clouded Leonard's cold, dark eyes. Alonzo returned the other man's stare without expression. Silent moments ticked by during the battle of wills.

The high school math teacher and football coach finally broke the impasse. "You came back to town and thought you'd replace Paul."

"That's not precisely the way it happened." Alonzo considered the other man's reaction to the news he was marrying Doreen. It was greater than disappointment and stronger than resentment. What was it—and how dangerous could it be?

"Where were you while Paul Fever was dying and Doreen needed someone to lean on?" Leonard became more agitated. "You weren't here and neither was her son."

Alonzo's temper stirred at the criticism against Doreen's son, who also was Alonzo's friend. "Paul didn't want Ean to know he was sick. You're aware of that."

"You're making excuses for him?"

"That's not an excuse. It's a fact. And I was here, Leo. You know that as well."

He'd returned to Trinity Falls after his high school friend wrote and told him he was dying. But he'd returned for Paul, not Doreen. He'd spent a lot of time with Paul. It was during one of those times that Paul had asked whether Alonzo had left Trinity Falls because he loved Doreen.

Leonard stood and paced the room. "What makes you think you're worthy of Doreen?"

"I could ask you the same thing." Alonzo struggled to maintain his implacable expression. His temper was rising. He tracked the other man's progress past his desk to his dark wood bookcase tucked into the corner near his window. Alonzo maintained his silence.

"I can tell you're hiding something." Leonard turned to face him. "What is it?"

Enough was enough. He didn't know Leonard's game and he wasn't playing it. Alonzo stood. "I *will* marry Doreen. I *won't* answer your questions. Get out of my office."

"You're right. You don't have to tell me." Leonard

wandered to the door. He stood with his hand on the knob and looked back to Alonzo. "But I'll figure it out. Whatever you don't want to tell me, I'm sure Doreen would be interested in knowing."

Alonzo watched Leonard walk through the open door. His features remained impassive but his temper burned.

Does Leonard know something about my past? He acted as though he did.

What about Doreen? If Leonard told her about his past, would she turn away from him? Terror iced his temper. Alonzo sank onto his chair. He'd tried to convince himself to leave his past behind, but now Leonard threatened that. Should he tell Doreen himself or continue to hope his past would remain a secret?

Alonzo knocked hesitantly on Darius's open office door in *The Trinity Falls Monitor* office Friday afternoon. He waited for the newspaper man to look up. "How are you settling into your new office?"

Darius spun his executive chair away from his computer monitor. A welcoming smile brightened his movie star good looks. His right arm swept the room, encompassing the stacks of files, competitor newspapers, and reports spread across the top of every desk and file cabinet in his office. "I'd say I'm pretty well settled in."

"They might have some trouble getting you back out." Alonzo considered the organized clutter that had invaded his friend's office. The other man looked pretty busy. Maybe this hadn't been a good idea. He took a step back, searching for a graceful exit.

Darius gestured toward one of the two gray padded

visitor's chairs in front of his wood laminate desk. "Have a seat, Sheriff. What's on your mind?"

He should have known the former newspaper reporter would sense a cover-up. Darius's expression sobered when Alonzo pulled the door shut.

He crossed the room and took a seat. Did Darius realize his office smelled like newsprint? Separate from the clutter on his desk were personal mementos. On a shelf above his computer monitor stood a photo of Darius, posing with Ean and Quincy after a Heritage High School football game. On the far side of his keyboard was a framed photograph of Peyton sitting on the lip around Wishing Lake. She was laughing into the sun and her copper curls were bouncing on a breeze.

Alonzo turned to Darius. "I don't know where to start."

"What's troubling you?" Darius held Alonzo's gaze as though the newsman could read his mind.

Alonzo drew a deep breath, exhaled, and filled his lungs again. "I don't think I'm good enough for Doreen."

Darius didn't answer right away. Alonzo struggled to remain still under the other man's steady scrutiny. "When did you decide that?"

He'd expected Darius to ask why he felt he wasn't good enough for Doreen. The former reporter's question caught him off guard. "It was after we started planning the wedding. Doreen said she wasn't going to wear white, of course, because ours will be her second marriage. I started thinking about the things I've done as a law enforcement officer."

"You think you're not good enough for Doreen because you're in law enforcement?"

"I did some things while I was a metropolitan police

officer." The words burned his throat like acid and stirred memories he prayed every night to forget.

"Have you spoken with Doreen?"

"No." Alonzo answered even before Darius had finished asking.

"I didn't think so." Darius leaned into his desk, holding Alonzo's gaze. "I have no idea what you've been through or what you're going through now. I don't know the man you were. But I'm proud to call the man you are a friend. And I know that man makes Doreen happy."

It would be so easy to accept Darius's words. "But as you said, you don't know what I've done."

"Alonzo, whatever's weighing on your mind may need more than a friendly conversation." Darius searched Alonzo's expression. "Have you considered speaking with a priest?"

The idea of taking his demons to the church turned his blood cold. But perhaps Darius had a point. Wasn't he looking for absolution? Would the church grant it to someone with his past? He had to find the courage to try. It was his only hope of finding happiness with Doreen.

Alonzo stood. "I think I do need some sort of spiritual counsel."

Darius rose also. "You should also speak with Doreen. She's the only one who can tell you whether you're good enough to be a part of her life."

"You're both basing your judgments on who you think I am." It tormented him that he didn't have the courage to tell them the truth.

Darius spread his arms. "Alonzo, we can only measure the person you allow us to see. And that person is a good and generous friend." A grin flashed across his face. "And perhaps a talented actor."

Alonzo was surprised he could smile. "I'll take your advice about speaking with my priest."

He shook Darius's hand before leaving. Absolution wasn't supposed to be easy. Wasn't the pain part of the penance? He'd find the strength to get through it as long as in the end, he could be with Doreen.

"Good morning, Father. Thanks for meeting with me." Alonzo shook Father Steven Meadows's hand Saturday. The priest had the callous, rough palm of a hardworking man.

Father Steven had been assigned to their parish about five years earlier, a year before Alonzo had returned to Trinity Falls. He was of average height with a wiry build. His full head of hair was salt-and-pepper gray. But his smooth nutmeg skin and quiet energy made it difficult to pinpoint his age.

"Of course, Sheriff." Father Steven led Alonzo to the two blue-cushioned armchairs in a corner of his spacious rectory. "How are your wedding plans coming?"

"Fine, Father." Alonzo took the seat the priest gestured toward. It was a comfortable chair, but he was too tense to relax. "Benita's worked miracles getting everything ready in such a short time."

"Today is May sixteenth." Father Steven settled onto the other chair. "Your wedding is exactly five weeks from today."

Alonzo inclined his head. "Everything's in place.

Our last critical task was identifying groomsmen and bridesmaids."

"Who are they?"

"Juan, Jack, and Darius agreed to stand with me. Megan, Ramona, and Audra will be Doreen's bridesmaids."

"Excellent choices." Father Steven nodded. Curiosity gleamed in the older man's dark brown eyes even as he waited patiently for Alonzo to speak his mind. But Alonzo felt a need to stall.

He broke eye contact and looked around the large room with its beige carpeting. Paintings and posters dressed the off-white walls with images of religious figures praying, walking, or offering comfort. The vivid artwork added color to the otherwise monochromatic space. A wall of bookshelves lined one side of the room, stacked with theological and philosophical texts, including Dr. Martin Luther King Jr.'s *A Knock at Midnight*. On the other side, a rectangular maple wood conference table stood surrounded by six matching chairs. In its center, a thick white candle sat on a green doily.

Alonzo returned his attention to the patient priest. "I need your advice, Father."

"How can I help you, Alonzo?"

He stood to pace away from the coffee tables and armchairs. "I'm not good enough to marry Doreen."

"Why do you think that?"

"She's dedicated most of her life to improving our community." Alonzo paused, his back to Father Steven. "She's been a positive, nurturing force. But in the line of duty, I've done things I regret."

"Like what?"

Alonzo's shoulders slumped. The priest was going to make him say it. "I've killed people."

There was a beat of silence as though the priest was absorbing Alonzo's words. "Why have you come to see me? What can I do for you?"

"I've felt, the closer we get to our wedding day the more my past comes between Doreen and me." Alonzo paced again.

"Has Doreen done something to make you feel this way?"

"No, she doesn't know about that part of my past." He dragged his hand through his hair. "But every time I think of all the good she's done and is doing, I feel as though the blood I've spilled is coming between us."

"You committed these acts in defense of others." Father Steven's quiet voice didn't reveal his feelings about Alonzo's actions.

"That doesn't make the people any less dead, Father." Alonzo flexed his shoulders to ease the strain tightening his muscles. What was the priest's judgment? Did he agree that Alonzo didn't deserve Doreen? Should he call off their wedding and leave her life?

"The job you chose is a courageous and selfless profession, Alonzo. You put your life in jeopardy to protect us and our community every day."

"That's my point, Father." Alonzo turned toward the priest. "I'm supposed to protect lives, not take them."

"Ecclesiastes, 'To every thing there is a season and a time to every purpose under Heaven.'" Father Steven held Alonzo's gaze as he recited the verse. "'A time to kill and a time to heal.'"

"'A time to break down and a time to build up.'" Alonzo sighed as he concluded the quote. "Doreen's dedicated her life to building, but my career has been spent breaking down."

Father Steven leaned forward on his chair, still holding Alonzo's gaze. "A good man—or woman—doesn't seek to end someone's life. But sometimes to protect one life, we're forced to end another's."

Alonzo crossed back to the armchairs and reclaimed his seat. "But do I have the right to bring this kind of darkness into Doreen's life? Despite my past, am I good enough for her?"

"The only person who can give you an accurate answer to that question is Doreen." Father Steven sat back on his chair. "Ask her."

Alonzo drew a deep, bracing breath, then exhaled. The scent of lavender filled his senses. He pushed himself to his feet. "Thanks for your time, Father."

He shook the priest's hand again, then turned to leave. The what-ifs plagued him with every step that carried him from the room. What if he never told Doreen about his past? What if he found the courage to tell her about the people he'd killed?

What if, in response to his past, Doreen returned his ring and asked never to see him again?

⌒⌒CHAPTER 24⌒⌒

Books & Bakery was packed Tuesday afternoon. Benita carried her turkey-and-cheddar-on-wheat-bread sandwich to the last empty seat at the food counter. "Welcome home, Quincy. I heard you were in town for Doreen and Alonzo's wedding."

Quincy shifted on the bar stool beside her to better meet Benita's gaze. "And I heard you're the one keeping the ceremony on schedule."

Benita glanced around. "Where's Ramona? Am I taking her seat?"

"No, she's meeting some friends from the mayor's office for lunch." Quincy returned to his roast beef on rye. An empty soup bowl had been shoved to a corner of his tray.

Some of the pleasures of eating at Books & Bakery were the scents. The confection sugar, chocolate, and freshly baked bread coexisted nicely with the vegetables, soups, and coffees.

Benita bit into her sandwich, enjoying the rich taste of homemade bread. As she chewed, her eyes roamed the familiar and not-as-familiar faces around the café. The low murmur of multiple conversations and bubbles of laughter surrounded her. It wasn't any wonder people flocked here for breakfast, lunch, and snacks: good food, good atmosphere, and great prices.

Benita swallowed her sandwich and turned back to Quincy. "How have you and Ramona settled into Philadelphia? You must love it there."

"I miss Trinity Falls." Quincy's voice was flat.

"You're kidding." Benita gave him a wide-eyed stare. "You now live in the fifth-largest city in the country and you're telling me you miss little Trinity Falls? Why?"

"I have friends here."

"You'll make friends in Philadelphia." Although after three years in L.A., she still didn't have friendships that were nearly as close as the ones she'd left behind. In Trinity Falls, you could pick up friendships where you'd left off. In L.A., she had trouble even forming them.

"Philadelphia isn't Trinity Falls."

Benita frowned. Quincy had lost her. "Isn't that the point? Isn't that the reason you left Trinity Falls and accepted the faculty position at the University of Pennsylvania?"

"Not exactly." Quincy shrugged an impatient shoulder. "I thought a faculty position at Penn would offer more research opportunities."

"I'm sure it does." Benita felt an obligation to defend Ramona's desire for something more than what this small town had to offer—although it seemed that Ramona was hesitant about staying in Philadelphia. "It also has cultural attractions and opportunities you'd never find in Trinity Falls."

"We have our own cultural attractions." Quincy adopted a stubborn tone. "We have beautiful parks here."

"Philadelphia has parks, too. And four major league sports franchises."

Quincy snorted. "I'm a fan of the Cleveland teams. For that matter, I'd rather attend a Heritage High or TFU game. At least I care about those teams."

"I don't understand you, Quincy." Benita shook her head. "You finally make it out of Trinity Falls, get a job at a prestigious university, and you're complaining that you want to come back?"

"Ean did it." Quincy gave her a smug look. "He gave up his partnership at a well-renowned law firm in New York and returned to Trinity Falls."

"I never understood that, either."

"Trinity Falls is home, Benita."

"That doesn't mean you have to live here." She waved a hand to encompass the bookstore. "If you get home-sick, you can return for a visit."

Quincy searched Benita's features. She wondered what her high school friend was looking for. "How happy are you in Los Angeles?"

Benita relaxed into a smile. "Palm trees, beaches, perfect weather. What's not to love about L.A.?"

"I can think of a few things." Quincy sipped his soda. "Earthquakes, smog, water shortages."

Benita gave him a pitying look. "Hollywood, Universal Studios, Disneyland."

Quincy counted off on his fingers. "High cost of living, high crime, congested freeways."

Benita scowled. "I have a great apartment—"

"Here you could afford a house."

Benita continued, ignoring Quincy's interruption. "And a successful career—"

"Which you could obviously manage from anywhere."

Benita bit back a sigh of irritation. "I'm not the one who wants to return to Trinity Falls."

"Maybe you should." He shrugged wide shoulders. "You have family, friends, and a boyfriend here. They're more valuable than professional sports franchises or cultural attractions."

Quincy's words had the tug of truth. Benita fought it.

"Trinity Falls bores me." Although it hadn't bored her during this visit. Between planning Doreen and Alonzo's wedding, helping Vaughn produce his play, and coordinating the university dinner for her great-aunt, her schedule had been frantic—and interesting and fun. The realization shocked her.

"When was the last time you attended an NBA game in Los Angeles?" Quincy challenged her with a look.

Benita hesitated. "I've never been to a game."

"Why not?"

Benita shrugged a shoulder. She stared at what was left of her sandwich. "I didn't want to go by myself."

"That makes a difference, doesn't it?" Quincy stood to leave.

"But you have Ramona. The two of you can tour

Philadelphia together." Just like she and Vaughn could attend an NBA game together.

"That part's been a lot of fun. But Ramona and I don't have to live in Philadelphia to explore it."

Benita mulled that over. The university professor had a point. Quincy and Ramona didn't have to move to Philadelphia to enjoy the city's attractions. The City of Brotherly Love was within driving distance of Trinity Falls, albeit a long drive.

"I think Ramona could love Philadelphia." Benita looked up at Quincy. "Isn't it worth at least an effort for her sake?" Why couldn't Quincy and Vaughn at least try the big city lifestyle for the women they loved?

Quincy lifted his tray from the counter. "I haven't told Ramona that I want to come back to Trinity Falls. I'm waiting for the right time."

Ramona would probably take to the big city like a duck to water, if given the chance. Growing up, that's one of the few things she'd had in common with the other woman—an impatience to escape from their small hometown.

"I hope the two of you can work it out." Benita reached out to squeeze Quincy's thick forearm.

"So do I." Quincy's smile was wistful. Benita could see the love the university professor had for the town's former mayor. Once again, the pinch in her gut felt like envy.

Benita returned to her lunch, although she didn't have much of an appetite left. She'd realized the similarities between her relationship with Vaughn, and Quincy and Ramona's relationship. Ramona had wanted to leave

Trinity Falls. Quincy left with her but now he regretted the decision. In contrast, Vaughn was immovable on the subject of leaving Trinity Falls because, like Quincy, Vaughn believed Trinity Falls was where he belonged. All Benita wanted was for Vaughn to give L.A. a real chance. But could she live with herself if like Quincy, Vaughn ultimately regretted it?

✑CHAPTER 25✑

Benita pulled into a front-row visitor parking space in the assisted living residence's lot Wednesday afternoon. She stepped out of her Acura and hurried to the passenger side of the car to assist her great-aunt. But Ms. Helen already had climbed out of the passenger seat before Benita reached her.

The retired chemistry professor stood staring at the building in front of them. "What is this place?"

Benita turned her attention to the sprawling gray and white, wood and stone residence. The architecture combined modern living with Victorian character. A wraparound veranda welcomed visitors. There was whimsy in the stone turrets and wood trusses that crowned the building. A firm spring breeze ruffled the leaves covering the stately maple trees that dotted the well-manicured lawn. Benita had fallen in love with it as soon as she'd seen the brochures.

"This is The Villages at Sequoia Alms." Benita squinted against the sunlight as her gaze moved over the bay window on the second floor. Natural light must flood that room during the day.

"It's an old people's home." Ms. Helen's words were stiff.

"It's an assisted living residence." Benita searched her great-aunt's profile. She felt the tension coming off her relative like smoke from an inferno. "Isn't it beautiful?"

"What are we doing here?" The elderly woman's dark eyes were cold and distant as they held Benita's gaze.

"I thought we'd take a tour." Benita sensed the first whiff of unease.

"Why?"

Benita chose her words carefully. "Aunt Helen, I'm not comfortable with you living on your own."

"Why not?" Some would label it stubbornness. Others would call it determination. Whatever quality helped her great-aunt earn a doctorate in the age of Jim Crow, Benita heard it in her voice.

"You're getting older."

"We've all been getting older since the day we were born. You're getting older, too."

"You know what I mean." A breeze ruffled Benita's hair. It carried the scent of new flowers and fresh earth.

"No, I don't." The same breeze teased tendrils of hair free of Ms. Helen's chignon. "Why are you suddenly concerned?"

"Actually, Aunt Helen, I've been worried for a while." It was a relief to get that off her chest.

"You've been here since March twenty-first. It's now May twentieth. In the past two months, have I fallen?"

"No." *Why would she ask me that?*

"Have I set the house on fire?"

"No." Benita had a sense of the direction this conversation was taking.

"Have I had any car accidents or given away all of my money to questionable charities?"

"You know you haven't."

"And so do you." Ms. Helen adjusted the shoulder strap of her purse. "So your only cause for concern is my age—a number. Well, darling, that's not good enough to convince me to indulge you."

"Let's at least take a tour of the residence." Benita waved an arm toward the veranda. "You haven't even seen it."

Ms. Helen jabbed a finger toward the structure. "I'm not stepping one foot into that place."

"But we've driven all this way." Benita wanted to stomp her foot in frustration. She'd researched a dozen nearby assisted living facilities, interviewed their directors, reviewed their literature and Web sites. The least her great-aunt could do was tour one facility.

"That's the other thing." Ms. Helen's voice shook with outrage. "This old age home isn't even in Trinity Falls. It's in Sequoia."

"It's not far from Trinity Falls." Why wouldn't her great-aunt at least give the place a chance? "You'll make new friends here who are your own age."

"I like the friends—young and old—that I have in Trinity Falls." Ms. Helen crossed her arms over her small chest. "You just don't get it, do you, Benny? If you'd stop looking at the number of years I've been on this earth, you'd have to admit that I'm quite capable of taking care of myself."

"Aunt Helen—"

"I'm not finished." Her tone was stern. "With the friends I have, I don't need to move into an old age home. The difference between living on my own in Trinity Falls and living in this so-called assisted living facility is that, the people who check on me at my home make the time to do so because they love me. Not because I'm paying them to look in on me as they can."

She hadn't meant to upset her great-aunt. How could she explain that she'd had the best of intentions? "Aunt Helen, I know your friends stop by to check on you and help around your house. But your house is still a lot to take care of on your own."

"It's my house." Ms. Helen raised her right hand, palm out. "Benny, as long as you're not going to listen to me, I'm going to stop talking. You can tour the old age home if you'd like. Unlock the car and I'll wait for you here."

Benita looked from the large assisted living facility to her tiny great-aunt's rigid back as Ms. Helen waited beside the passenger door. She considered the parade of people whose habit it was to stop by her great-aunt's house every day, starting with Ean and Megan, who checked in at six o'clock in the morning at the end of their jog. Alonzo arrived at noon, Doreen at four o'clock, and Darius after work around six in the evening. There were others, like Vaughn, Audra, and Jackson, whose visits were more random. But still, they stopped by every day.

Her great-aunt had a point. These were her friends

who loved her enough to want to check on her welfare. Then they'd stay to help with repairs like changing a lightbulb, replacing a wooden step, clearing her gutters, or mowing her law. There wasn't a need for her great-aunt to uproot her life. No one could care for her more or better. It was time for Benita to eat crow.

She pressed a button on her keychain to deactivate her alarm and unlock her car. She opened the door for her great-aunt. "I'm sorry. I was wrong."

Ms. Helen looked from the door to Benita. "No more talking about old age homes?"

"I promise. Besides, the way your friends hold court for you, I shouldn't mess with a good thing."

Ms. Helen chuckled as she settled onto her seat. "You should have such good friends when you're my age."

Benita froze as her thoughts sped forward. She'd never have the kinds of friendships Ms. Helen had even if she lived the rest of her life in L.A. All of her really good friends were in Trinity Falls. Without Vaughn, Benita's future in the Golden State looked very bleak.

"How would you feel about being neighbors?"

Ms. Helen frowned. "What do you mean?"

"I'm thinking of making an offer on Doreen's house."

"You're moving back to Trinity Falls?" Ms. Helen's jaw dropped.

"I might be." Benita closed her great-aunt's passenger door, then circled the hood to get behind the car's steering wheel.

It was time she stopped fighting it. Everyone was right. Trinity Falls was home. It was time to claim it—and Vaughn.

* * *

Ramona let herself into Foster Gooden's office suite. The university was as silent and empty as a tomb this late on a Thursday afternoon.

His administrative assistant looked up from her computer. A smile brightened her severe features. "Mayor— I mean Ms. McCloud. It's good to see you."

"It's good to see you, too, Treena. Thank you." She glanced toward Foster's open door, then back to the other woman. "I have a three o'clock appointment with Foster."

"Oh, yes." Treena waved a hand toward the doorway. "Please, go in."

Ramona gave Treena a parting smile before knocking on the open office door.

Foster rose and circled his desk. His arms were open as he approached her. "Ramona. Welcome back."

Ramona crossed into the office. "It's good to be back."

Foster hugged her, patting her back like a favorite uncle before he stepped back and released her. He gestured toward a royal blue cushioned chair at the small circular table in the front corner of his office. "Come in and have a seat. How are you?"

"I'm well, thank you. How's everything with you?" Ramona sat, crossing her legs and folding her hands on the table.

"I can't complain." Foster reclined on the chair opposite her.

Ramona arched a brow. "That doesn't sound good. What's going on?"

Foster waved a hand. "Things are tough in academia right now. Higher ed enrollment is down all over Ohio. Budgets have been cut to the bone."

They chatted for a while about higher education in Ohio and Trinity Falls University specifically. As they talked, Ramona studied Foster's office. It was bright. In addition to the overhead lights, he had a lamp beside his desk and another stood on its surface. The walls were painted white. His desk, conversation table, and bookcase were made of honey-toned wood, and his file cabinets were made of cream metal. The table where they sat was stacked with copies of *The Chronicle of Higher Education*. Several of the pages were flagged with sticky notes.

Foster waved a hand dismissively. "But that's more than you ever wanted to know about TFU's enrollment."

Actually, it was. Ramona straightened on her chair. "Quincy told me that he'd come to speak with you a couple of weeks ago, but he didn't tell me how your conversation ended. I'm dying of curiosity. Could you tell me?"

Ramona forced a winning smile past the trepidation powering her pulse. This is where Foster was supposed to say that he hadn't seen Quincy. Ethel Knight had been wrong; it wasn't Quincy she'd seen leaving Foster's office nine days ago. In fact, he was hurt that Quincy hadn't stopped by to say hello. Ramona held her breath, waiting for Foster's response.

The older man's beetled eyebrows knitted. "I don't think that I should tell you, Ramona. The news really should come from Quincy."

Ramona froze. Her pulse thundered in her ears. *Ethel had been right.* She'd been afraid of that, which was the reason Ramona hadn't confronted Quincy sooner. She hadn't wanted to face the myriad of reasons her boyfriend would have met with his former boss without telling her.

She'd suspected Foster would be too circumspect to give up the information easily. And to think Quincy hadn't told her that he'd met with TFU's vice president for academic affairs or what the meeting had been about. Her lover, who was notorious for not being able to keep secrets, was keeping secrets from her. *Unbelievable*. If Ethel hadn't mentioned spotting Quincy coming out of Foster's office, Ramona would still be in the dark. She'd waited almost two weeks for her absentminded professor to mention a meeting with his former boss. He'd never said a word. Now here she was, checking up on him like some modern-day Mata Hari.

"Could you at least tell me if it's good news?" Ramona leaned forward, clasping her hands together as though she was hoping really, really hard. But for what was she hoping?

"Oh, it's good news indeed." Foster grinned. "Very good news. But I don't want to ruin the surprise. Besides, he asked me not to mention it to you."

So Quincy had plotted to keep her in the dark deliberately. *Unbelievable*.

Ramona gritted her teeth into another winning smile. "You won't ruin the surprise if I guess. You're going to allow Q to return to TFU as a tenured professor, aren't you?"

"You've guessed correctly." Foster laughed. "I'm thrilled that Quincy will be returning to TFU. He's one of our best professors. His leaving was a great loss to the university and to our students."

And Quincy's lying to her also was a great loss. Ramona found the strength to smile through the pain.

"That's wonderful news, Foster. You've made Quincy—both of us—very happy."

Foster beamed. "You've both made me very happy, too. Do you know when Quincy will make his decision?"

Quincy hadn't made his final decision yet? Was it his intent to discuss this opportunity with her? If so, what was he waiting for? Divine intervention?

Ramona coughed, trying to dislodge the lump of anger growing in her throat. "Oh, don't worry, Foster. We're going to discuss Q's return to TFU at length tonight."

Foster rubbed his hands together. "Then I'll look forward to receiving his answer bright and early Monday morning."

Ramona's smile was growing stiff. She made a show of looking at her watch, although she couldn't read the time through the red wash of anger floating before her eyes. "It's been wonderful catching up with you, but I'd better go. I'm sure you have a ton of work to get through and I have some stuff, too."

Foster rose. "I look forward to hearing from you and Quincy Monday."

"Absolutely." She stood from the table, then shook Foster's hand. "Take care, Foster. Thanks again for your time."

She was looking forward to hearing from Quincy tonight. He had a lot of explaining to do.

⤜⤚CHAPTER 26⤙⤛

Doreen secured the café's kitchen Thursday afternoon, then adjusted her purse strap on her shoulder. After three years, she still couldn't determine which was the busiest day of the week—Friday or Saturday. She turned, intending to search for Megan to wish her friend and boss a good evening. She hesitated when she noticed Nessa walking toward her.

"I'm sorry, Nessa, the café's closed." Doreen adjusted the purse strap on her shoulder.

"I'm not here for a meal, Doreen." The town council president dug into her oversized navy leather purse. She pulled out a familiar ivory linen envelope. "What's this about?"

Doreen recognized the stationery at a glance. "It's an invitation to my wedding."

"I know that." Nessa looked from the envelope to Doreen. "Why did you send this to me?"

Doreen checked the bronze Movado wristwatch Ean had bought for her several Christmases ago. It was just after three o'clock. In the distance, she heard the faint sounds of conversation and laughter from the bookstore customers. They were mostly retirees and TFU students at this time of the day.

"I'm getting married June twentieth, Nessa. You're welcome to attend both the wedding and reception if you'd like—or not." She walked past Nessa, intending to keep going. But Nessa's next words stopped her.

"Are you that desperate for gifts that you'd invite your enemies to your wedding?"

Doreen stiffened. She faced Nessa. "I hadn't realized we were enemies."

"Maybe 'enemy' is too strong of a term." Nessa put the envelope back into her purse. "But we aren't friends. So why did you invite me to your wedding?"

"Why not?"

"Is it really that easy for you?" Nessa's dark eyes reflected her puzzlement and frustration.

"Why are you making it so hard?" Doreen searched Nessa's thin brown features. "You make everything hard. Vaughn wanted to perform his musical in the community center. You rejected his request without discussing it with members of the council or me."

"According to our bylaws, I'm not required to discuss decisions on nonessential matters with you."

"That's just one example." Doreen gripped her purse strap, using it to hold on to her temper. "Why are you trying to alienate me on even the smallest of matters? Wouldn't it be easier for us to get along?"

Nessa smirked. "Who told you that being mayor, even of a small town like ours, was supposed to be easy?"

And with that single question, Nessa Linden in all her spiteful glory was back.

"I know we're not friends and you never intend us to become closer. But I sent you an invitation to my wedding anyway because one of us should at least try to make an effort."

"So you think you're a better person than me?" Nessa's eyebrows stretched up her forehead.

"Don't twist my words." Doreen gestured toward Nessa's oversized navy purse, which carried the wedding invitation. "Come or don't come. It's up to you. I don't have an ulterior motive for inviting you."

Once again Doreen turned to walk away and once again Nessa's words stopped her.

"You're always so charming and likable." Nessa didn't make that sound like a compliment. "The voice of reason for the winning side of a community issue."

"Is that the way you see me?" Doreen gave Nessa a wide-eyed stare.

"Yes, and so do a lot of other people." Nessa's response was vicious.

"Thanks." Doreen smiled and walked away.

There wasn't anything she could do about Nessa's or anyone else's perception of her. She could only be true to herself—which meant admitting at least to herself that she was enjoying Nessa's confusion over her wedding invitation.

Doreen was still smiling miles later as she drove home from Ms. Helen's house Thursday afternoon. Although Benita was staying with the elderly woman, Doreen continued to stop by Ms. Helen's home every day around four P.M. She enjoyed the former university professor's company. And, as a bonus, today Benita had made a bid on Doreen's former house. If all went well, soon Doreen wouldn't have to worry about the house's maintenance. Great news, indeed.

Singing along with the radio, Doreen pulled her Honda Civic into the garage of the home she now shared with Alonzo. She collected her purse before climbing from the car and walking toward the mailbox. That's when she noticed Leonard waiting for her at the bottom of the driveway.

"You've already moved in with him?" Leonard sounded as though he'd been betrayed.

"What are you doing here?" Doreen stopped halfway between her garage and the mailbox.

She studied Leonard as he scanned the two-story white and black colonial-style home behind her. The high school math teacher and football coach had lost weight. His blue denims and black long-sleeved jersey were loose on his frame.

Leonard returned his attention to her. "Are you really going to marry him?"

"Yes, I am. And I want you to leave." Doreen didn't want Leonard to be here when Alonzo arrived home. She could imagine the sheriff and the high school teacher getting into an altercation, news of which would spread like wildfire from Alonzo's neighbors to the entire town.

"Dorie, I need to talk to you. Let's go inside." Leonard gestured toward the front steps.

Had he lost his mind? "I'm not letting you in. Go home, Leo."

Leonard expelled an irritated breath. "How well do you know Alonzo?"

"Leo, you broke up with me—"

"Is that what all of this is about?" He smiled. "I'll take you back, Dorie."

"I'm not interested in a relationship with you." Doreen beat back her own annoyance. "You broke up with me because I wanted to be mayor. You wanted me to choose between my dreams and yours. That's not the kind of relationship I need."

"But *Alonzo* gives you what you need?" Leonard sneered.

"Yes, he does. I can depend on him in a way I can't depend on you."

"He'd been out of your life for more than forty years." Leonard gave her a sly look. "What was he doing all that time?"

"The same thing we were all doing, working, growing, planning for the future." Doreen checked up and down the street.

How many neighbors were in their homes, enjoying the show? Most people were still at work, but she was certain one or two neighbors were home. After all, she was. Doreen looked across the street. Had a curtain moved in the window or was she being paranoid?

She didn't need this type of attention. She could already hear Nessa's lecture on a proper mayor's public persona. And how would this affect Alonzo? But there was no way she was letting Leonard into their home. Fortunately, they were the only ones outside, which was surprising. It was a beautiful late spring afternoon. Doreen could feel the advent of summer.

"What do you know about Alonzo, specifically during those years he was away?" Leonard's question reclaimed her attention.

Alonzo's nightmares and his odd, moody behavior

flashed across her mind. Doreen slapped the memories away and the doubt that came with them. "Alonzo hadn't been absent the entire time. He returned to Trinity Falls often to visit his family and friends. Paul and I saw him several times a year."

"And what did he share about his life?"

"What are you implying?"

Leonard inclined his head toward the home behind her. "Let's go inside and talk."

"About what?" Doreen crossed her arms. "What can you possibly have to tell me about my fiancé?"

A flash of anger moved over Leonard's soft brown features. "He's not good enough for you."

"What?" The accusation took her by surprise. Coming from Leonard, it shouldn't have.

"I would've married you."

"And that would have been a mistake."

"Marrying Alonzo isn't?"

"Of course not." It was a struggle to control her voice. "Alonzo encourages me to be the person I want to be. You tried to make me into the person you want me to be."

"You make it sound as though I forced you to do things you didn't want to do."

Doreen sighed. She was suddenly tired of everything. She was tired of Leonard trying to convince her to reconcile with him. She was tired of Nessa trying to cause conflicts where none existed. She just wanted Leonard to leave so she could have some time alone before Alonzo came home.

"We're just not right for each other, Leo." She spoke as gently as she could. "I'm going to marry Alonzo. You have to accept that."

Leonard's dark eyes studied her for silent moments. "I never stopped loving you."

She felt nothing. "I'm in love with Alonzo. It's time you moved on."

Doreen walked back into the garage. She pressed the power button to lower the door, shutting out Leonard. Alonzo could bring in the mail later. For now, she just needed to sit and unwind. Between Nessa and Leonard, she'd had enough drama for the day.

CHAPTER 27

"Benita, it's Tommy Poole." The Los Angeles theater producer sounded as though he'd just introduced himself to a throng of giddy tweens.

Benita's heart had jumped when Tommy's name had appeared on her cellular phone's caller identification. She hadn't expected to hear from him this quickly. She took a deep, calming breath, drawing in the scents of the broiled salmon and mixed vegetables she was making for her great-aunt's Thursday dinner.

"Hi, Tommy. Have you read the script I sent you?" Benita braced her hips against the nearby kitchen counter to support her suddenly shaky knees. *Why am I so nervous? I don't have anything to lose, whether or not Tommy's interested in Vaughn's musical.*

She pictured her business acquaintance seated behind his glass and sterling silver desk in his company's fifth-floor office suite in Beverly Hills. The last time she'd seen him, he'd been wearing deceptively casual but undoubtedly expensive tan khakis and a pale pink polo shirt. His shock of white hair had been cut in an asymmetrical style that had given his ice blue eyes an unnecessary emphasis. She'd wondered from time to time how many facelifts he'd had to achieve that near-plastic expression.

"Where did you get this script?" Soft music played in the background as though Tommy was listening to a compact disk on his office sound system.

"I told you. A friend wrote it." Benita glanced at the clock suspended from the kitchen wall. It was almost five P.M., which mean it was coming up on two o'clock in Beverly Hills.

"A friend from Trident Falls?" Tommy's tone was dubious.

"*Trinity* Falls, yes." Why couldn't her L.A. associates remember the name of her hometown? "Why are you asking?"

As she checked on the salmon and vegetables, Benita pictured the area surrounding Tommy's office. She envisioned the palm trees rising against cloudless blue skies, exclusive shops on Rodeo Drive, the congested sidewalks along Sunset Boulevard, and the contrasting architecture that lined Melrose Avenue. It was a galaxy away from Trinity Falls.

"I'm just surprised that something of such high quality came out of that town." The producer chuckled.

Benita's back stiffened. *That town?* "I'm from this town, Tommy. What are you trying to say?"

"Yes, well, you're not there anymore, are you, darling?" His tone was dismissive.

Benita shrugged off her irritation and crossed to sit at the table. "So you like the script?"

"It's brilliant." Tommy's enthusiasm almost made up for his thoughtless words. Almost. "The writing is clever and unique. The story's original. The pacing is great and it has good tension. I'm interested in producing it."

"Wonderful." Benita's senses heightened with the smell of a new deal.

She'd known Vaughn's talent would attract power players in the theater world who were looking for the next new voice. Perhaps his work would also appeal to movie producers. Benita made a mental note to investigate that.

"Although we may need a few character adjustments." Tommy's comment brought Benita's imaginary celebration to a halt.

"What kind of adjustments?" *Keep an open mind, Benita.*

"The dialogue will need to change." Tommy yawned as though the discussion barely held his interest. "If these characters are poor people from a poor country, their dialogue should be more . . . authentic."

Was that code for 'illiterate'? "What makes you think these characters are poor? The hero and his neighbor are farmers. But from the brief description Vaughn gives us, they're not struggling."

"That's the other thing. They should be struggling. We should feel their desperation." Tommy's arrogance was on full display.

Benita rose and counted to ten. She paced around the kitchen table. "I think you're focusing on the wrong things. This musical is a tribute to the myths and folklore of the author's parents' culture. That's the only aspect of the characters that's important to the storytelling."

"But we don't want viewers to question the credibility of the story."

Benita almost burst out laughing. "People who attend this play will have to suspend their disbelief. You do realize water nymphs and fairies don't exist, right?"

When they'd first met, Benita had been in awe of Tommy Poole. The older man had seemed so wise and worldly to the young and inexperienced woman Benita had been. But over time, Tommy's sheen had tarnished. The opinions and perspectives he sometimes voiced were almost criminally biased. Today especially, she wasn't afraid to speak her mind to him. Maybe it was the two months she'd spent in Trinity Falls during this visit, which was the longest amount of time she'd been home since she'd relocated to L.A.

"I'm well aware that water nymphs and fairies don't exist." His voice slapped at her. Men like Tommy didn't like to be talked down to.

Funny, neither did women like Benita. She stopped pacing. She was done playing games. "The script isn't changing, Tommy."

"If you want me to produce it, it will."

"Then you won't be producing it. Thanks for your time." He sure did think a lot of himself. Benita started to disconnect the call when the producer's voice stopped her.

"Benita, wait. I'm just asking for minor changes."

"As I explained, this play is a tribute to the author's parents, not some blaxploitation project. You'll produce it as it's written or not at all." In the past, she might have caved in to bullying by Tommy and people of his ilk. The old Benita measured success in deals made and money paid. Funny how that changed when you remembered where and who you came from.

"Aren't you at least going to take my offer to your client?"

"My client would agree with me." *My client doesn't even know I'm shopping his work.*

After a beat of silence, Tommy gave in. "Fine. Extend an offer to your client. The script will remain as it was written."

Yes! "I'll discuss your offer with my client and get back to you." Benita disconnected the call.

Then she did a victory dance around Ms. Helen's cozy kitchen, jumping up and down and shaking her hips. She knew Vaughn's talents were meant to be enjoyed by thousands, millions even. She couldn't wait to see his face when she gave him the good news. She was breathless and impatient with excitement.

But she needed to slow down. Vaughn would take some convincing that Tommy Poole's offer was a good thing. She'd have to pick the right time to tell him. Even then, she'd have to hope for the best.

"There you are. I was starting to worry."

Ramona looked up at Quincy's greeting. She pulled her gaze from the devastatingly handsome image he made in his teal T-shirt, slate gray shorts, and beautiful smile. *How can he still get to me when I'm this angry with him?*

Without a word, she secured the front door of their rental cabin. It was more about buying time for herself than a concern about possible crime.

"Where have you been?" Quincy's smile was welcoming. His words were light as he approached her.

Ramona stepped away from the door to meet him halfway. In hindsight, she wished she'd asked Quincy that same question nine days ago, right after he'd met with Foster. Unless he came clean with her now, how could she ever trust him again? She stopped in front of the sofa in the family room. Quincy stood less than an arm's length from her. He pressed his lips against her cheek. Ramona's heart cracked.

Why didn't you tell me you were going to ask for your old job back?

She swallowed to dislodge the lump in her throat. "Have you seen Foster?"

Quincy's smile faded. "Foster? Why do you ask?"

Ramona stepped back. Was he going to lie to her again? "He asked me to give you his best. And he's still waiting for an answer about your faculty position."

Surprise swept across his ruggedly handsome features. "You saw him?"

"Why didn't you tell me you were going to ask him for your job back?"

Quincy turned away from her. He shoved his fists into the front pockets of his shorts. "I was waiting for the right time."

Ramona gaped at his broad back. "You were waiting for the right time? Well, you missed it. It came and left. Now you're dealing with this time."

He faced her again, his forehead furrowed in confusion. "What do you mean?"

"The right time would've been the minute the idea entered your head to ask Foster for your tenured faculty position back." She jabbed a finger toward the multi-colored area rug. "That would have been the right time, Q."

"I didn't want to just spring this on you." Quincy dragged a broad hand over his clean-shaven head. "I wanted you to know I had a plan."

"You've created an entire plan that involved Foster agreeing for you to return?" Ramona straightened in surprise.

"Yes." Quincy nodded like an eager puppy.

"And you've done all of this without even *once* consulting with me?" A red haze of anger returned to cloud her vision again.

For a beat, Quincy seemed at a loss for words. "Honey, I didn't want to get your hopes up until I knew that Foster would agree."

Ramona wrapped her arms around herself. Fine tremors of anger shook her body. "I thought we were a couple, Q. I thought we were trying to build a life together."

"We are." He looked hurt. But not as hurt as she felt.

"Then why are you making plans for our lives without talking with me first?"

Quincy spread his arms. "I wanted to know if my idea would work. I wanted something to offer you as an alternative."

"What if I enjoy living in Philadelphia? Suppose I didn't want to leave? Did that ever occur to you?"

Quincy circled the sofa. "I didn't do this to upset you."

"Well, you managed to anyway."

Quincy stopped pacing. He set his hands on his hips and faced her squarely. "What if I'd come to you and said I wanted to move back to Trinity Falls but first I need to know whether Foster would rehire me?"

"Then we would've had a basis for our conversation." Ramona waved a stiff hand between the two of them. "But you went off on your own, without even telling me what you were thinking. I had to find out from someone else that my boyfriend met with his former boss. Do you know how unsettling that was for me?"

"Who told you?" Quincy frowned.

Ramona blinked. "What difference does that make? You have no right to be angry with the person who told me. You should be disappointed in yourself that *you* didn't tell me."

"Do you really enjoy living in Philadelphia?" Quincy looked troubled.

Ramona threw up her hands. "That's not the point, either."

"But do you?"

"No." Why couldn't he see how wrong his actions had been? Was this really acceptable behavior to him? "I'm homesick, too, Quincy. I want to return to Trinity Falls, as well. But that's not the point."

His eyes widened in surprise. "But if I did something that benefits both of us, why are you angry with me?"

Ramona's head was about to explode. "Because you designed your plan without taking me into consideration. We're supposed to be in this together. We're supposed to be a couple. But you acted on your own. And the fact that you can't see that you were wrong and why your actions hurt me tells me a lot about how you view our relationship."

Fear entered Quincy's coal black eyes. "What are you saying?"

"I wonder if you and I even have a relationship. Or have I been deluding myself this entire time?"

Ramona turned away. She hurried into the bedroom and closed the door behind her, ignoring Quincy's pleas for her to talk to him. They'd done enough talking. Now it was her turn to come up with a plan.

Dinner was almost ready when Doreen heard Alonzo's key in the door Thursday evening. She'd grown to love that sound over the three weeks that they'd been living together. But tonight, in addition to a burst of happy anticipation, she felt a flicker of dread. She wasn't looking forward to telling him about her conversation with Leonard.

Alonzo's footsteps stopped in the kitchen's doorway. Doreen turned from the counter where she was cutting vegetables for the salad.

"Hello, *mi amor*." His smile made her toes curl in her fuzzy pink slippers.

He was as handsome as ever despite the clouds in his eyes. When was he going to tell her what was causing them? She hated to pile one more thing on him. But the sooner she told him about Leonard, the sooner they could put the other man and his jealousy behind them.

Doreen crossed the kitchen to welcome Alonzo with a kiss. He drew her closer to deepen their caress. Doreen caught her breath as he swept his tongue over the seam of her lips and teased them apart. *Oh, my.* Leonard who?

Alonzo lifted his head and gazed down into her eyes.

Doreen's body pulsed with awakening desire. She cleared her throat. "How was your day?"

Alonzo gave her his slow smile. "It's getting better."

"Good. I'm glad." Doreen rested her hands on his biceps. She had the feeling his arms were the only things keeping her upright.

"Something smells delicious."

"We're having chicken for dinner. It should be ready in a few minutes." Doreen locked her knees, then eased out of his loose embrace. "There's something I need to tell you first, though."

Alonzo let her go. His smile dimmed but didn't fade. "That doesn't sound good."

"Everything's OK. I handled it. But I wanted you to know that Leo stopped by today. He was waiting for me when I got home from Ms. Helen's." She tried for a casual tone but didn't quite pull it off.

Alonzo's expression grew cold. "He was in our house?"

"No, no." Doreen rushed to reassure him. "I spoke with him in the driveway."

Some of his anger dissipated. "What did he want?"

Doreen shrugged as she wandered back to the counter. "He wants to reconcile with me. I told him that would never happen, even if I weren't marrying you."

"Did he accept that?"

Doreen shook her head with her back to Alonzo. She resumed cutting vegetables for their salad. "He kept saying that I don't know the real you. He said you have secrets."

"He said the same thing to me."

Doreen dropped the knife she was using to slice

carrots and turned to her fiancé. "You spoke with Leo? When?"

"He came to my office last week." Alonzo braced his shoulder against the entryway to the kitchen.

Doreen's eyes widened. "What did he want?"

"To warn me against marrying you. He said I wasn't good enough for you." His gaze was hooded, as though he wanted to hide his expression from her. *Why? What was he thinking?*

"Why didn't you tell me you'd spoken with him?" Doreen braced her hips against the counter and crossed her arms.

Alonzo shrugged again. "It wasn't important."

She expelled an exasperated breath. "Yes, it was. If I'd known Leo had spoken to you, I'd have been better prepared when he showed up in our driveway."

"Why would you need to be prepared to see him?"

Doreen scowled. "How would you have felt if I hadn't told you that I saw Leo today?"

"That's different." Alonzo straightened from the entryway. "I'm not the one Leo wants to marry."

"That's not the point. We shouldn't be keeping secrets from each other."

"All right. Fine." Alonzo dragged a hand through his thick, wavy hair. "I'm sorry."

Doreen considered Alonzo. She'd thought he was tired. But this wasn't fatigue. This was something more. Why wouldn't he confide in her? She was about to become his wife.

She straightened from the counter and crossed to

him. "You've been in a strange mood for months. What's wrong?"

"Nothing." He wouldn't look at her.

Doreen grew chilled. Was Ramona right about Alonzo and Quincy? Both men were acting out of character, seemingly growing cooler within their relationship. Why? What had changed?

"Alonzo, I need to know." Doreen hesitated, taking a deep breath. "Are you reconsidering our wedding? Are you getting cold feet?"

"Of course not."

"Then why won't you tell me what's wrong?" Doreen wasn't convinced. "Why are you keeping secrets from me?"

Alonzo gave her a sharp look. "Why would you ask me that? Has Leo convinced you that I'm not good enough for you?"

Doreen stepped back. "Where did that question come from?"

"Are you doubting me now that you've spoken with Leo?"

Was Alonzo even listening to her? Could he hear himself?

"Of course not."

"Maybe you're right, Doreen. Maybe this wedding is a mistake." Alonzo turned and left her.

Doreen stared after him, speechless. She couldn't pull her thoughts together. She heard his footsteps, carrying him up the stairs. Doreen stumbled to the table. She sank onto a chair, not wanting to fall before she fell down. From where had Alonzo's outburst come? Why would he ask her to marry him if that wasn't what he wanted? What had she done wrong—and how could she fix this?

CHAPTER 28

"Is *Mystic Park* about us?" Benita watched Vaughn closely later on Thursday. She'd catch any movement, muscle twitch, or shift in his expression that tipped his hand one way or the other about the autobiographical nature of his play.

"Do you see a similarity?" Vaughn didn't appear at all sheepish. He seemed more amused—and a little tired.

The music professor had had a long Thursday: several summer semester classes and a concert band practice even before tonight's rehearsal. Overall, the rehearsal had gone well. The only glitch had been their female lead's absence, a pretty major glitch. Vaughn had been stressed enough without Benita pointing out that she'd once again been right. Instead, she'd given him an I-told-you-so look, then stepped into the role for the night. Benita was more than capable of the substitution. She'd sung and danced her way through musicals in high school and the first two years of college.

They'd stayed after rehearsal to review the musical's

props, costumes, and advertisements. Benita had waited until they'd discussed all of those items before voicing her suspicions about Vaughn's play.

"Come on, Vaughn. In your play, Mama D'Leau is based on my mother, isn't she?" Benita wouldn't be distracted from the debate at hand. She leaned against the base of the stage, facing Vaughn where he sat in the front row of the left section of audience seats.

"Does that make you the water fairy?" His smile was a teasing taunt.

"Am I right?" Benita wouldn't allow him to divert her with his sexy smile and teasing eyes. She had him. He was sending her a message with his play.

"What if you are?" Vaughn settled back onto the folding audience seat. He propped his right ankle onto his left knee. "What is our story in the play?"

"Just like Mama D'Leau won't let the water fairy live on land with the mortals, you blame my mother for convincing me to leave Trinity Falls." Benita waited for Vaughn's reaction. Again, he didn't give away his inner thoughts with so much as a muscle twitch. The silence stretched on for almost a solid minute.

"The play isn't about us, Benny." Vaughn rose slowly to his feet. "Although I can see why you'd think it was."

"Maybe you didn't realize you were writing about us." Benita straightened away from the stage. "But I want you to know that my mother isn't keeping me from Trinity Falls. I left on my own."

"And you left me."

She stepped back from the pain in his voice. "Come with me."

"You blame Trinity Falls for your parents' divorce, but you're wrong." Vaughn packed up his suitcase. "Your parents grew apart. Trinity Falls had nothing to do with it."

"How can you say that? There was even less to do in this town when my parents lived here." Benita collected her purse, tote bag, and coat. "Maybe they'd still be married if there'd been more to hold their interests in this town."

"If your theory was correct, everyone in Trinity Falls would be divorced." Vaughn escorted her from the auditorium. "The fact is Trinity Falls's divorce rate is well below the national average."

"How do you know that?"

"I just do."

In silence, Benita preceded Vaughn down the narrow staircase from the second floor to the main lobby. It was almost ten P.M. She was getting used to Trinity Falls University at night. The lamppost lit their way across the campus Oval to the university parking lot on the other side of the street. A few shadowy figures walked in groups away from the library, a sure sign that summer semester was under way.

Benita glanced at Vaughn from the corner of her eye. His expression was an unreadable mask in the shadows. "I never meant to hurt you by leaving. I was following my dream. But I never said you couldn't come with me."

"Then Los Angeles will change both of us."

"What do you mean?" Her eyebrows knitted.

"Like I said, Benny, you're not the same person when you're in Los Angeles."

"How am I different?" He'd told her this before, but Benita had had no idea what he'd been talking about.

"You're more relaxed in Trinity Falls. When we're together, I have your attention." Vaughn checked both ways before heading across the street. "In Los Angeles, you're always checking your cell phone and e-mails."

"That's because I'm working." Benita spotted her car under one of the lights.

"You're always looking around to see if anyone famous is nearby."

"Working." She sang the word as she pulled her keys from her pants pocket.

"You're not always working, Benny. And if living in Los Angeles can do that to you, it can change me." Vaughn stopped beside her car and faced her. "I love you, but I don't want that to happen."

"Where does that leave us? I'm on water and you're on land?" She made a reference to one of the key songs in his play. "I love you, too, Vaughn. But my life isn't a musical."

"Neither is mine. Good night, Benny." Vaughn turned and walked to his car.

Benita watched him for a few seconds before climbing into her Acura. Whether he'd intended to make the script about them, he must recognize the similarity in their love stories. It was time she heeded the message of *Mystic Park*, Vaughn's fictional Trinity Falls, and live where her love is. She was going to finalize her offer on Doreen's house.

* * *

Vaughn approached the counter at Books & Bakery Saturday morning. The scents of baking bread, confectioners' sugar, and coffee assailed him. Ean, Quincy, and Darius already were there and finishing breakfast. Megan and Doreen stood on the other side of the counter, keeping the men company.

Darius looked up as Vaughn took the empty bar stool beside him. "Hey, Vaughn. Interesting that you're here. You don't usually join us."

A surprising number of customers had arrived early at Books & Bakery to enjoy breakfast at the café tables. The diners ranged from retired couples, students on summer semester, and couples and families enjoying breakfast out. The couple reviewing the map appeared to be tourists. That wasn't surprising considering it was Memorial Day Weekend.

"I'm looking to make some changes in my life." Vaughn returned his attention to Darius.

"How are things with Benita?" The newspaper man gave him a concerned look.

Vaughn paused to breathe through the pain in his chest. "We've broken up for good this time."

A chorus of regrets circled him. He appreciated his friends' concern, but it only made him feel worse. As it was, he was holding on to his composure by a thread.

"At least you're not alone." Darius waved his hand to encompass the group seated at the counter. "Everyone here is experiencing relationship problems. Well, everyone except me."

Ean frowned. "Megan and I aren't having trouble."

"Yet." Darius sipped his coffee.

Ean's scowl deepened. "What does that mean?"

Megan reached across the counter to squeeze Ean's shoulder. "Don't encourage him."

"You're on borrowed time, E." Darius continued without invitation. "You're going to have to polish up that proposal pretty soon."

Quincy snorted. "This from a man who declared his love in a bathroom."

"At least it was the ladies restroom. Did you know they have scented lotions and potpourri in there?" Darius pinned Megan and Doreen with a look. "You ladies have much nicer bathrooms than men."

Doreen turned to Vaughn. "What can I get you?"

He decided to splurge. "May I have steak and eggs, please?"

"Sure. Coffee?" Doreen laid his silverware and napkin before him.

"Please." Vaughn nodded.

"I've got it." Megan squeezed Doreen's shoulder. She offered Vaughn a cup of coffee as the other woman disappeared into the kitchen to make Vaughn's breakfast.

Vaughn glanced at Darius as he added creamer and sugar to his coffee. "If your relationship with Peyton is fine, why are you having breakfast with us?"

Darius jerked a thumb toward Quincy. "Q sent a nine-one-one. Ramona hasn't spoken to him since she ripped him a new one Thursday night."

It was Saturday morning. "You went a whole day without her talking to you?" Vaughn's eyes widened with concern. "What happened?"

Quincy rubbed a hand over his face. "She found out I'd talked with Foster about getting my old job back."

"The problem is he hadn't spoken with Ramona first." Ean shook his head in disbelief.

"Oh, man." Vaughn sighed.

"That sums it up." Darius propped his forearms on the counter.

Vaughn looked at Megan, Ramona's cousin. "Do you have any insight on this situation?"

Megan refilled Darius's coffee mug. "After speaking with Ramona, I suggested to Quincy that he stay with Ean and me for a while."

From bad to worse. Vaughn looked at Quincy's bent head. "Good luck, Q." He couldn't think of anything else to say. "What about Doreen? Everything's fine with her and Alonzo, right?"

Megan glanced cautiously toward the kitchen. "The wedding may be off."

"Oh, no." Vaughn looked around the counter. Everyone looked upset by the news, especially Ean. "Does Benita know?"

"Doreen spoke with her yesterday." Megan leaned a hip against the counter. "She's confident it's pre-wedding nerves. She's following up with the wedding preparations as though it's going to happen."

Vaughn stared into his mug of coffee. That sounded like Benita. She would trust everything to work out. She wouldn't give up. If only she'd taken the same positive approach with Trinity Falls and not given up on them.

"I'm going to ask Ramona to marry me." Quincy's announcement startled Vaughn. Judging by the expressions on his friends' faces, Quincy had surprised everyone.

Darius recovered first. "Maybe you should wait until she's speaking to you again."

Quincy scowled at the newspaper man. "I'm serious, D."

"So am I, Q." Darius's tone was firm.

"I've been thinking of proposing to her for a while now," Quincy confessed. "I just thought I should wait for the right time."

"Quincy, this isn't the right time," Ean warned.

"I think it is," Quincy insisted. "She thinks I don't see her as an equal partner in our relationship. I think asking her to be my wife will prove to her that I do."

"Quincy." Megan's voice was sharp. She held Quincy's gaze. "Do you have any idea how angry Ramona is with you right now? She's so angry with you that you're staying with Ean and me. That's how angry she is with you right now. Do you understand?"

"Yes." Quincy looked depressed.

Megan folded her hands on the counter in front of him. "Then do you really think *this* is the time when you should propose marriage to Ramona?"

"No." Quincy rubbed his forehead. The enormity of his situation seemed to have crashed onto him at one time.

Megan reached over and rubbed his shoulder. "It's OK. She'll calm down eventually. She always does."

Crisis averted, Vaughn's friends changed the subject. They asked him about *Mystic Park*, summer semester, and his brothers. *Mystic Park* was going well. Summer semester was light, and both of his brothers were returning to Trinity Falls for his play. Before he knew it, Doreen returned with his breakfast.

Megan straightened from the counter. "What's next for you once *Mystic Park* is over, Vaughn?"

Vaughn turned to Doreen. "I'm hoping to buy a house. I'd like to make an offer on yours, Doreen."

"Oh." Doreen exchanged looks with Megan and Ean before turning back to Vaughn. "Someone's already put an offer on my house. I'm sorry."

Vaughn's eyebrows rose. "Already? That was fast. I hadn't realized it had gone on the market."

Again, Doreen looked to the others before answering him. "The person made the offer before it was listed."

The others in the group regarded him with inscrutable expressions. "May I ask who made the offer?"

"I'd rather wait until the sale is final before giving the name." Doreen refreshed his coffee. "I promise to contact you first if, for some reason, the sale doesn't go through."

"I'd appreciate that." Vaughn considered Doreen's smile. It didn't mask the concern in her eyes. The others looked away when he turned to them. Then Megan changed the subject.

Was he being paranoid or were they hiding something?

Alonzo was waiting outside of Leonard's house when the high school mathematics-teacher-cum-football-head-coach pulled onto his driveway late Thursday afternoon. It was poetic justice since Leonard had lain in wait for Doreen when she'd come home from work exactly one week ago today. From his position leaning back against the railing attached to Leonard's house, Alonzo watched the smaller man climb from his car.

"Am I supposed to be intimidated by you, Alonzo?" Leonard slammed shut the driver's side door and circled the trunk of his brown Ford sedan.

"The only reason a person would say that is if he were intimidated." Alonzo remained still, tracking Leonard's progress with only his gaze. He still wore his sheriff's uniform. His arms were crossed at his chest. His legs were crossed at his ankles.

"Should I be?" Leonard leaned against the passenger side of his car. He set his soft black briefcase on the ground beside him.

"Yes."

Leonard's neighbors were either still at work, still at school, or in their houses. The picturesque street was deserted this final week of May. Alonzo had known it would be. He'd driven past Leonard's house a couple of times in the past week while he figured out how he would deal with this wannabe rival for Doreen's affections.

"Are you threatening me, Sheriff?"

"I'm educating you, Leo. But don't worry. There are just two simple lessons. Lesson one: stay away from my house."

"It's a public street."

"Lesson two: stay away from my woman."

Leonard narrowed his eyes. "Does Doreen know you're here?"

"See, that's the thing, Leo." Alonzo kept his voice nice and easy despite the inferno of fury burning inside him. "Nothing about Doreen is any of your concern. So there's no reason for you to think about her beyond the fact that she's your mayor." And he knew just how much Leonard loved that, considering he'd tried to prevent her from being elected.

Leonard held Alonzo's gaze in silence for several seconds. "Whatever you're hiding must be cataclysmic for you to try to get me to forget that I'd once had an intimate relationship with the woman you think you're going to marry."

"And you must be pretty desperate to make up stories about me." Alonzo straightened from the rail and approached Leonard. The other man stiffened as though anticipating an attack. Alonzo hoped it would never come to that. He hadn't gotten into law enforcement for the violence. And he'd had more than enough of it over the years.

Alonzo stopped an arm's length from Leonard. He wasn't stupid. He straightened to his full height, which was considerably taller than the other man. "Lesson one: stay away from my house. Lesson two: stay away from my woman." Alonzo stepped back and tipped his hat. "Have a nice night."

He turned and walked away without a backward glance. Alonzo had parked his car around the corner so he wouldn't tip off Leonard. It was a lot to go through just to get some guy to leave his fiancée alone. But love made you stupid. Real stupid.

Speaking of stupid, now that he'd dealt with Leonard, how was he going to mend the busted bridge between him and Doreen?

* * *

"How was your day?" Two afternoons later, Alonzo greeted Doreen at their front door with a kiss and a glass of lemonade.

"Fine. Thanks." Doreen accepted both before moving farther into their home. She'd finished a Saturday at Books & Bakery, and a quick visit with Ms. Helen and Benita.

"Is something wrong?" Alonzo locked the front door as he watched her walk away from him. She seemed preoccupied.

"I'm just tired." Her voice carried to him as she disappeared into the kitchen.

Alonzo winced. That was the same excuse he'd given her for the past two and a half months. What was it they said about payback? It was true. He sought her out in the kitchen. Doreen stood at the counter, pouring herself more lemonade. She replaced the pitcher in the refrigerator.

"Doreen, could we talk?"

"I'd welcome it." She crossed to the circular ash wood table and sank onto a chair. "What would you like to talk about: canceling our wedding, my moving out of your house, or your threatening Leo?"

I should have known the gutless wonder would go running to Doreen. Alonzo closed his eyes briefly. Some people learn best through repetition.

He squared his shoulders, then took the chair on the other side of the table from her. "After I say my piece, you can decide which of those things you want to discuss first."

A cautious expression settled into her brown eyes. "All right."

This is what dread feels like. His muscles had seized. His heart had stopped. His tongue lay like cement in his mouth. Alonzo still didn't know where to begin his story. He could only pray that inspiration would guide him. "I fell in love with you in high school, although I didn't know it was love until college. You brought people together. You put a spotlight on issues in the community that needed to be addressed. Every action you took had a positive reaction in Trinity Falls."

"You give me too much credit." Doreen raised a hand, palm out. "I didn't do anything alone. A lot of people helped me, including you and Paul."

"But you were the driving force. You were the one who got us started and kept us going."

"That's debatable, but it's not what we're talking about right now."

"All right." Alonzo stood and crossed the kitchen. "I went into law enforcement because I wanted to have a positive impact on the community, too. But it didn't work out the way I'd hoped."

"What happened?" Her voice invited his confidences.

Alonzo hesitated. His gaze was on the view outside his kitchen window. But in his mind, he saw his old beat in Miami. "Instead of helping to build a community, in the course of my career, I've taken lives."

Doreen gasped. "Alonzo, how?"

He kept his back to her. He couldn't bear to see her rejection when he told her the truth. "One of the victims was an abusive ex-husband, holding his ex-wife and three-year-old daughter hostage. The second was a bank robber. The third was a home invader. After that, I decided to leave the big city to become a small town sheriff's deputy."

His tension built to almost screaming proportion as he waited for Doreen's reaction. Was this where their story ended for good? Why would someone like her—someone who creates and builds—want anything to do with a man who had blood on his hands? Would they remain friends at least? Or wouldn't she want any part of him?

"Alonzo, I'm so sorry." Her hand settled gently on his shoulder.

He started. He hadn't heard her move. "So am I." Alonzo turned to her. "The memories of the lives I took are always with me. Always. But the recent police shootings have made them even harder to contain."

Doreen shook her head fiercely. "Those killings weren't anything like your experiences. You didn't kill unarmed people under questionable circumstances. You shot armed and violent offenders who were directly endangering you and other people."

"It was still murder." Alonzo turned from her.

"What would have happened to the woman and child who were being held hostage by her ex-husband?"

"He was threatening to kill his daughter if his wife didn't leave with him." Sometimes with the memory came the fear and tension from that scene. Alonzo clenched his fist to keep the feelings from building.

Doreen squeezed his shoulder. "How many customers were in the bank when the robber struck?"

"Nine employees and ten customers." Through the grace of God, no one else had been killed or injured. But he imagined the danger had taken an emotional toll on all of them.

"What about the home invasion?"

He understood her questions, but reliving these memories was hard on him.

"It was a family of six." Alonzo paused as images from that day raced across his mind's eye. "The parents were in their midthirties. They had three children, ages ten, seven, and three. The wife's mother lived with them."

Why is she rubbing my back? Alonzo had expected that Doreen would have started packing by now.

"Alonzo, you're in law enforcement."

"That's not a license to kill."

"No, it isn't." Doreen's voice was patient. "It's a directive to protect and to serve. You had to draw your gun to protect that mother and her baby daughter, the employees and customers in that bank, and that family."

"I often wonder if there had been another choice." He'd never spoken that uncertainty aloud.

Doreen stopped rubbing his back. She wrapped her arms around him and hugged him from behind. Hard. "I'm so sorry you had those experiences. But, Alonzo, I don't think you had another choice. A lot of lives were at stake."

She's hugging me. Alonzo barely heard Doreen's words. He was too stunned. Instead of turning away from him, Doreen was literally embracing him. Did this mean she was willing to accept all of him, including his past?

Alonzo turned in her embrace. "This is the reason I've been so distant. I was afraid that, once you learned what I did, you wouldn't want to marry me."

Doreen's eyes filled with sadness and confusion. "Alonzo, I know what you do for a living. I don't like to think about the danger you've been in or the images you must have seen. But I'm not naive."

Alonzo was weak with relief. He leaned back against the counter. "You're not canceling the wedding?"

"No, I'm not canceling our wedding, although you've been a real pain in the neck." Doreen rose on her toes to give him a quick kiss. "I love you. I want to spend the rest of my life with you."

"And we'll spend those years making only happy memories."

"That's a promise." Doreen sealed it with a kiss.

⌒⌒CHAPTER 29⌒⌒

Benita followed Vaughn into his apartment Friday evening. In eight days, *Mystic Park* would take the stage. It would be the show's debut performance. But if Benita's negotiations worked, it wouldn't be its last. This seemed like the best time to tell Vaughn about Tommy Poole's offer, when she had other good news to share as well. But Benita didn't know what to tell him about first: the L.A. theater producer or her buying Doreen's house.

"How was your class?" She lowered herself onto the sofa, watching while he settled beside her.

"Something tells me you didn't come here to ask about my music class." Vaughn gave her a curious smile. "What's going on?"

"You're right." Benita held both hands up, palms out. A huge smile stretched her lips. "Great news. I found a theater producer in L.A. who's interested in performing *Mystic Park*."

Vaughn didn't respond. He returned her gaze as though

she were talking a foreign language. Several seconds ticked by. Finally, Benita spoke again. "Did you hear me?"

"I don't think I did." Vaughn sounded so serious. His eyes were cool and distant. "Did you send my musical to a producer in Los Angeles?"

Benita's smile wavered. "Yes, and he's very interested in it. Very interested."

"But why would you have sent it to a producer in Los Angeles when I specifically asked you not to do that?" Vaughn's voice was tight with control.

"*Mystic Park* is a fantastic musical. It deserves to be seen in additional venues." Benita felt her first stirring of unease.

"Son of a—" Vaughn surged off his sofa and paced across the room to the fireplace. "You're a piece of work, Benny."

"Vaughn, an *L.A.* producer wants to produce *your* musical. Doesn't that mean anything to you?" She thought he'd at least be flattered by the producer's interest.

"I'm producing my musical on my own. Why should I care what this guy thinks?"

"For one thing, it's additional validation of your work." Benita smoothed her right eyebrow. She was becoming impatient. "A lot of people would be flattered."

"I know what you're doing." Vaughn pinned her with a cold gaze. "It's not going to work."

"Vaughn, I—"

"You thought I'd be so impressed and flattered by this L.A. hotshot's approval that I'd change my mind about leaving Trinity Falls, didn't you?" His voice shook with temper.

"I didn't send your play to an L.A. producer to convince you to move." *Why is he so angry?*

"You're lying." Vaughn swept his hand in the air as he paced to his bay window on the other side of the room.

Benita stiffened. That was uncalled for. "No, I'm not."

"This is what you've been planning all along. How could I not have seen it?" He paced away from his window and started toward his fireplace. "You wanted to help me with *Mystic Park* as part of your plan to convince me to move to Los Angeles with you."

"I did consider that at first." Benita crossed her arms and legs, uncomfortable with the truth of his accusation. "But I don't feel that way now."

"You hounded me to send my proposal to a producer once you found out I'd completed the musical."

"Only because your talent deserves a broader audience." *Stubborn man.*

"And when I wouldn't send it out, you offered to do it for me."

"Because it's a great script and a wonderful score."

"I told you not to send it, but you went behind my back and did it anyway."

"Vaughn, I'm proud of what you've done and I admire your talent. I may have started out to—"

"I can't believe your audacity." Vaughn dragged a hand over his clean-shaven head. "Don't you think I'm qualified to make my own decisions?"

"Of course I do." Benita wanted to stand, but she didn't believe her shaky legs would support her.

"Then why did you disregard my wishes?"

Benita spread her arms. "I wanted to help you."

"For Pete's sake. You wanted to help me?" Vaughn stared at her as though he'd never seen her before. "This is why we can't be together."

Benita gasped. His words were like knives in her heart. "How can you say that?"

"You think you know everything. No one else's opinion matters. You're the great Benita Hawkins and you know what's best for everyone."

Benita surged to her feet. Enough was enough. "I chose that L.A. producer because I knew he'd be interested in your story and open to a musical. So that was calculated on my part."

"It's always about you—"

"Listen to me!" Benita set her hands on her hips. "Initially, I did hope this producer's interest would convince you that you had greater opportunities in L.A. But the fact of the matter is, Vaughn, you don't have to live in L.A. for your musical to be performed there. But *Mystic Park* deserves to be seen in other markets: New York, L.A., San Francisco, Chicago, Kalamazoo."

"Whether *Mystic Park* is seen in other venues is my decision, not yours." Vaughn stopped pacing to glare at her. "And I've finally realized I can't be with someone who's constantly making decisions for me."

"You're right. I'm sorry I overstepped my boundaries." As Benita collected her purse all thoughts of Doreen's house—now her house—had flown from her head. She hurried toward the door before the tears fell. "I'll tell the producer you're not interested."

Benita let herself out of Vaughn's apartment and jogged to her car parked in front of his garage. If she hadn't believed their relationship was done before, she believed it now. He'd been so angry. She hadn't thought he'd be that angry.

She deactivated her car alarm, which unlocked her doors. With shaking hands, she let herself into her Acura and collapsed behind the steering wheel. She'd wanted to help him. Instead her actions had pushed him away for good. Their relationship was over, forever over. How ironic, now that she'd finally moved back to Trinity Falls.

"Are you lost?" Ramona spoke from her reclining position on the sofa in the center of the rental cabin's great room.

Quincy locked the front door behind him and strode to where Ramona lay on the couch reading a home decorating magazine. It was the first Saturday afternoon in June. Ramona hadn't spoken to him in more than two weeks.

During that time, Quincy had accepted sanctuary with Megan and Ean. They'd been great hosts, but it was time for him to reestablish his place with Ramona. The first week, Quincy had given Ramona her space. But the second week, he'd called and stopped by every day. She'd frozen him out. He was growing increasingly concerned that she would never let him back in. He couldn't allow that to happen.

"Enough is enough, Ramona." Quincy stopped beside the sofa. "I didn't come home to spend the time apart from you."

Ramona turned a page in her magazine. Her attention was glued to its glossy paper. "We're still not even. Your not spending time with me isn't the same as my finding out you're making plans to stay in Trinity Falls without me."

"You *want* to move back to Trinity Falls." That much he'd put together from the stingy words she'd given him over the past fifteen days.

Ramona looked up from her magazine and pinned him with her ebony stare. "That's not the point."

"Then what is the point? Explain it to me." Their disagreement had gone on for two weeks too long. It needed to end today. He wanted his Ramona back. He missed her too much.

Ramona closed her magazine. She sat up, swinging her long, bare legs over the side of the couch. She was wearing a white crop top and short purple shorts. Her hair hung loose and tousled around her shoulders.

She shifted on the sofa to face him. "You made me believe that you thought I was more than a decoration."

Quincy frowned. "Of course I do."

"Then why are you treating me like one?"

Quincy's eyes widened. "What do you mean?"

Ramona drew her fingers through her luxurious raven hair. She seemed weary and frustrated. "Instead of coming to me so that we could decide together where we're going to live, you decided on your own as though I don't have the intellect to contribute to the discussion."

"That's not what I was doing." Quincy was shocked at her interpretation of the situation. "I wanted to have a plan to offer you."

"We're a couple. We should've figured it out together." Ramona's sigh was thick with confusion. "Instead, you decided you needed to be the man with a plan."

Quincy risked sitting an arm's length from Ramona on the sofa. "I'm sorry, Ramona. I thought I was helping by coming up with a solution on my own."

"Suppose we didn't have the same solution?" She shrugged. "I want to come home to Trinity Falls. But what if I didn't?"

"Then I'd need another solution."

She arched a brow. "Another one you came up with by yourself?"

"No, we'd figure it out together, you and me."

Ramona inclined her head. "Make sure you always remember that."

"I promise I will. I'm sorry I upset you. It was never my intention." He searched her eyes, hoping she believed him.

"I understand. Just don't make that mistake again, please." Ramona started to rise from the couch.

Quincy caught her arm. "There's one more matter I need your input on. It's just a question."

Ramona sat again. Her ebony eyes were bright with curiosity. "What is it?"

Quincy pulled the ring box from his front cargo shorts

pocket. He opened it, holding the case toward her. "Will you marry me?"

Ramona gaped. She stared, motionless, at the princess cut, nine-carat diamond as though it would do a song-and-dance routine for her.

Finally, she threw herself into his arms. "Doctor Quincy Spates, you're a fast learner."

Quincy's smile was unsure. "Is that a yes?"

Ramona's laugh was buoyant and free, like a rushing brook. "Yes, you ridiculous man. I'll marry you." She leaned back in his embrace. "I love you so much. And I love the way you love me."

Quincy's heart swelled in his chest. "You've just made me the happiest man of the century. I love you, Ramona McCloud. Forever and always."

"She's not coming. I can't believe Ginny's not coming." Vaughn sounded on the verge of hyperventilating.

It was six-thirty on *Mystic Park*'s opening night, June thirteenth. Curtain call was seven P.M. Cast members and stagehands had been asked to arrive backstage by five-thirty P.M. As five-thirty became six o'clock and six o'clock had grown to six-thirty, the volunteers had accepted that Ginny Carp, their play's immensely talented but grossly unreliable female lead, wasn't coming.

Benita had ignored the furtive glances cast in her direction. It was apparent that the cast and crew expected her to replace Ginny for tonight's performance just as she had each time Ginny had been late or missed rehearsal altogether. However, the knots reproducing in her stomach were sending another message.

"The stagehand came back a few minutes ago." Benita stood beside Vaughn as they looked out over the audience, each willing Ginny to appear; better late than never. "He said no one answered the door and it didn't look as though anyone had been home."

They hadn't stood this close or spoken as many words to each other in more than a week, not since Benita had told Vaughn about the theater producer who was interested in his play.

"Do you think she's on her way?" Vaughn checked his watch.

"No, and neither do you." Benita checked her wristwatch as well. They were running out of time. Guests were beginning to arrive. Darius escorted Peyton and Ms. Helen into the auditorium. Jackson and Audra followed them in. Benita was going to be sick. She could only imagine how anxious Vaughn felt. "She's still not answering her phone, either."

"I can't believe she's not going to show for the performance."

"I warned you she was erratic. She keyed Darius's car, for heaven's sake." Benita crossed her arms. She felt her heart thundering against her chest. "Do you remember when I suggested we get understudies?"

Now probably wasn't the best time to remind Vaughn of the road not traveled. But she really hated being put in this position.

Vaughn turned to her, his expression desperate. "Yes, I remember."

"I hate when I'm right."

"So do I." He glanced over the audience again before facing Benita.

"I know what you're going to say." She glared at him, more from fear than anger.

"I don't have any right to ask you."

"No, you don't."

"But I am asking, Benny. Will you fill in for Ginny one more time?"

"This isn't a rehearsal. It's the actual performance. There are people watching." Benita's muscles were tight with panic. A sharp pain in her temple signaled a tension headache was building.

"I know you're not comfortable performing. But you're a natural and you have a beautiful singing voice."

Vaughn was laying it on pretty thick. She was still angry with him. His accusations about her contacting the L.A. producer were ugly and uncalled for. But as angry as she felt, she still couldn't bring herself to destroy his opening night. Tonight was the realization of his dream. A lot of other people also had worked hard and made great sacrifices to get to this night. She couldn't let any of them down.

"I really hate this." She rubbed her eyebrow.

"I know. I'm sorry, but I'm not asking just for me."

"I know." Benita spun on her heels and hurried toward the dressing room before she changed her mind. "Just make the announcement that I'm filling in for Ginny."

"I will." Vaughn followed after her.

Benita clenched her fists as her body started to shake with nerves. "The costume probably won't fit."

"We have time to make adjustments."

That depended on the extent of the alterations. Benita had never even tried on the costume. She'd refused to believe Ginny wouldn't turn up for the performance. She should have known better.

This was one of her worst nightmares come true. At least once it was over, she'd never have to spend time with Vaughn ever again.

Three hours later, Vaughn stood on stage with Benita and the rest of the *Mystic Park* cast as they accepted the audience's standing ovation. Despite Ginny not showing up, the night had been better than he'd ever hoped. Once the applause died down, Vaughn led the cast, musicians, and crew backstage for the after party.

"Congratulations, everyone. Congratulations." Vaughn stood in the front of the break room and raised his voice to get the group's attention. The room grew quiet. "I'd like to thank you all for a wonderful performance tonight. You were all great: actors, musicians, and crew. You deserved the audience's ovation and another round of applause."

The room erupted in cheers and handclapping.

Ethel Knight shouted above the cacophony. "You deserve another round of applause, too, for that phenomenal script and those songs."

More cheers, and this time foot stomping joined the applause.

Vaughn raised his hands again and called for order. "I asked a lot of you to prepare this show in just seven weeks. But you pulled it off and your performance was better than I'd even hoped. Thank you."

He waited for the din to quiet down. "Special thanks

to our last-minute water fairy, Benita Hawkins, who filled in for our female lead and provided us with an outstanding performance."

The roar of approval almost brought down the house. Vaughn was thrilled for Benita, especially considering how nervous she'd been.

"Thank you, Benita, for saving the show." Simon Knight shouted the words above the cheers, and the noise grew even louder.

Vaughn smiled as Benita's golden brown skin took on a pinkish hue. He wanted to talk with her. He needed to tell her how much he appreciated her finding the courage to do the live performance. If it weren't for her, his dream of producing *Mystic Park* would not have been realized tonight.

He worked his way across the room, stopping often to offer congratulations and to accept them. There was an electric current in the room. It was made of excitement, success, victory, and relief. He'd felt it before in other performances he'd been a part of. It was heady. It made people chatty, giddy.

Vaughn finally made his way to Benita's side. He noticed right away that she seemed neither chatty nor giddy. "Thank you again so much. You really went above and beyond for the play."

"I'm glad you were able to bring your musical to the stage." Benita's smile didn't make it to her eyes. "It was the realization of your dream. And, judging by the size of the audience, it also was a very successful fundraiser." She started to turn away from him.

Vaughn caught her arm. "I'm sorry for the things I said the last time we talked."

"Are you?" She walked away from him before he could say another word.

Vaughn didn't know what he would have said if she'd stayed but he would have liked to have found out. Instead he watched her disappear into the crowd of cast members, stagehands, musicians, friends, and family.

Darius's hand on his shoulder startled him. "Well done."

"Thanks." Vaughn turned to offer his friend a smile.

Darius jerked his chin in the direction Benita had disappeared. "She was fantastic."

Vaughn's smile was much more natural this time. "Yes, she was."

"Were you able to resolve your issues or are you breaking up?"

Vaughn glanced over his shoulder. "I guess we're breaking up."

⌒⌒ CHAPTER 30 ⌒⌒

Alonzo's wedding day was perfect: cloudless blue sky, gentle breeze, and scores of friends to wish them well.

Someone pinch me.

Alonzo stood with Darius, Juan, Jackson, and Father Steven on a low platform in an open clearing near Pearl Lake at Harmony Cabins. Vaughn sat at a baby grand piano, playing "Air," by George F. Handel, for the wedding processional.

All of the bridesmaids carried hand-tied bouquets of purple roses and soft white calla lilies. They wore different variations of the same basic Chardonnay dress. Audra appeared first, walking the path that led from the main cabin. Her version featured capped sleeves and ended at her knees. Ramona's dress was sleeveless with a high waist and a hemline above her knees. Megan's dress had a cinched waist, three-quarter-length sleeves, and ended just below the knees.

After the bridesmaids were in position, Vaughn changed the music to "At Last," sung by Etta James. It was the perfect song for them.

And then Doreen appeared.

Alonzo's heart stopped. Doreen was an ethereal vision in her full-length ivory sheath gown. She was glowing as she walked alone down the path to join him. In her hands, she carried a hand-tied bouquet of ivory roses. Her soft smile was steady. Her brown eyes were full of love. She came to him and he took her hands. Alonzo's heart was full.

Father Steven began their wedding ceremony. "Dearly beloved, we are gathered here today to join this man and this woman in holy matrimony."

The priest's words faded into the distance as Alonzo gazed down at Doreen. He'd truly never seen her look so lovely. Her beauty would not be accurately captured in their wedding photos. He'd have to try—

"I have an objection." Leonard's voice was strong and clear as it cut across Father Steven's officiating.

Stunned, Alonzo turned to look out over their guests. His eyes landed on Leonard, standing near the back of the gathering.

Benita was rushing toward the wedding crasher. "Leo, how did you get in here? You weren't on the guest list."

Leonard set his hands on his hips. "I have a right to speak my mind."

"Sir, the wedding ceremony no longer asks for any objections." Father Steven addressed Leonard in a calm and reasoned tone. He might as well have saved his breath. "That part of the script is now obsolete."

"It shouldn't be." Leonard jerked his arm free of Benita's hold. "I object very strenuously to this marriage. What do we know about the sheriff?"

Alonzo stepped forward. "Leo—"

Darius stopped him with a hand on his arm. "We'll handle this. That's what groomsmen are for."

Darius, Juan, and Jackson stepped down from the low platform and marched toward Leonard. Ean joined them. Benita stepped aside as the four men approached.

Leonard glared at the group bearing down on him. "I have a right to speak my piece."

Ean scowled at his former high school football coach. "That's where you're wrong, Leo."

Darius agreed. "This isn't a public hearing. It's a private ceremony. And you're not welcome here."

The four men surrounded Leo. They escorted him firmly and respectfully away from the ceremony and presumably to the parking lot.

Alonzo glanced at Doreen. She appeared shaken and upset. He wrapped an arm around her and drew her closer to his side. She thanked him with a warm if unsteady smile.

He looked at the guests seated in the folding chairs arranged in front of the platform. Most of them looked surprised and confused as the groomsmen and Ean took Leonard away from the clearing. A few appeared excited by the scandalous interruption of the wedding ceremony. How long would it take them to spread tales of Leonard's outburst? But it was Nessa's expression of cold contempt and superiority that dampened Alonzo's spirits and cast a shadow over their day.

Benita joined the platform with Doreen and Alonzo. "I'm so sorry. Leo must have snuck in with a group that had an invitation. I take full responsibility for this. I'm very sorry."

Doreen took Benita's hand. "This wasn't your fault. And I refuse to let this destroy our day."

"Leo planned this to try to ruin it." Alonzo turned to Doreen. "Please excuse me, sweetheart. I won't be gone long."

"And you won't be going alone." Doreen lifted the hemline of her gown out of the way. "I'm coming with you."

Alonzo decided against wasting time trying to talk Doreen out of joining him. Instead, he helped her from the platform. As he strode after Leonard, he heard Benita trying to explain the events to their guests.

He caught up with Leonard a short distance from the clearing. The five men were walking quietly toward the parking lot. Leonard seemed to be clothed in a satisfied silence.

"Leo." The sound of Alonzo's voice brought Leonard, Ean, and the groomsmen to a stop.

"Alonzo, what are you doing?" Ean looked from his mother to Alonzo at her side.

Alonzo came to a stop an arm's length from the group. He held Leonard's surprised gaze. "If you were hoping to spoil our wedding day, you failed."

Leonard narrowed his eyes. He turned to Doreen. "Are you sure he's the man he claims to be? Dorie, what do you really know about him and his past?"

"Shut up, Leo," Doreen snapped. "With every syllable you utter, you make me more and more relieved that I had the good sense not to marry you. And stop calling me Dorie. It's a stupid nickname."

Alonzo chuckled. He wrapped his right arm around Doreen's slim waist. She was so gorgeous. This is what he needed to reclaim his wedding day. Ean, Darius, Juan, and Jackson moved away from Leonard to stand with Alonzo and Doreen.

Alonzo looked again to Leonard. The other man's face bore an angry flush. Alonzo smiled. "As you drive away from Harmony Cabins, I want you to keep one thing in mind: within the hour, Doreen and I will be Mr. and Mrs. Lopez, and I will be the happiest man on the planet."

"And I will be the happiest woman." Doreen raised up on her toes to kiss his lips. "Let's go get married."

Alonzo allowed his bride-to-be to lead him back to the clearing. He was aware of his friends following them. A soft breeze played with the leaves in the trees around them. The sky was a perfect, cloudless blue. Good friends surrounded them.

His wedding day was once again perfect.

Vaughn waved to catch Jackson's and Darius's attention when he saw them walk into the sports bar Monday afternoon. The gesture gave him a glimpse of his silver Timex wristwatch. What time was Benita leaving for Los Angeles? Had she already left? He couldn't dwell on the image of Benita once again leaving him. He needed a distraction of lunch with his friends.

He, Ean, and Quincy already had secured a high table with a good view of several televisions. A server arrived minutes after to take the five men's drink orders.

"So, it's official." Quincy looked around the table. "I'm returning to Trinity Falls University this fall."

Congratulatory comments rained down on the professor of African-American history. Jackson and Ean delighted in slapping Quincy on the back.

Vaughn raised his voice to interrupt the well-deserved cheers. "He's not just returning to TFU. He's retained his tenure and he's the new history department chair."

"Wow, Q, that's wonderful," Jackson said.

Ean shook his head in amazement. "Must be clean living."

"Or he has naughty pictures of someone," Darius theorized.

More jokes and laughter followed until the server returned with their drinks and took their food orders. Everyone requested salads to go with their chicken wings, burger, or fish sandwich.

Vaughn watched the server leave. "What did Ramona say?"

Quincy smiled with relief. "She's thrilled. She's already making plans for me to succeed Foster when he retires."

"If he retires." Jackson added sugar to his iced tea.

"He's been there a while." Darius sipped his root beer. "So, Q, what have you learned from this tragic and completely avoidable experience?"

"I know. I know." Quincy lowered his glass of ice water. "I have to discuss important life decisions with my life partner."

"No." Darius waved his hand. "You need to listen to your friends when they tell you that you have to discuss important decisions with your girlfriend."

Quincy shook his head. "You know, I wouldn't wish on anyone the misery I experienced when Ramona was angry with me. But if anyone could use that kind of comeuppance, it's you, man."

Darius seemed shocked. "What are you talking about? I've been by your side this whole time."

Quincy snorted. "Yeah, gloating because everything's going so well with you and Peyton."

Darius sobered. "It hasn't always been that way."

"That's an understatement," Vaughn agreed.

Their food arrived. The friends ate lunch accompanied by more banter, updates on national events, and rumors circulating town. They also watched sports highlights on the televisions mounted to the walls. When the check arrived, they split the bill, tipped the server generously, then prepared to leave.

Vaughn took one last deep drink of his iced tea. "I'd better hurry. I'm meeting an agent to look at realty listings."

Darius stopped to face Vaughn. The group stood in the bar's back parking lot. "You really don't know who bought Doreen's house, do you?"

"No, who bought it?" *And why should I care?*

Darius shook his head. "Benita."

Shock rocked Vaughn back on his heels. *Benita*. She was staying in Trinity Falls. Their last bitter argument and every horrible thing he'd said to her came back to him. His face burned with shame.

"When?" He could barely form the word.

Darius frowned in thought. "About a week before your musical."

Helplessly, Vaughn turned to his friends. They didn't look surprised. "Why didn't someone tell me?"

"We thought Benita wanted to tell you." Jackson shrugged.

Vaughn imagined her sitting on his sofa the day they'd had their final argument. She'd glowed with happiness. He'd thought it had been about the theater producer.

"She probably had." Vaughn clenched his teeth. "I'm such an idiot."

"No arguments here," Darius agreed.

"What are you going to do?" Jackson asked.

Vaughn looked blindly around the parking lot. His mind was shooting off in a million different directions. Panic gripped him. "I'm going to apologize. But I'm not sure how. I've got to make it good, though. Something tells me I'll only get one chance."

⮰⮰ CHAPTER 31 ⮱⮱

Running footsteps sounded behind Benita on the jogging path in Freedom Park Tuesday morning. She shifted to her right, allowing room for the other person to pass on the inside of the trail. She'd moved back to Trinity Falls but was keeping the safety tips she'd picked up during her three years in Los Angeles.

The other jogger didn't pass her, though. Instead, his long, lean presence remained on her left. "Morning."

At the sound of Vaughn's voice, Benita stumbled over nothing. Vaughn's hand shot out, catching her upper arm to steady her.

"Thanks." Benita glimpsed his sweat-darkened navy T-shirt and black running shorts. Her gaze paused on the black knapsack on his back. *What was that about?*

"Are you starting or almost done?" Vaughn asked the same question Benita had gasped when she'd arranged to happen upon him on the trail two months earlier.

"Starting." *How many of these encounters will I have to survive before they stop hurting? Would they ever stop hurting?*

"So am I."

Benita scowled at the path in front of her. They both knew she was stuck with him. It wasn't as though she could speed off. Vaughn could outrun her in his sleep.

Benita drew a deep breath, inhaling the scents of grass and earth. The late-June weather was warm and sunny. There were a few other joggers and walkers—familiar faces now—on the broad dirt path. They exchanged nods and smiles of greeting, everyone from the speed walkers to joggers and hard-core marathon trainers. Another difference between Trinity Falls and L.A.

"What. Do you. Want?" Benita refused to look at him. Seeing his sweat-dampened T-shirt clinging to his torso, knowing she couldn't touch him would hurt too much. She had the answer to her question whether his mesmerism was deliberate or a product of his charms. It was definitely his charm. He couldn't fake this.

"I thought we could keep each other company while we jogged."

Was he kidding? She couldn't take this. She just couldn't.

"Please. Leave." Benita wiped moisture from her eyes. Was it sweat or tears?

"Benny—" His voice, laced with concern, was muted beneath the pounding in her ears.

"Please." Benita slowed. She couldn't battle the jogging trail and Vaughn. She didn't have the stamina.

A familiar path came into view on Vaughn's left. He took her wrist and tugged her along. "Come with me."

"No." She pulled against him, but she might as well not have bothered. She felt like the animated character Gumby following in Vaughn's wake.

He pressed a button to pause his stopwatch as they

moved deeper onto the path. Benita didn't want to admit her gratitude when he slowed to a walk. They traveled past mostly white ash, beech, and big elm trees, and only a few evergreens. It was quieter here. She heard the birds singing from the treetops and the rustle of squirrels and chipmunks in the undergrowth.

Benita dug in her heels. She was nearly face to face with the old oak tree on which she and Vaughn had carved their initials so many heartaches ago. "I don't want to be here."

"We can stop now." Vaughn faced her. Just looking at his handsome features and knowing they could never be together tore open her heart.

Benita looked away. "Let me go."

"That's just it, Benny. I can't."

She frowned at him. *What did that mean?* "What are we doing here?"

"I have something for you." He started to take off his knapsack without releasing her wrist.

"You should let me go if you want to take that off." A reluctant smile curved her lips.

Vaughn searched her eyes. "If I let you go, you'll leave."

She held his gaze. "I promise I won't."

Without hesitation, Vaughn released Benita's arm. He used both of his hands to shrug off the knapsack. He reached into it and withdrew a plastic bag, which he offered to her.

Benita looked from Vaughn to the bag. She took it, then pulled out a notebook. She read its cover: Benita E. Hawkins, 1999 to __ .

Benita's head snapped up. Her eyes were wide on Vaughn. "You stole my diary!"

"I'm sorry. I—"

"You're sorry?" Outrage flashed through her. She could barely think. "If you were sorry, you'd have returned it fourteen years ago."

Her mind raced with all the things she remembered writing in her journal. What about the things she'd forgotten about? *Oh, my word.*

"Benny, I—"

"All of my most personal thoughts are in here." She waved the book under his nose. "I wrote about the first time we . . . How could you? That was personal."

Vaughn viced his hands around her upper arms and drew her to him. "You wrote that you'd love me forever."

Benita stilled. "I can't believe you read my diary."

"I was desperate, Benny." His shoulders slumped. "Your parents had just divorced. They were both leaving Trinity Falls and you were leaving with them. I wanted to know what would happen to us."

"Why didn't you just ask me?"

Vaughn released one of her arms to run his hand over the back of his neck. "I needed to be sure. I thought whatever you'd written in your diary must be true."

"So you found my diary and kept it?" Benita's anger drained. Now she struggled with confusion. What was he saying?

"Through all these years and all of your relocations, those words—'I'll love him forever'—have given me hope." Vaughn released her arms, but his gaze still held her. "And, yes, I wrote *Mystic Park* about us."

"I knew it." Benita narrowed her eyes.

Vaughn crossed his arms over his dampened T-shirt. "And now I have an even greater reason to hope."

"What?" Benita stepped back.

"You bought Doreen's house." He took a step toward her.

"It's across the street from Aunt Helen's."

"You wrote that you'd love me forever. I wanted to believe your diary entry so badly." Vaughn took her hand. "But there were times when I lost hope. When I found out you were the one who bought Doreen's house, I felt like the governor had granted me a stay of execution."

"Why?" Benita blinked back tears. She gasped when Vaughn went down on one knee. "What are you doing?"

"We've waited long enough, Benny." He took both of her hands with his. "You're my forever love. Marry me, please? I don't want to be apart from you anymore."

A slow-building roar of approval sounded behind them. Benita looked around and saw her morning jogging and walking companions watching them from a distance.

She shook her head. "There really isn't any privacy in Trinity Falls, is there?"

"Does that bother you so much?"

"No, because I don't care who knows that I love you like crazy." She tightened her grip on his hands and tugged him to his feet. "It took me long enough, but I've finally found my home, and it's right here in your arms."

Don't miss a Finding Home novella in

A CHRISTMAS KISS

Coming in October 2015!

Here's a sneak peek!

⟋⟋CHAPTER 1⟍⟍

"Picture this." June Cale made her pitch for the Kwanzaa presentation from the threadbare seat in front of her boss's desk at the Guiding Light Community Center. It was Monday morning, the second day of November. They were running out of time. "Saturday afternoon before Thanksgiving, our community room is set up like an auditorium. A makeshift stage is built in front of the room. Doctor Quincy Spates, professor of African American History at Trinity Falls University, stands on the stage. From a podium, he leads a free discussion on the seven values of Kwanzaa."

Benjamin Brooks, the center's new director and her boss of two months, lowered his coffee mug. As usual, his handsome sienna features were hard to read, emotionless. *The Iceman.* "How does a free presentation raise money for the center?"

"It's not a fund-raiser." June adjusted the project folder on her lap. "Doctor Spates's discussion is a community-engagement event. The goal of this event is to help strengthen our relationship with the community, which will—hopefully—make it easier to persuade them to support the center."

June considered her boss's conservative blue tie and the snow-white linen shirt that hugged his well-muscled shoulders. They both looked expensive—and out of place in the worn and faded office. Why had Benjamin Brooks really returned home to Trinity Falls?

Like his youngest brother, Vaughn, who was a professor of music at Trinity Falls University, Benjamin Brooks was a dangerously attractive man. His dark brown hair was cut neat and close. His square jaw was clean shaven. Piercing ebony eyes beneath thick dark eyebrows dominated his chiseled features. June's tripping pulse wasn't all due to nerves.

Yes, Ben Brooks is a good-looking man. But right now, I want to shake him silly.

"Has Quincy agreed to do the Kwanzaa presentation?" Benjamin wrapped his coffee mug between his hands. Was he trying to warm them? His office was like an ice box.

"I asked him to hold the date. But I need to confirm with him." June's nerves were tingling again. Benjamin was a lot less enthusiastic than she'd hoped.

"You're not giving him much time. Today's November second." Benjamin's gaze settled somewhere behind June. She assumed he was consulting the twelve-month calendar his predecessor had posted to the wall. "The Saturday before Thanksgiving is November twenty-first, less than three weeks away."

"If you approve of the idea, I'll invite him today." June waited for him to say the words.

June had approached Quincy when she'd started her position as deputy director and fund-raising manager in

August. He'd agreed to hold the date. However, she hadn't wanted to confirm the event until her new boss had settled in after his September start date. With one center crisis after another, time had slipped away and the November date had rushed up on her.

"What else do you have?" Benjamin settled back on his gray cushioned chair. He seemed underwhelmed.

June regrouped. "Picture this. The community room transformed into a winter wonderland. Traditional Christmas dishes and desserts served in a winding buffet line while Christmas carols and secular pop songs provide music for a dinner dance." June saw it in her mind's eye. The image made her smile.

"Didn't a special community fund-raising committee just host a party for the center?" Again, Benjamin appeared less than impressed.

"That was in January. It was a twentieth anniversary party for the center." June had heard around town that the event had been an incredible success.

"We shouldn't host a fund-raising party in January, then another in December. That's overkill." Tension seemed to hover around Benjamin like a cloud. *Why?*

"Going forward, I think we should host a Christmas dinner dance. Then, the center's anniversary in January could be our annual online day of giving."

"What's that?"

"Giving Tuesdays are national examples of days of giving. We'll focus all our energies on one day, the center's birthday, and ask people to either make a donation online or mail a check. I'm working on a process for the project."

"It sounds like a good idea." Benjamin nodded as he sipped more coffee.

"Great. Then I'll move forward with the Christmas dinner dance." The anxious butterflies in her stomach settled down.

"I don't want to do a Christmas celebration." Benjamin waved a hand, dismissing June's proposal. "Everyone's doing that."

"Who else is doing a Christmas fund-raiser?" June searched her mind but couldn't think of a single organization in Trinity Falls that was doing a similar event.

"Books and Bakery."

"Megan hosts a Christmas-themed store event similar to her Halloween party and story time. But it's not a fund-raiser." Megan McCloud was the owner of Books & Bakery. Her themed events were highly anticipated in the community.

"Close enough."

June couldn't disagree more. "Our event will be very different from Books and Bakery's."

Benjamin was shaking his head even before June finished speaking. "We should avoid events that are even remotely similar to long-established traditions like Books and Bakery's Christmas celebration."

June was almost speechless with disappointment. She tried a different approach. "One of the reasons I think a Christmas dance would be successful is that the January birthday party brought in a lot of money and increased attendance for our other events."

"Come up with something else, June." Benjamin's tone was flat with finality.

June took a moment to moderate her tone. Her gaze circled his office. It was Benjamin's ninth week on the job. Why was he making such slow progress toward moving all the way into his office? Shelf spaces and cabinet surfaces were bare. Faded patches on the walls revealed where his predecessor had hung framed photographs and plaques. When would Benjamin do the same? The only personal item in his office was a framed photograph of two young children. His son and daughter? They were beautiful.

She turned back to her new boss. "Do you have any suggestions?"

"I'm sure you'll think of something."

June was glad one of them thought so. "May I at least go forward with the Kwanzaa presentation? As you said, we need to give Dr. Spates time to prepare, provided he agrees to do the presentation."

Benjamin seemed to hesitate. "Sure, the presentation should be fine."

June stood to leave. Her gut burned with frustration. At the threshold of his modest office, she once again faced Benjamin. "We need a year-end event, something spectacular to engage the community. I spent a lot of time developing the proposal and budget for the Christmas dinner dance."

Benjamin leaned into his desk. "I appreciate your time and efforts. Perhaps some of your work could be applied to your new idea."

His message was loud and clear: her dinner dance was a nonstarter. *Come up with something else.* But did he have even one clue of what went into coming up with and executing these events?

"I'll see what I can do." June walked out of Benjamin's office.

Her heart wouldn't be engaged in any other idea, though. She'd wanted to raise money for the center but she also wanted to celebrate Christmas. Why was The Iceman being such a Scrooge?

Benjamin's cellular phone rang, interrupting his contemplation of the semi-empty refrigerator in his townhouse Monday evening. Welcoming the reprieve, he allowed the fridge's door to swing shut and fished his phone from the front pocket of his gray slacks. He recognized his ex-wife's telephone number on the identification screen. *Perfect.*

He counseled himself to keep calm as he accepted her call. "Hello, Aliyah."

"Ben, how are you?" She sounded hesitant. It had been almost a year since their marriage had ended, Christmas Eve's Eve. Still, in the seven months since their divorce had been finalized, neither of them had gotten used to the coldness of their new relationship.

"What is it, Aliyah?" He didn't want to chat or catch up. He wanted this call to be over, the sooner the better.

"When last did you hear from the children?" Aliyah's voice was tense.

"It's been a while." Benjamin had spoken with their nineteen-year-old son, Terence, and eighteen-year-old daughter, Zora, perhaps two weeks ago. He'd last seen them about ten months ago when he and Aliyah had helped them move into the residence halls at The Ohio State University. "Why?"

"They've stopped returning my calls."

"They aren't returning mine, either." When Benjamin did reach them, their conversations were frustratingly brief. He didn't know which was worse, their silence or the one-sided conversations with their monosyllabic responses. "They're upset about our divorce. They don't understand why we won't get back together."

"They know now," Aliyah reassured him.

"What do you mean?" Benjamin needed to sit down. He moved into the living room of his small, two-story townhouse.

His black leather recliner was one of the most uncomfortable pieces of furniture ever created. In fact, he'd bought his furniture—the black television stand, coffee table, and entertainment system, and the matching black leather sofa—to fill the room. Comfort hadn't been his first priority.

"I told them I'd had an affair." Aliyah's words were low with shame. "I didn't like what our breakup was doing to your relationship with them. It wasn't fair that they blamed you for our divorce."

"How did it go?" Benjamin sank deeper into the stiff recliner.

The discussion must have taken a lot of courage on Aliyah's part. Benjamin couldn't bring himself to express his gratitude for her confession, though. The wound her betrayal had caused was still too fresh. He couldn't get past it or the fact that, if Aliyah hadn't had an affair, they wouldn't need to tell their children about it. He wouldn't have had to leave his job. And he wouldn't have returned to his small hometown of Trinity Falls in northeast Ohio to start over.

"Telling them was difficult and ugly. And now they're not speaking to me." There were tears in Aliyah's voice.

"I'm sorry." Surprisingly, it was the truth. He was sorry their children were giving her the silent treatment. She'd been a faithless wife, but there was no denying she was a loving mother.

"So am I." Aliyah paused. "Thanksgiving is less than four weeks away. I thought they'd come home for school break."

"What makes you think they won't?" This would be the first Thanksgiving he'd spend without his family in nineteen years. Benjamin rubbed his chest to ease the weight crushing his heart.

"Well, for one thing, they're not returning my calls." Aliyah's words wobbled around a forced chuckle.

"They'll come around." It was time to get off the phone. He couldn't control his emotions much longer.

"What are you doing for Thanksgiving, Ben?"

Benjamin gritted his teeth. Why was she asking? What did she expect to hear? "I'll probably spend it with my brothers."

"I'd forgotten that Zach had moved back to Trinity Falls as well. Now all of the Brooks brothers are back in town."

Benjamin didn't find her observation amusing. He loved Trinity Falls, but he'd had a family and a life in Chicago—before the woman who'd promised to love and cherish him until "death do us part" had cheated on him. Repeatedly.

"I hope you and the kids enjoy Thanksgiving. I'll call." Benjamin pushed himself up from the recliner.

"Spend Thanksgiving with us." Aliyah's request rushed down the cell phone connection.

Benjamin froze. "You want us to be like a family again?" *She must be kidding.*

"I want the kids to spend Thanksgiving at home. I also want them to see us getting along."

Benjamin rubbed the back of his neck. "What about Larry?"

Larry Cox had been Aliyah's lover for almost two years. He'd also been Benjamin's boss at Hughes & Coal Corp., the Chicago-based financial investment company for which he'd worked for almost twenty years.

"Larry and I aren't seeing each other anymore." Aliyah's admission was surprising.

She'd waited until their divorce to break off her extramarital affair. What, if anything, should he read into that?

"I'll call you and the kids on Thanksgiving Day." He started to end the call.

"Ben, please. They're not speaking to me." Aliyah's voice broke. "I'm not too proud to ask for your help."

"There's nothing I can do for you. Terry and Zora need time." Benjamin touched the screen to end the call.

Hopefully, time was all he needed as well to banish the bitterness and anger in his heart. June's pitch for the center's Christmas dinner dance came to his mind. Benjamin shook his head. How could he approve the event? He wasn't exactly in the Christmas mood.

June's cellular phone rang just as she entered her home Monday evening. She fished the device from her purse as she locked her door. The caller identification listed her son's name.

"Wow, two phone calls in one week." June kicked off her shoes, then crossed the entryway of her colonial home. "To what do I owe this bountiful pleasure?"

"Real funny, Mom." Noah's words held suppressed laughter. "How're you doing?"

June hung her emerald winter coat in the closet before walking to her family room. She collapsed onto the welcoming cushions of her foam-green love seat, a match to her sofa and armchair.

"About the same as I was when we spoke yesterday. How are you?" She turned up the volume on her Mom Hearing. She and Noah had always been close. But this evening, June sensed something more than that behind his attentiveness.

"Are you settling in okay in Trinity Falls?"

June's brows knitted at the concern she heard in her child's voice. *Why is he still worrying about me?* "Noah, I've told you I'm fine. This is your freshman year. You should be focusing on your classes."

Her heart swelled with pride that her son had earned a full academic scholarship to Columbia University in New York. She gazed at the photos lining her fireplace mantel and the ones mounted to the walls. With very little effort, she relived events from her son's birth to young adulthood: first day of kindergarten, first communion, confirmation, pee wee football, high school graduation and moving onto Columbia's campus. She blinked away tears. *Has any son ever made a mother prouder?*

June swallowed the lump in her throat. "How are your classes?"

"They're all right." There was an echo behind Noah's voice and muted conversations in the distance. He must be using his cell phone in the hallway again. *Is he getting along with his roommate?*

June arched a brow. "After ten weeks of classes, the

best review you could give me is 'all right'? Are you keeping up with your readings?"

"Yes, ma'am. It's hard, but I'm making it work." His sigh stirred all her maternal instincts. *Is he getting enough sleep? Is he eating right? He gave up football. Is he still finding time to exercise?*

June took a breath to ask him all of these questions again, but Noah spoke first.

"How was the Books and Bakery Halloween party?" His tone was too casual.

"It was nice. I had a good time." *Didn't we talk about this yesterday?*

June had attended Books & Bakery's annual Halloween party and children's story time on Saturday, which had been Halloween. Trinity Falls's residents had crowded the bookstore and café. They were dressed as historical figures, or popular characters from comic books, novels, movies and television. June had gone as Florence Nightingale. She'd always admired the historical figure. She still wasn't sure what Benjamin had been. Dressed in jeans, flannel shirt, and a tool belt, he'd claimed to be a handyman. June and Megan McCloud, Books & Bakery's owner and the organizer of the Halloween event, had given him a D for effort.

"Are you sure you had a good time?" Noah persisted.

The virtual lightbulb came on in June's brain. *I'm going to ground him.* "How long have you been using Darius to check up on me?" Silence. "Noah?" She used her best warning tone.

"I didn't ask Darius to spy on you, Mom. I promise. You told me you were going to the party. And Darius told me some people have been giving you a hard time.

I was worried something might have happened at the bookstore."

"Noah, I can—"

"Take care of yourself. I know." He sighed and June pictured her eighteen-year-old son taking on the weight of the world. "But just like a mother worries about her son, a son worries about his mother."

June was momentarily speechless. *Look at him, using my words to turn the tables on me.* "Noah, I appreciate your concern, but I need you to remain focused on your future."

"I wouldn't be as worried if you were still living in Sequoia. Sequoia is familiar."

June rose and paced across the room to the fireplace. "Neither of us expected Making an Event would file for bankruptcy the week Darius and I moved you into Columbia."

She should have realized the marketing and event-planning company for which she'd worked for the past fourteen years was getting ready to close its doors for-ever. But she was a single parent, working a demanding job, and helping her son prepare for college.

"I guess Mayor Lopez offering you the job with Trin-ity Falls's community center was like good news, bad news." Noah still sounded troubled.

"It was all good news." She injected even more con-fidence into her voice. "We must remember to count our blessings instead of our burdens. This job is an exciting change. It's a promotion. The pay's better. I was fortu-nate to sell our home quickly and for enough money to put a decent down payment on this one."

"I remember what it was like when people in Sequoia

rejected you. I don't want you to go through that again."
The pain in her child's voice ripped her heart in two.

"It's not the same, Noah." She wasn't a young woman
on her own with a baby to protect. She was a much more
mature and battle-tested woman who'd single-handedly
raised an impressive young man. "I already have friends
in Trinity Falls."

"People who aren't that friendly are there, too."

"What can I do to convince you that I'm fine?" June
paced back across the room and dropped onto the sofa.

"Tell me if people are giving you a hard time."

"What will you do?"

"I might not be able to do anything, but I at least want
to know. Promise me."

Tension drained from June, bringing forth a smile.
"Well, if you want to know about the difficult people
I'm dealing with, let me tell you about my new boss."

"Is he as bad as Miss Gina?" Noah's voice sounded
lighter. She pictured the smile on his handsome, young
face.

Gina Carter owned Making an Event. She was a nice
person, but her lack of planning had often caused chaos
for June and the rest of the staff. At least she could
reason with the older woman. Benjamin Brooks was
distractingly attractive. But once you got past his good
looks—no easy feat—he also was distressingly unreasonable.

"He might be worse." June was only half joking. Or
maybe she wasn't joking at all. "But first, tell me about
your chemistry professor. Did you meet with her about
your class project?"

"Yes, ma'am." Noah launched into an amusing account of his meeting with his professor to get clarification

on his chemistry report. Thankfully, the anecdote, which had a happy ending, seemed to distract her son from worrying about her. At least for now.

June listened to Noah with one half of her mind while the other continued to brood over her boss and an idea for their year-end fund-raiser. Ever since Benjamin had shot down her Christmas dance idea that morning, she'd been struggling to come up with a substitute event. But The Iceman wasn't being helpful. He knew what he didn't want, but he had no idea what he wanted.

Was it the event itself or the Christmas theme that he was opposed to? Did he have something against the holiday?